THE
FOREVER
KISS

THEA DEVINE

THE FOREVER KISS

ℬ
BRAVA

KENSINGTON PUBLISHING CORP.
http://www.kensingtonbooks.com

BRAVA BOOKS are published by

Kensington Publishing Corp.
850 Third Avenue
New York, NY 10022

All Kensington titles, imprints and distributed lines are available at special quantity discounts for bulk purchases for sales promotion, premiums, fund-raising, educational or institutional use.

Special book excerpts or customized printings can also be created to fit specific needs. For details, write or phone the office of the Kensington Special Sales Manager: Kensington Publishing Corp., 850 Third Avenue, New York, NY 10022. Attn. Special Sales Department. Phone: 1-800-221-2647.

Brava and the B logo Reg. U.S. Pat. & TM Off.

ISBN 0-7582-0399-3

First Kensington Trade Paperback Printing: June 2003
10 9 8 7 6 5 4 3 2 1

Printed in the United States of America

THE
FOREVER
KISS

Prologue

Dundee Hospital Station, South Africa
October 1899

The colonel did not believe in coincidences. He didn't believe in fate or luck or a person having a double somewhere on earth.

But he did believe that Ducas Sangbourne was dying, and that the man standing beside him in the shadow of the hospital tent looked enough like him to be his twin.

Except that was impossible. He had known the man next to him for years, knew his life, his childhood, the grinding poverty in which he'd been raised, for which enlistment in the army was the means to an end. Had fought beside him during the Indian Mutiny and at Khartoum, and here, at Talana Hill.

And now this: a dying man, an uncanny resemblance, and the rare and fateful opportunity to make use of those two convergent facts.

Except he didn't believe in fate. He didn't know what to believe. And the man beside him was silent in that way he had as if he were taking apart every level and nuance of their previous conversation, and carefully examining the risks and ramifications.

He was staring at the dying man, perhaps even more

nonplussed than the colonel at the unbelievable resemblance.

Everything about what the colonel had proposed was unbelievable. And in spite of that, it was his choice, his decision, and he didn't have to do anything if he didn't wish to.

He hadn't been going to decide until he had actually seen for himself the remarkable resemblance between the dying man and himself.

He felt nothing, staring at the man who could be his twin. And that surprised him. Or did it? Was it not an axiom that everyone had a look-alike somewhere? It was wishful thinking to want to believe that somehow he, Dar St. Onge, orphan of the world, and erstwhile death-defying soldier of fortune, was some distant relation of this man. It was a longing and yearning to have the bedrock of a family behind him instead of the empty maw of an orphanage childhood.

And he knew it.

The army had become his family instead, the colonel as close as he had to a father. And now this man, this other, this duplicate . . . of him. Who had lived another life, a different life, a privileged life.

A life the colonel now wanted him to step into, and pretend . . .

To be something, someone, he was not.

To convince this man's loving family that their son had come home to them safe from the wars.

And to root out a traitor . . .

The man was dying; white, bloodless, limp and lifeless, he lay on a wooden pallet, taking a sip of water now and again from an orderly.

"They can do nothing more for him now," the colonel said, his voice low. "It's only a matter of time. Hours, perhaps. No more than a few days."

There was not a nuance of expression in his voice. This was one of his men still, and he ws honor bound to treat him so near death, no matter what circumstances might prove otherwise. "The orderlies and nurses have been encouraging him to reminisce; you will have to feign amnesia, but you won't be walking into the situation blind."

"No, just with blinders," Dar said wryly. "God, it's uncanny . . . it's eerie watching someone who could be your second self in the throes of death."

"Don't look, then. I just wanted you to see. . . ."

He nodded. He still didn't know. Seeing the man and how close the likeness, and weighting that against what he owed the colonel, and his own skirt-the-edge-of-death recklessness, he still didn't know.

To walk in another man's shoes, into his life, his family, into all that he was that was unknown was a risk beyond the realm of imagining. And yet, and yet . . .

He lifted the curtain of the tent to look at the man once again.

Closer than close, despite the pallor, the gauntness, the height—it was like looking at the ghost of himself.

It aroused his curiosity even though he knew it would come to naught. He was a child of the poorhouse, raised in squalor, educated in hardship, graduated to military, and now a merciless operative, the one the colonel called when the job must be done.

This was his life, his home, his niche. The man on the pallet was an aberration. He dropped the curtain and turned to follow the colonel out of the tent.

And he still didn't know. . . .

Chapter 1

Sangbourne Manor, Cheshamshire, England
November 1899

It was the blood. That gypsy blood pounding through her body that would never let anything go. And it was the house, Ducas's house, a magnet, with the gas- and candlelit windows that beckoned deep in the night, especially when Lord and Lady Sangbourne were entertaining.

They were always entertaining. Lady Sangbourne had an insatiable need to surround herself with people all the time, fascinating people. People about whom you could find things out if you were clever enough and if you followed the lure of your gypsy blood.

Oh, there was something about the way it thrummed deep within her, blotting out her mother's every attempt to turn her into the lady her father wanted her to be.

But then, her father didn't know that her mother was a frequent visitor to Sangbourne Manor, because he himself was such an infrequent visitor to the house in Cheshamshire.

And this he didn't need to know—that his exotic, alluring Gaetana was frequently the paid entertainment. They feasted on her, the wild gypsy dancer, as they gossiped about her, she who had enticed an earl and held him still in her thrall and they paid her to come to the Manor and dance for them. And she went, following the call of her nature, and in spite of the fact the Earl kept her like a queen.

It was the blood. It could not be denied. Not in her mother, not in her. And so Gaetana danced, giving herself to whatever voluptuous pleasures were on the menu on any given evening at Sangbourne Manor, and giving herself to her lover, the Earl, at his command.

Gaetana on the inside and Angene, her changeling daughter, on the outside, looking in, squirreling away secrets.

So many secrets. Her gypsy blood reveled in the secrets. Secrets were knowledge, secrets were power, and Angene knew it with every fiber of her gypsy soul.

And besides, what else had she to do until Ducas came back from the war? Dear God, Ducas, throwing himself in harm's way in a godforsaken country thousands of miles away for no reason she could ever understand.

Ducas with his persistent tongue and honeyed promises.

Her body twinged just thinking of it. It was the blood; no decent woman would even conceive of doing what she intended to do when Ducas returned.

And he would return. There was not a doubt in her mind. And then . . . and then—she would become his mistress and enslave him forever, the way her mother had captivated the Earl.

The thought made her breathless.

How stupid of him to go to war. It wasn't his war. And it was so far away that it could take him years to return. The idea of it yawned like an abyss, dark as the night that enfolded her. Perhaps that was why she so loved the night: there was always the promise of a new day, and with it, Ducas's return.

But until that day, it was the house that drew her, and the sense that at night she could be close to him by just touching the cold stone walls, and by learning everything she could about those who were involved in his life.

By lurking in the shadows . . .

It was the blood: there was a turbulence in her that could not be tempered by all the good breeding of the man who had sired her, nor by a hundred lessons with the best tutors in deportment and manners her mother had employed.

She was what she was: daughter of a gypsy dancer and an aristocratic Earl, and the fact she was creeping along the outers walls of Sangbourne Manor was proof enough which part of her held sway.

And then there were the secrets, the delicious sensual secrets about the games that adults played.

Games that quickened her blood, because she and Ducas had played at those games, had skirted the ultimate conquest and surrender, with the full understanding and promise that someday, somehow, it would happen.

But for now, she moved noiselessly through the trees and into the bushes that fronted the windows of the grand parlor where the games would begin.

The dining first, hours of it with five or six courses of elegantly prepared food and the best china and silver; they began early in the country, on the evenings when they played their games. After dinner, the men would retreat for port and polite conversation as the tension and anticipation escalated to an unbearable degree. And finally the men would join the ladies for the evenings' entertainment—this night, they would welcome yet again Gaetana the gypsy, well paid for her sensual dances, for her time, for her body.

A never-ending fascination, watching the aristocracy, as they ate, drank, eyed each other, flirted, paired off, disappeared; sometimes they imported girls from the village to service the gentlemen while the ladies went off with the goat boys and shepherds into the fields.

Or they would hire high priced courtesans for a more elegant and willful seduction.

Or they took each other up and off in private rooms in a variety of interesting combinations as they would do this night.

And the queen of all this rampant lasciviousness was Ducas's beautiful exotic mother.

Gaetana would never talk about her, nor anything that went on at Sangbourne Manor. Secrets were safe at the Manor, kept beyond the grave in a devil's bargain to shield the sins of the sinful. No one would tell, ever, about the things that went on there, the weekend-long things, the forbidden things.

Things perhaps Ducas had been a part of. Things, because of that, Angene had to know because she was certain they were things that would give her the power she needed to convince him to become her lover, forever. She was a bastard child of dubious lineage; she wanted, she could hope for nothing more.

As she peered into the tall, multipaned windows of the dimly lit grand parlor, she saw her mother dancing to a wildly strumming guitar, her skirts held high, her feet and legs bared to all. And the look on her face—the transcending look of joy that she could finally be herself, even among these heathens who had no idea of her life, her lore, her heritage.

It didn't matter. Gaetana did not need to pretend in these wild hours. She could follow the dictates of her heart, her blood, and no one would tell.

In that curious honor among like-minded hedonists, her mother's secret was safe.

Angene was the only one who knew—and she harbored a tumultuous desire to be among these libertine people, her hair, her skirts, her desire flowing free.

If only Ducas would return; Ducas understood her. Handsome, reckless Ducas with that irresistible combination of haughty aristocrat and primitive stable boy—and that tongue, that insatiable demanding tongue . . .

But wait—her mother's voluptuous dance was finished,

and the guests—three couples in all, excluding Lord and Lady Sangbourne—were clapping loudly and appreciatively.

She knew what came next in the sexual quadrille: these country weekends seemed to be almost a set piece, depending on the guests. In tonight's little play, the lights would dim, a gentleman would rise and select the lady of his choice, who was not his wife, and away they would go into the shadows to explore the unfettered nature of men and the naked response of women.

Lady Sangbourne directed the scene, standing tall and slender in the center of the room, dressed in her habitual green, with her long thick hair that deliberately grazed her waist bound carelessly away from her narrow face; did she not know how much men loved long hair to curtain their sins? Yet she was always the last to go into the shadows.

She knew everything, Lady Sangbourne, and didn't blink an eye as her husband chose his companion for the night . . .

Gaetana?

Angene's heart sank. This she had never witnessed before, this wholesale taking of her mother, in spite of her allegiance to and her love for the Earl. But none of that ever counted here. And certainly not tonight, if her mother's expression was any indication.

The air was thick with expendable lust, and every last guest only wanted that evanescent moment of surrender. Instinctively Angene understood that the crux of the evening was the pleasure point, nothing more, nothing less, and not even her mother was immune to the call of her blood.

She sank against the wall, her heart pounding painfully. This reality was not pretty, not even romantic. But then, wasn't it what she wanted for herself? To give herself wholly and completely to Ducas, and to live, outside constraints, as the one and only desire of his heart forever?

Was there a forever when it came to the nature of men?

Would *she* entertain Ducas's friends and companions, and would he just as cavalierly hand her over to whoever wanted her for a night? Was this the life she wanted to commit to, in her overwhelming desire to be with Ducas?

It did not bear thinking about . . . she couldn't. He might be dead for all she knew, on that foreign battlefield, dead with no remains to be buried and mourned over . . . and this was worse than anything that might come of their life together.

Oh, dear Lord—Ducas . . .

Silence descended, the curious silence of the deep dark night, where the merest rustle of a leaf could set the blood thrumming. Not a star burned; the moon drifted behind a tail of clouds; every detail of the landscape merged into another so that suddenly there was only the flat black of nothingness around her.

There was nowhere to move, no landmark to guide her back home. In a breath, she was a prisoner of the dark, caught in that abyss of emptiness, that cold black hole she so dreaded. The cold began to seep into her bones. An owl hooted somewhere in the trees, underscored by the wind rustling through the leaves that sounded like bats, flurrying over her head.

She was trapped there for sure, her long, thin woolen cloak her only protection against the night, against predators, against death, and there was nothing she could do, nowhere she could move, she was blind as the night, and there was no other choice but to curl up against the cold stone walls of Sangbourne Manor for cold hard comfort until daylight.

She wouldn't sleep; she was too cold, too saturated with fear.

Too aware of the endless noises in the night. Close. Subtle. Scared.

She slept.

The howling of a dog awakened her.

Dawn. Cold. Dank.

Jingling. A rasping rolling sound. Horses. A carriage

emerging out of the fog that hovered just beyond the drive in front of Sangbourne Manor.

Dreaming. Too early in the morning for visitors . . . and besides, they were all still tumbled in their ruttish rest.

If she moved quickly, she could get back to her house before her mother returned.

Only, limbs stiff from the cold. Can't move. Not yet. Slowly, slowly . . . no sound—if anyone caught her here, her mother would abandon her to the wolves . . . the carriage door opening—who . . . ?

A stranger. Wait—someone leaning on him . . .

Slowly easing out of the carriage—was it? The stranger, giving him a cane. A familiar stance, a bend of the body, the rumble of a word, the timbre of a familiar voice . . .

Oh, God—was it? Or was she dreaming? Ducas? *Ducas?* As if she'd conjured him to reality out of her dreams. Injured? Maimed? She couldn't see clearly as she crouched, peering through the lower branches of the hedge in which she'd cowered the entire night.

Oh, mighty Lord in heaven, he must not see her here, not like this, not now . . . There could be no explanation, ever, for her skulking around his house like this. . . .

She ducked back into the bushes, and watched him walk slowly and painfully on the arm of the stranger up to the front door.

A jangling bell in the distance. Scurry of footsteps. The door opening. She couldn't see anything—it couldn't be him, could it?

But it must be . . . a word, a welcome, and he limped into the house.

The fog rolled up across the lawn, catching in the brittle branches of every tree and bush. Thank heaven for the fog—while they were all occupied by the surprise of his return, she could slip and slide away without anyone noticing, a swirling shadow swallowed by the mist.

But dear heaven, this was so unexpected, he couldn't be

back yet, could he? She felt so disoriented by the arrival of this man who looked like Ducas. It was so soon after he'd gone, so unreal, coming out of the fog.

She didn't know what to think, what to do, as she slipped away from Sangbourne Manor as quickly as a wraith.

She had to get home, she had to think, she had to plan. *But you don't have to do anything. Not yet, not now. Ducas is home. . . .*

It was the blood.

Or the lack of it.

Constable Croyd didn't need to know anything more. It was yet another mysterious animal death in an intermittent series of them around the countryside. Never enough to arouse suspicions. Oh, every few weeks, someone would report an animal gone, drained of its lifeblood, with no earthly reason why or how.

Never any bites, tears, or marks. Just the animal, drained and dead.

They would notify him, as he had long ago instructed, and then they would cut up the carcass and bury it, with the proper precautions, just in case.

They never said in case of what, but Croyd knew. In the depths of the countryside, superstitions abounded, and while there was nothing about the deaths of the animals that could remotely be construed as suspicious or supernatural, no one ever wanted to take the chance that something had been . . . overlooked.

Even now, Croyd wondered if there was something he had overlooked. This newest animal demise was closer to home than usual. One of the Sangbourne tenant farmers, actually.

And the Sangbournes were an odd lot, to his mind. That son going off to South Africa on the turn of tuppence. The mother, so exotic, so beautiful, keeping to herself, even while she played bountiful lady of the manor. And Sir Eustace, of whom everyone was so fond, except they believed he'd been a little sun-touched all those years ago when he'd met and decided to marry Lady Veleka somewhere in the remote and erotic Far East.

There was one story about which no one would ever know the truth.

But what truth? The Lady Veleka was cordial and generous, as Sir Eustace's wife should be, and just that little bit distant. And on top of that, a little strange. And the strangeness was the thing that Constable Croyd was watching, in his own quiet, unassuming way.

He couldn't quite define it, or put his finger on just what it was. But there was something about Lady Sangbourne that nagged at him. So he watched her. Quietly, subtly. Never in any way that would reveal he was even aware of her, but he watched her.

And now he had an excuse to go to the manor, for surely Sir Eustace would want to be aware of what had happened on one of his tenant farms. Probably the farmer had sent word already, but it would be good for Sir Eustace and his lady to know that the law was following these mysterious killings as well.

Just in case. Their being so close to home, so to speak. *The lord and lady should be aware,* he thought.

With all due precautions.

It was like walking onto a battlefield blind, with every sense heightened, every nerve screamingly alert.

And yet, what could be more normal than the entrance hallway of Sangbourne Manor in the early morning hours when no one was awake, and the butler was stumbling sleepily down the hall, having been awakened by the odd jangling of the bell so early in the morning.

The butler knew him immediately. The first test passed. His eyes skewed suspiciously to Dar's companion, Alton, and then back to Dar. There was no question in his mind, on his lips. Not a single doubt that he was Ducas Sangbourne come home.

So now the subterfuge began.

"Mr. Ducas . . ." The butler's tone was apologetic, shocked, deferential, and foggy with sleep. "We had no idea, we didn't expect . . . no one sent word—if we'd only known . . . do let me . . ."

Dar didn't move. The butler stopped in mid-motion and looked at Alton.

"He doesn't know you," Alton interposed quickly. "He remembers nothing. He was badly wounded at the battle of Dundee, he spent two months at Cumberside, and even then . . . nothing. The doctors there could only do so much. It was thought best to bring him back to Sangbourne Manor, to what was familiar, to see if it would would shock his memory. But you must not hope—the doctor says it may never happen."

"I see."

Dar said nothing. It was better to say nothing, that was the strategy: to take Ducas's place, and to navigate the tricky waters of his life as expediently as possible, "kill him" again, as it were, and get out before the family found out that Ducas was really dead.

"I see," the butler said again, his tone more considering, his reserve snapping back in place. "Mr. Ducas, I am Holmby."

Dar could see him looking for any sign that he was recognized. "Holmby," he said slowly. "Holmby?" He shot a glance at Alton. Alton nodded. "Holmby, then."

Alton said, "He really doesn't remember—anything."

"Inconceivable, " the butler muttered, and then, "I must wake the family. Will you stay with him in the library?"

"For as long as necessary," Alton said, shooting a glance at Dar.

The library was a cold book-lined room with stiff sofas and a long table that fronted a floor-to-ceiling window that framed the flaming sunrise.

Dar sat gingerly on one of the couches and looked around. Sat down right in Ducas Sangbourne's life—one that was so diametrically the opposite of his own, one filled with luxury and servants, and beautifully bound books and elegant furniture.

And parents.

There were parents; this he knew from the colonel who had given him a précis of Ducas's background obtained from the records and from the information gleaned by the attendants who had nursed him. He knew about Ducas's beautiful and intense mother, his scholarly and gentle father, about Sangbourne Manor, and the neighboring village.

All this he knew, and then he knew what he himself had sensed as he limped into the Manor hall—the thick scent of lust and unbridled emotion, overlaid with a cool deliberate constraint.

It was so palpable, it was almost tangible, and yet there was nothing in the shadowy corners of the hallway and library to even warrant such conclusions.

But he never ignored his senses.

"What do you think?" Alton whispered.

"I'm in way over my ears," Dar muttered. Way over his heart and deep into his emotions already about the complications of this mission. He hadn't even considered he might have strong feelings about Ducas's parents, or even the consequences of his deceiving them so cruelly.

On the battlefield, in discussion, it had been such an abstract thing. Sitting in the beautifully appointed library, waiting on the butler, the parents, he comprehended it was something else quite again, and that there were pitfalls he never even considered.

It would be too easy to fall into the trap of becoming their son, for one thing. Too easy because it was something he had yearned for all his life: parents, a home, stability, love.

And Ducas had had it all, had betrayed everything he held dear, and given his life in the process, so that he, Dar

St. Onge, could step into Ducas's life, and briefly give back to his family what had been taken from them. And then, when he was integrated, when he fulfilled his mission, when he was ready to leave them, he would kill Ducas all over again.

Hell. Shit.

So be it. This was war, and Ducas was suspect, and no matter what his upbringing, no matter how much he was loved and coddled in his sphere, justice must be done.

He heard a woman shrieking in the distance as footsteps pounded down the stairs. The mother—it had to be the mother.

"Ducas? Ducas—where are you? Dear heaven, where *are* you?"

". . . library, mum . . ." the butler's voice faintly behind her, and a moment later, she appeared in the doorway in a swirl of green satin and lace.

Dear God, she was beautiful. And younger than he would have thought. And that hair—thick, dark, down to her waist. Holding out her arms, her hands, with their long tapered fingers beckoning him as he rose to his feet as she entered with melodramatic flair.

He knew her, from everything the colonel had told him, he knew her. And it was so hard not to go to her, as Ducas's ghost, and let himself be enfolded in her arms.

"He doesn't know you, my lady," Alton, finally speaking, said.

Her flashing green eyes speared him. "How so?"

"His memory, my lady. Gone. Utterly. I have all the reports and papers here. It was thought best to send him home and see if being among familiar faces might be of some benefit—or comfort."

He didn't have to say, *for you.*

She made a move, and the tall gray-haired man standing behind her with his hands on her shoulders, immediately restrained her.

"Veleka."

So that was her name. And he was Sir Eustace, Ducas's father.

"I want to hold him, he'll know me then, he will . . ."

"Veleka, my dear, you didn't believe Holmby, so let us listen to . . . this gentleman—"

"Alton, sir . . ."

"—Alton . . . who has accompanied our son home." He moved her into the room, to the sofa opposite the one in front of which Dar stood; the butler drew the curtains so the rising sun would not glare in her eyes, and everyone sat down, slowly, gingerly, while Veleka's hot green gaze poured all over him.

"Sir. Mr. Ducas was wounded at Talana Hill, took a very bad hit on his head, was in the hospital for these two months, unconscious, and came out of it with no memory of who he was or what had happened. The doctors thought it best to send him back home. It might help, it might not. There's no way to tell."

"I see," Sir Eustace murmured.

"Well, it's just not possible," Veleka said, jumping to her feet. "He will remember everything, I will see to it. I will make it happen." She was at Dar's side instantly, taking his hands, gazing into his eyes. "It will happen. How could my son not remember all that there is to remember? His life here was happy, fulfilled, his need to go to war the patriotism of a son of England. And now he will be repaired, I swear it."

"As you say, my lady."

"And you will be rewarded for bringing him home to us. Eustace, my darling . . ."

"Veleka, you are being melodramatic as usual. Alton is welcome to stay as long as it takes Ducas to become acclimated again. We would be grateful for the help, actually. This is the last turn of events we could have expected, and I'm rather at a loss how to cope with it."

"As you say, sir," Alton murmured.

"Excellent. Then Holmby will show you to Ducas's room—I'm sure you've been traveling for hours, and need to wash and refresh yourselves. And let us then all convene for breakfast at nine o'clock."

"Nine-thirty," Veleka said, her tone fraught with meaning that Sir Eustace immediately understood.

"Oh, God, yes, our guests. Very well. Nine-thirty." Sir Eustace rose up and came to Dar, and touched him on the shoulder. "I'm grateful to have you home, Son."

"Gentlemen," Holmby now, taking charge.

"Nine-thirty," Veleka said.

"Understood, mum." Holmby motioned to the steps. "This way, my lord."

My lord . . . Dar shot a glance at Alton. Dear God, my lord. One thing to know it, another to hear it. Alton raised an eyebow and nodded, and they both followed Holmby out to the hallway and the winding mahogany staircase.

Twenty-foot ceilings, at least. A Persian runner two inches thick on the steps. Wood burnished to a satin sheen. Soft light from a clerestory window as dawn broke, sending thin fingers of sunlight tiptoeing across the jewel-colored carpet. The walls, a soft ivory of age and elegance. The landing carpeted in exquisite oriental rugs laid one over the other at angles to each of two doorways on this side of the landing.

Everything quiet, hushed, infused with the scent of beeswax and a hint of smokiness from the morning fires already lit in bedroom fireplaces.

Perfection, in a way that only the impoverished could dream of. It was like a novel come to life. A dream. Dar's reality now.

And it was already too easy to forget just why he was here.

Holmby led them to the far side of the landing and opened the last door on that wall. "My lord."

En garde . . . Dar looked at him blankly again.

"Your room, sir."

"Oh. Yes. Of course." *Not too much. Restraint in every-thing. Don't give away anything. If you're in doubt, pretend you don't know, you don't remember.*

God, what a tightrope walk . . .

He entered the room. The curtains, heavy dark velvet, were drawn. The room was luxurious, the walls a deep, rich wine color. There was a full tester bed with matching velvet hangings jutting out from one wall. An ornate table and deeply tufted upholstered chair by the window. A matching table and chair by the fireplace. A mahogany dresser against another wall, alongside a discreet door. A huge matching armoire against the third wall. The same rich jewel-toned carpets on the floor as were on the landing.

Every piece of furniture seemed oversize, opulent, rich.

And too perfect. And cold.

Dar didn't know quite what to do now; Holmby was watching him so he sank into one of the chairs and stared around him with the feigned curiosity of a child.

The environment of the man whom I would be. Not what I would have chosen, but then—I don't know what I would have chosen when my bedroom has been the battle-field and my mattress a sleeping bag. . . .

He schooled his expression. He could have no opinion. He could know nothing. Holmby was watching, almost as if he weren't quite sure, maybe they all weren't *quite* sure—and then he looked at Alton.

Alton shrugged. "I can't emphasize this enough . . . he just doesn't remember anything. He will never be as he was. At least, that is the doctor's opinion, but who really can know what might trick his memory back to life."

"I will explain that to Sir Eustace," Holmby murmured. "The water closet and dressing room are through that door. My lord's luggage, what there is of it, will be brought up directly. There is clothing if he wishes to change."

"Thank you. I'll see that he's downstairs at nine-thirty."

Holmby closed the door softly. Dar shook his head as Alton started to speak, mouthing, *not yet,* and motioning him to take the chair by the fireplace.

Only then did he let out his breath. The first hurdle passed. And so many more to come.

Chapter 2

They were all so spoiled, so accustomed to having everything their own way, and it was a problem with no immediate solution.

They had gotten too comfortable the way they were and no one wanted to change. Of course, it took something catastrophic like Ducas's loss of memory to make that crystal clear to her, but now she understood—something *was* going to change: the way they would treat Ducas—nothing would be the same now he had returned and his memory was gone.

Merciful hell, she was so scared for Ducas and what this meant for him—for her. Her beautiful son, present in body but not in mind. She hadn't yet comprehended the breadth of this shock, or even how this could have happened. Or what the ramifications would be.

How could this have happened? Ducas was strong, smart, canny, elusive, and he would never have let himself fall into a situation that would be so injurious to him. It didn't bear thinking about, and there was nothing she could do about it anyway.

So she needed to calm down, to contain herself, and de-

cide what next to do. There were her guests to consider—
she couldn't quite chase them out the door, even on the
heels of Ducas's return. They would stay at least another
day, and so they would bear witness to her grief.

So be it. Soon enough everyone would know anyway,
whether they heard it from her guests, or from Gaetana,
lady gracious, who would spread the news to the village as
soon she could bear to pull herself out of Sir Eustace's bed.

The bitch. She would never know that it was she, Veleka,
who ordained the coupling with her husband, and not Sir
Eustace's unrequited passion run amok.

It didn't matter now anyway. Nothing mattered but
Ducas. And Eustace had understood that instantly. He
would leave her alone. For now, in any event. Until she as-
sessed how much damage had been done.

Damn it all to hellfire. Nothing ever went the way she
wanted it to, nothing. Things like this turned everything inside out, and it was all because they were unprepared, so
lapped in luxury, so unwilling to do what needed to be
done. As if Ducas had been their servant. As if they had no
responsibilities.

She was sick of it all, sick of her life, of the ongoing ne-
cessity for propriety and manners, sick of their friends, of
the pretenses and pursuits that made life in the country
moderately tolerable, but mostly, she was sick of the wild
untamed blood of the gypsy who taunted her, dancing for
Sir Eustance and claiming him as her own.

Utterly sick of that. And Sir Eustace skulking off on the
odd afternoon to see her. Well, he was going to get rid of
her now. That was finished. Did he *really* think she didn't
know?

She knew everything. *Everything.*

The only thing she didn't know was what to do about
Ducas. The complications, the ramifications seemed insur-
mountable. And add to that, still another stranger in the
house, because she couldn't dismiss the Alton person when
he could be of service to Ducas.

Ducas knew him, insofar as he could know anything; and this man had known him on the battlefield, had accompanied him from halfway around the world. He knew the situation, he had dealt with Ducas for thousands of miles of travel and companionship.

He had the advantage of Ducas's own family, a fact that rankled her.

What to do, what to do?

She felt a great overwhelming yaw of dismay at what she had lost in her son. All the memories, everything they had shared. He knew nothing, according to Holmby, not a blink of recognition as he entered his room, as he gazed at his furniture, as he stepped back into his life . . .

This just could not be. She wouldn't allow it to be. *She* would school him in his past, and he would get it back, all of it, he would, because there was no other choice as far as she was concerned.

If he remained like this, it would be as if he were dead. She might as well bury him, and she would move hell and earth before it came to that.

Something in her chest heaved. *Ducas . . .*

No!!—there was only one choice, and it was all up to her—to do everything in her power to bring him back to life.

"Sir . . ?"

Dar held up his hand, and leaped to the door. No sound without. He cracked it open. Silence. The hallway was quiet, empty, shadowy. Not a light in sight. Not a servant about.

He let out a breath and eased the door closed. "Now . . ." But he didn't know what now either. It was enough to have gotten past the front door without arousing any suspicion. And it was going to strain every ounce of his cunning to play a man without a memory while simultaneously trying to unearth Ducas's secrets.

What manner of man was Ducas Sangbourne, after all?

There were no clues in his belongings: it was all standard issue army in his suitcase, which would soon be brought to the room. There was nothing personal. No mementos, no letters from a loved one, no pictures, no souvenirs. Everything militarily correct. As if Ducas Sangbourne was a man without a past—or the perfect soldier of the Empire, focused solely on Queen and country.

Even this room, as luxurious as it was, revealed nothing about the man's personality or his likes or dislikes. Probably it was the mother whose hand had furnished the room. Probably it was the mother who dictated everything in this house.

"Where to begin?" he murmured.

"Maybe not, sir," Alton said tentatively. "Someone could come at any moment."

"Nevertheless—" Dar started at the bed, and went on to look in, under and around, every piece of furniture in the room. "Even if we find nothing out of order on the surface . . . I have to start somewhere."

But there it was, as if every vestige of Ducas's presence had been obliterated when he went off to war.

"Do you think they'll let me stay, sir?" Alton asked as they rummaged through the dressing room, where all they found were several neatly hung suits, shirts, and some grooming implements.

That was the plan, after all; to convince them that Dar would be helpless without this one familiar face to turn to. But the colonel couldn't have conceived the force and vitality of the mother, who looked as if she could move mountains if she were to determined to do so. And Ducas's recovery was theoretically one immovable mountain, the kind of challenge she would take on as her own.

For that alone, he needed Alton to run interference.

"We'll have to convince them that would be the best course."

"Right, sir. I'll do what I can."

Treacherous situation any which way, Dar thought, prowling the room in frustration. The mother was too sharp, too intense. And he had no inkling what else to expect, or how much time he might have to root around in Ducas's life before things got hot.

He pulled the curtains back to look out the window. The view was what he expected: sweeping lawns, immaculately tended gardens and bushes, the too bright morning sun blaring down.

He dropped the curtain just as someone pounded at the door.

"Ducas..!"

The mother. Of course. He nodded to Alton as he lowered himself into the chair by the window and schooled his expression, and Alton admitted her.

She swirled in like a sandstorm, followed by a footman carrying his mingy two pieces of luggage. "Ducas—" she started, and then took one look at his face and stopped abruptly. "I cannot believe this." She whipped around to Alton. "It cannot be that he doesn't know me."

"It is, mum."

A shudder went through her. Her back was to Dar; the footman had gone into the dressing room and was unpacking the suitcases, and he took that moment to covertly study her.

She was younger than he'd expected, and rail thin. Up close, her dark hair was astonishing, thick, wavy, lustrous, just grazing her waist. She was still dressed in her emerald morning gown, and in profile, she was classically beautiful. Her hands moved expressively when she talked and in her clipped aristocratic tones, he caught the faintest hint of an accent. And in her passion, she radiated a nervous energy that was so potent, it was almost tangible.

This was a woman to be reckoned with. She wouldn't leave it alone, and she would never leave Ducas alone until she forced his memory back somehow. Which made everything instantly infinitely more complicated.

He blanked out his expression again as she turned to him. "Ducas—"

He looked at her curiously, and she stamped her foot, grabbed his hands and looked deep into his eyes.

Her gaze was hypnotic, her will as fierce as a lion, and had he not had combat experience, if he had never endured captivity and torture in his career, he never could have maintained the slack expression of someone mentally unconscious in the face of such ferocity.

But he knew all that, and in that one off-guard moment, he knew her for the adversary she was, and she almost caught that intelligence in his eyes. Almost. It flashed in and out and was gone, and his eyes went blank, unknowing, seeing only the reality in his mind.

And Veleka, standing before him, her emotions warring with logic and the seemingly irrefutable reality.

Finally, she took a deep breath. Logic won. The reality won. And Dar comprehended that he had crossed another threshold in her acceptance of him as her memory-deprived son.

She had not let go of his hands, and now she squeezed them tightly.

"You *are* Ducas, they told you that you are Ducas Sangbourne, did they not?" she demanded.

He looked at her with that same distant curiosity and shrugged; her lips thinned, her grip tightened. "I will address you as Ducas. And you will answer to that name. You are my son, and I will have you back, do you hear me? You will come back. There is no other course. But right now, you will come to breakfast. You will be with your family and our friends. And then—" her voice hoarsened, "—and then, we will see what we will see."

Everyone knew Gaetana Benviste and her daughter, Angene. They were neither outcasts nor part of the community. They just *were,* a mother and daughter living in a beautiful half-timbered two-story house a mile outside of town, near by Sangbourne Manor.

Everyone was aware of Gaetana's heritage and her story—how the Earl of Wentmore fell deeply in love with her at first sight, and imported her from some nomadic gypsy camp in the mountains of some Slavic country to the staid confines of a sumptuously furnished house in Cheshamshire.

She had acclimated so well, they said. She kept to herself, she had raised her out-of-wedlock daughter with all the propriety of the putative wife of an earl, and educated her to that station. She dressed well. She didn't try to insinuate herself where she wasn't wanted. She was chaste and discreet, and if she indulged in any way outside of her relationship with the Earl, no one knew it.

But now Angene knew it, and it was a sore secret. She had crept back to the house very early in the morning, well ahead of her mother's return, and she waited for her in the parlor, swathed in quilts on the couch beside a roaring fire, her bones utterly saturated with the damp cold of her untenable knowledge.

Ah—what had she expected? The Earl visited little enough; and her mother was still young, her blood hot and passionate.

But Sir Eustace . . . ! Oh, he was the last person Angene had imagined her mother would want. This had to be the reason that Gaetana would never speak of her evenings at the Manor.

She was so confused. No, she wasn't. Ducas was home. And Gaetana had paired with Sir Eustace. How could there be anything confusing about two cataclysmic events in one night that could change everything.

She was so cold . . . and Gaetana was taking forever to make her way home. She didn't even know what she would say to her when she came in.

Yes, Mother, I know all about Sir Eustace, and by the

way, Ducas is home, so you cannot have another liaison with his father.

Oh, yes, her mother would be completely amenable to that.

How could Lady Sangbourne have permitted such a thing?

She hated adults and their forbidden seductions. She hated men and the games they played.

Oh, but Ducas—Ducas . . . she didn't hate him . . . even if Gaetana did. Mustn't forget that. Gaetana had never liked Ducas or his blatant pursuit of Angene.

And now he's home . . . and as soon as he can, he'll come to me—

"Angene . . . ?" Her mother's voice, sharp as a needle, lancing into her thoughts. "What are you doing here?" She stood at the door of the parlor, her shawl draped over her head, and an expression of pure fury on her beautiful face.

She struggled to sit up. "Mother." Composure now. Her mother didn't know where she had been or what she had seen. Only, she wasn't sure she could ever look at her mother the same way ever again.

Well, she had to. "Are you just back from the Manor?" she managed to ask.

Gaetana glided into the room with her dancer's walk and rubbed her hands over the fire. "Just, blast them all to hell. Oh, yes, I'm back from the Manor, from where I was summarily dismissed like a servant while the other *welcome* guests are settling down for a nice hot breakfast. Yes, I'm back, the paid entertainment who was paid and sent away. The gypsy at the back door is good enough for the bed but not for the table, and so she is back in her own house, through the *front* door, blast them all to hell . . ."

She was shaking with anger, her blood pounding through her veins, fierce with the need for retaliation. "Never again. Never, ever again . . . Curse that bitch Veleka. Curse Sir Eustace. Curse their blasted blood born son and may his memory never return . . ."

"What?" Angene leaped off the couch. *"What?"*

"Listen, you." Gaetana turned to face her. "Something's happened."

Confessions now, from her notoriously closemouthed mother?

"Ducas is back."

She had to react; her mother didn't know that she knew, and she had to feign joy, shock, surprise—whatever seemed natural at such a stone-hard announcement of her dearest desire.

Gaetana held up her hand. "Contain your joy. He's lost his memory, praise heaven, he has suffered the revenge of the righteous. Apparently he was wounded and unconscious for some months, and they finally sent him home. I curse them all, and I rejoice in his misfortune: he doesn't remember *anything* . . . and bless the merciful saints, he won't remember you."

Breakfast was fraught with tension and long emotional silences, all of it made worse because of their visiting friends who were uneasy and uncomfortable with the whole situation. Conversation was difficult, if nonexistent, and the burden of making everything seem as normal as possible fell on Veleka, who was teeming with frustration.

Dar watched her covertly, her nervy hands, her fierce eyes, her forced good manners as she explained the circumstances of Ducas's return even as he sat there with an austere expression on his face.

He almost felt sorry for her. He almost wished he didn't know what he knew about Ducas and that he hadn't had to take over Ducas's life. War was hell, and Veleka would be a casualty and Ducas would have to die again.

"Madam?" Holmby was at the door of the dining room, looking grave.

"Yes?" Her answer was too terse and high-pitched.

"The constable."

Everyone looked up, a little nonplussed. Veleka looked

around at them and then at Sir Eustace, who shrugged. "Tell him to go away. No. Tell him to come in."

Croyd appeared a moment later, looking abashed. *A typical country constable*, Dar thought, *decent, reliable, and fully aware of his station.*

"So sorry, mum. I wasn't aware you were to breakfast."

"What is it?"

"Another killing, mum—Sir Eustace—one of your tenants' sheep this time."

Veleka took a deep breath. "You disrupted breakfast to tell us about the death of an animal?"

"Yes, mum. In the same way as the others. You know."

"I don't know," Veleka snapped. "Eustace, really . . . the last time it was a cow, for heaven's sake."

"Exactly so, mum. Drained, you know. The same kind of thing."

"Thank you," Veleka said through clenched teeth. "We'll have someone take care of it."

"With precautions," Croyd reminded her.

"If we must," Veleka muttered. "Holmby, show him out."

"What was that about?" Lord Lanthwaite asked languidly as he reached for yet another scone.

"The man has nothing else to do in this very small village but look for superstitious nonsense relating to the deaths of some chickens, or cattle and sheep over the past year or so in and around Cheshamshire," Veleka snapped. "Have I the right of it, Eustace? They seem to die of bloodletting, or something like that, and for some reason, Croyd has made it his crusade to discover if there is some human hand behind the deaths. It's probably some lunatic village farmhands, or a wolf roaming the hills. Someone should hunt it and kill it, for God's sake, and let us have done with his insistent visits. That man does annoy me, for the few calls he has made on that account. I apologize to you for all these unintentional disruptions."

"No, we should apologize to you for not leaving you to your reunion with your son," Lady Worsley said comfortingly from across the table. She looked at the other guests: her husband, and the Lanthwaites, and Tuttingtons, who were wallowing in the spectacle of Veleka losing control.

They shouldn't have stayed, even this long, in light of Ducas's return, but how delicious to witness all this emotion and anguish when Veleka was always the soul of sangfroid.

"We'll make ready to leave by tomorrow's train," Lady Worsley said. "If only we'd known sooner . . ."

How good of them to even notice, Veleka thought acrimoniously. She felt crowded, overrun, virtually unable to do anything for Ducas while all these *people* were here. While Croyd continued to pester her. While that Alton person had the run of her home.

Dar watched her, wondering about her guests, all of whom seemed to be just a little too conciliating, and reveling in her discomfort over this strange visit from Croyd just a little too much.

"Ducas, my dear—" She leaned across the table to him. "Nothing is familiar yet, is it?"

"No."

"I can't bear this," she murmured, looking around at her guests who were relishing this come-to-life penny dreadful enormously. The hell with them. She didn't care who was listening at that point. "It is my son and yet it isn't. It's like a ghost—you see it, but it has no substance. You reach out to touch it and there's nothing there."

"A ghost?" Dar said, mimicking her and looking around as if he expected to see one at the table. The guests leaned forward eagerly but Veleka was focused on him, solely on him. It was as if the guests weren't there, and Croyd had never come.

"No. No, my dear. Just a passing thought. This is your home. No matter what, here you'll stay, and here you will remember."

He shook his head. "I remember nothing. You could tell me anything."

"I'll tell you stories about your youth, my sweet, and all the good times we had. They will sound like fairy tales, but they're all true. You were the prince of our family. You made things possible. You were clever and inventive, and made everything in life bearable."

"Me." He said it in a flat expressionless tone.

"You," Veleka said. "So you must remember so that we can go on."

"I don't remember you," he said, his tone listless and slack.

"Oh!" She couldn't stand it. She was so easily frustrated. And now their friends knew, and Croyd was sniffing around, and she could do nothing for Ducas, and she felt like her world was falling away. She didn't care who was watching; she wanted this fixed, *now*. "Where is that Alton? Alton! *Alton!*"

Alton came running. "Mum?"

"He's impossible. Talk to him. *Make* him remember."

"You must have more patience, mum. It will take longer than a day."

"I don't have that time," Veleka said stormily. "I hate this."

"As we all do, mum."

"You were with him. He knows you. He can know other things. We just need to—jostle his memory."

"Well, we've barely begun, mum. We need to talk to him, to take him around, to show him photographs and family objects . . ."

"Yes, yes, of course—all of that . . . except, what is the point, when he seems to have lost all comprehension besides."

"Oh, no, mum."

"He used to ride," Veleka said abruptly. "Does he ride?"

"I should think he would still ride, mum."

"Take him out then and see if he rides. See if there is something left of my son to work with."

"As you wish, mum. Mr. Ducas?"

"Who are you?" Dar asked.

"I'm Alton, of course," Alton said patiently. "We traveled here to Cheshamshire together."

"Oh," Dar said. "That's right."

"We'll go for a little ride, my lord. It will clear your head, perhaps make things clearer for you."

"Do I ride?"

Veleka made a sound.

"I believe you do, my lord."

"Whose lord?"

"Mr. Ducas—"

Dar looked around him. "There's a ghost. That one—" he pointed his finger at Veleka, "—she said there's a ghost."

"I—" Veleka started to say and then broke off. "Take him to the stables, Alton. See if there's any little piece of my son still there."

She had never seen her mother like this. In all her years growing up in this elegant well-appointed house, she had never seen her mother in such a frenzy.

Blood will tell. Gaetana had tried so hard to fit into village life, she had never caused any gossip. Anyone who knew her would have taken her for the widow of a nobleman, so well did she comport herself.

She had been discreet and demure. And so the one time she had allowed her blood to rule her head, she had lowered herself to this, and all her devotion to Sir Eustace meant nothing. Only the titled were privileged to share their bodies and breakfast—the gypsy could only share Sir Eustace's bed.

So be it. She would deny her heritage no longer. She would release the demons and let the fire and ferocity burn everything in its path.

She sat in the living room, a shawl over her head, before a small altar filled with candles, murmuring incantations, looking up only when Angene entered the room.

"Stay away from that man." Her tone was dire and Angene cringed. Gaetana knew even before she did what she was going to do.

"I don't believe it; I don't believe Ducas is so far gone that he remembers nothing."

"He is that far gone," Gaetana said flatly. Ducas was a devil, in any event, dangerous, thoughtless, reckless. A man who exercised his *droit du seignor* like the conqueror he was.

And Angene had never been immune to him, despite all of Gaetana's warnings. Gaetana knew about that kind of man and what they did with women in the shadows, and she was certain Angene had done it all with Ducas before he decamped.

Which made it all the more difficult to keep her from him. She had no words to dissuade her willful daughter.

God, the passions of a woman—even she was not immune: only for her the consequences had come painfully clear. She had been put firmly in her place, and she wouldn't ever let them forget.

"Don't go to him, Angene. He won't know you."

"You can't be sure."

"I am certain."

"I am certain he'll know me," Angene said.

"It doesn't sound as if he is playing games, my girl. This is a problem involving the family and no one else."

"I don't care."

"I didn't think you would," Gaetana said, her voice laced with disgust. She had no words, no words at all to stop this folly. Just candles and curses. Paltry weapons at best. "And when he pushes you away, then what?"

"He won't."

"You can't know that."

"I will find out then."

"Stubborn girl."

"Like you?" Angene asked archly. "When Wentmore was in pursuit?"

"But Ducas cannot pursue anyone anymore. If anything, he will run the other way—and then what will you do?"

"Follow him," Angene said with all the confidence of youth. I'll be his mistress, just like you. . . ."

Finally, the lord and lady guests had no course but to excuse themselves and Veleka directed Alton to the back entrance which gave onto the gardens, and the track to the stables.

It was an overcast day, with clouds scudding across the sky, and the curious prescient silence that preceded a storm.

A little like Veleka's mood, Dar thought.

She was watching; he was as certain of that as he was of his name, watching as the groom came out of the stable with two of the gentlest horses, watching as he made a show of clumsily mounting his horse, missing the stirrup, sliding off the horse's rump, watching until Alton finally got him mounted and holding the reins in his hands.

"Not much advantage to continuing on like an imbecile, sir," Alton murmured.

"No, I think I'd better *remember* or I'll be imprisoned in that house."

"Good point, sir. Well, they do say there are activities that become second nature, even if you haven't done them in many years."

"Your muscles remember, you mean? Yes, well . . . so mine will, then. Ducas will not have forgotten how to ride. Veleka wouldn't let him in any event. She's as ferocious as a bear, that woman. She's so aware of every little detail about everything and everyone. We have to tread carefully around her. This is not a quick strike mission, but we must move as quickly as we can."

"Yes, sir. You should straighten up now."

Dar heaved himself slightly to one side. They walked the

horses toward the front of the house. Veleka was watching. He felt her gaze, avid and hot. She was following their progress room to room. Praying? Hoping? Nothing escaped Veleka. He felt a telltale prickling at the thought.

"She's watching you very closely from the house, sir," Alton said.

"I know."

"Well, then we'll keep going. Mr. Ducas will get it right this time." They walked the horses farther down the drive, to where they could take the long view of the house that they hadn't seen from the carriage when they drove up this morning.

It was a beautiful antique three-story building cast in white stone with wooden casements, dormers on the third floor, and set low to the ground. There were two wings on either side, spread like enfolding arms around to the rear of the house where they had exited to the terrace garden and the path to the stables.

This was the elegant home to which Ducas ought to have returned: filled with servants and good company, hunting and balls, and a proper marriage and proud parents. A world away from the filth and death of the trenches, and his covert descent into the underworld of secrets, lies, and traitors.

How could Ducas have abandoned all this? And for what?

Still, Dar had to play it out, give himself time to go through the motions of looking as if he were trying to jar his memory. Thank heaven, Veleka was so impatient. He had no idea how much time he had, or when she would start to notice the differences.

He didn't think she would be fooled for long.

He was almost certain she was watching him, so he acted as if he were still getting used to being in the saddle, but this time, he sat straight, correcting his hesitancies, taking it slow slow slow as they guided the horses down the drive toward the stables, and pulled up just before they reached the paddock.

"You did that very well, sir," Alton said. "Perhaps you could ride out yourself some morning and take a look around."

"Do you really think Veleka would let Ducas out of her sight for a moment let alone a half hour? She'd probably follow me."

"Aye, she probably would. Nonetheless, sir . . . we need to do something more today, and sooner than later."

"I think so, too. I think *you* should go in now while everyone's occupied and take another look in Ducas's room while I take this old girl for a trot around the paddock and pretend I'm still finding my seat."

"As you wish, sir." Alton headed into the stable and Dar veered his mount through the fence, and nudged him into a trot.

It suddenly occurred to him that it was the first time he'd been alone since he'd laid eyes on the dying Ducas Sangbourne in the hospital tent all those weeks ago.

It was a strange thought. Everything for this mission had been prepared well before the fact, as was to be expected. But all this time, from the moment he'd agreed to come to Sangbourne Manor, he had not been alone. Alton had been at the ready and waiting for the colonel's command and had been at his side ever since. Because the colonel had known Dar wouldn't say no . . . ?

The colonel knew him so well.

But he could not have known what Dar would find at Sangbourne Manor: the way Sir Eustace mercifully detached himself; the intensity of Veleka, and the way she was drawn to and repulsed by Ducas's impairment.

That worked to his advantage now; but his illness would only explain some of the differences between him and Ducas. Veleka *would* figure it out, and he had to work faster than that to discover the secrets of Sangbourne Manor.

Where to start was the question. What could explain why a man turned, without conscience, to murder and betrayal of his country? Turned from *this*—this heritage, these parents, this life. He'd never understand that as long as he lived: he would have killed for such a patrimony.

He heard the low rumble of thunder and he pulled the horse around and pointed her back to the stables. A simple ride, stretch the horse's legs after getting acquainted with the surroundings near the house . . . all of that—was Veleka watching and comprehending the story he was enacting for her?

The stable boy was nowhere around. Everything suddenly was dead silent, the air thick with the coming storm. He dismounted and went into the barn. It was unexpectedly warm in there, from the heat of a small, efficient potbellied stove. But no one was there. No one.

A flash of white, around the hayloft columns. A crack of thunder suddenly in the distance.

"Ducas!" The voice was musical, compelling, seductive. Behind him.

He whirled. "Jesus God—who's there?"

"Ducas—" A voice pining for lost love, a flurry of skirts just by the tack room. Lightning crackled.

He leaped toward the tack room. "Who are you?"

"You must remember . . ."

"I don't know who you are." He felt like a blind man, groping, feeling, missing everything. It was like talking to a ghost. He felt the dread of someone caught in a trap.

There was always a woman; why hadn't he realized Ducas would have one too. A seductive-sounding woman. Something unexpected to get in the way. Something unforeseen to trip him up.

"Who are you?" he asked resignedly. The rain started. Thunder rolled.

He could just see her in the dim light; she was beautiful, as any woman involved with Ducas would have to be. Well bred? Hard to tell, with her sinuous body draped in a translucent gauzy white. Someone who didn't have Sir Eustace's or Veleka's seal of approval? A likely guess.

"Oh, God," she whispered. "It's true. You don't remember?"

"I don't remember," Dar said brutally. He didn't need a woman complicating things, he didn't.

"Ducas . . ." There was such yearning in her voice.

Too easy to let that silky voice turn all his intentions to mush. "I *don't* remember, so I'd appreciate it if you would just tell me who you are."

"I can help you remember," she murmured.

"Maybe I'd appreciate that," he said warily, pacing closer toward her. She noticed. "But not right now. Who *are* you?"

Angene cocked her head and stared at him in the lowering light. She'd had to come; how could she not come? She hadn't believed Gaetana. And she wasn't prepared for for the fact that he was a stranger and yet he was exactly the same. That he wouldn't know her and yet, he had known her so well.

Nothing about him had changed, except that. The dark hair, the world-weary features, the beautiful mouth, the long lean body, so tall, so proud and erect, this was her Ducas, the man who had done everything but make love to her in the hayloft of this very place, the man on whose honeyed promises she had lived.

And there was nothing. Just the blank look of wariness out of those sharp intelligent eyes that she had loved so well.

This was a moment, she thought. Who was she? Such an apt question. She could tell him anything, she could tell him the truth. But if he didn't remember, she could tell him the lie, she could make her one powerful desire a reality.

And with that, she could be the very thing she had always wanted to be, and no one could disprove it, ever. And maybe, in the throes of Ducas's recovering his memory, he would make it happen in reality.

At best, she had little to risk and nothing to lose. And she had already learned that the less she revealed, the more intriguing she became to Ducas, and she saw it was no less so with this stranger whom Ducas had become.

"Tell me who you are." His voice was gentler now he was even closer to her. She really was quite beautiful.

She backed away still farther, almost to the stable doors, as thunder suddenly rolled and the rain came pouring down.

Lightning cracked again, limning her in eerie shadow.

"I wish you remembered," she whispered regretfully as she edged out the door. "I'm Angene. I'm your mistress." And she vanished like a ghost into the rain.

Chapter 3

The house was unnaturally quiet when Alton slipped in through the front door to avoid Veleka. It was getting toward one o'clock when everyone would come together again for the midday meal, and there was so little time to accomplish anything. But Dar was right: they had make use of every minute they could steal, whichever one of them was free.

He just had to not get caught. Thank God, everyone was occupied elsewhere, and Veleka was still distracted watching Dar from the library window. But the coming storm would put paid to that very soon.

Still, it was creepy slipping into Ducas's room alone. Deadly dark. No curtain drawn to let in what little daylight there was. No idea in his mind where he could search that Dar hadn't thought of.

And always, like a treacherous undertow, he felt a super-sensitive awareness of Veleka, stalking through her house, gauging every change in the atmosphere, and wanting to know where everyone was.

What could he discover in these opulent surroundings

that Dar might have missed in his quick but thorough examination of the room?

Secret hiding places, perhaps. Decorations that might conceal compartments. Things that unscrewed—like the heads of walking sticks, sometimes, that concealed weapons or a place to roll up and hide secret messages.

No, that kind of thinking was too over the moon, even for him. This wasn't a Sherlock Holmes story. The aristocracy didn't stoop to low-grade espionage tactics, for God's sake. Or the tricks of fiction writers. Ducas Sangbourne would have been cleverer than that.

If he were hiding something. And by God—why would a man rampantly murder a wagon house full of wounded British soldiers? And, if he were capable of that, how many more murders might he have committed over time . . . and was he involved in a consipracy to decimate the ranks of the army in the field together?

A man like that would leave nothing to chance. Nothing to his personal world that would point to his secret life.

Lord in heaven, where to even begin? Tap the walls, look for false bottoms, turn knobs, drawer pulls, tug on wall sconces, maybe there was a secret room somewhere? Test the footboard. Pull the bedposts. Maybe they unscrewed?

He tried the left footboard post, and was wholly shocked when he managed to twist it. His heart started pounding. He grasped the second post and unscrewed it.

A creaking sound. The mattress levering itself up, up, up on some kind of hidden mechanism. Not clear just what was underneath. Too dark to see and no time to look either; he'd made a discovery, he didn't know what it was, and he had to get out of there at the instant.

"Alton!!!!"

Too late. He knew that voice.

He whirled. No explanations possible. Nobody was asking either.

He didn't even know what he had seen—and then, in the blink of an eye, he saw nothing. . . .

* * *

He thought he imagined her. She was too perfect, too unreal. Like an apparition in the isolation, the intimacy of the rain. And no witnesses to the fact she had even been there.

Every sense prickling. The everlasting ceaseless prickling.

His mistress—no, Ducas's mistress . . . Should he even believe it?

Hell, what else could go wrong? Whoever she was, she wasn't someone to stay in the shadows. She was someone who was going to dog his heels, waiting for that mystery moment of remembrance when she could fully embrace him . . .

"So you rode—just a little bit," Veleka said over the crashing thunder as the guest assembled for lunch *en buffet*.

"They say that kind of thing comes back to you; that it's a different kind of memory," Dar said. "At least that's what Alton told me."

"Ah, Alton," Veleka murmured. "I hope you don't mind I sent him on an errand."

He shrugged.

It was odd, certainly, but just what Veleka might do. She hadn't at all liked having Alton to breakfast this morning, a man not of her class. And she'd want a graceful reason for him not to be at the table. And he, having no memory and no real connection to Alton, ought not even care.

"And nothing else is familiar?" she pressed him.

"Not yet." He didn't know what she wanted to hear. It was easier to say nothing, and Veleka seemed to expect it, seemed to be coming to grips with the idea that Ducas didn't have to be fully aware of his previous life at Sangbourne Manor to function.

"He rode," Veleka said to Sir Eustace and her guests as they all came to the table. "That's something. He even looked like himself on horseback. At least, after he got his seat. I could almost believe—" She shook herself. "Ah, well. It's something."

Silence fell, grew heavy with portent. Rain poured. Lightning flashed.

Veleka pushed her food around, slanting glances every now and again at Dar, as if she were expecting him to say something, or do something, while her guests stared at each other and her, and wondered what they should say. Or if they should do anything.

After an hour of this, she stood up abruptly. "You'll have to excuse me."

"My dear," Sir Eustace murmured, reaching out a detaining hand.

Veleka looked at Dar, who raised an eyebrow but otherwise said nothing. "No, I have to . . . You will excuse me?"

Sir Eustace nodded and Veleka swirled out of the room like green lightning. Sir Eustace looked at the guests. "She's like that sometimes. She's very sensitive, very upset over Ducas's situation, you know."

Lady Worsley said, "We know . . . it's awkward for all of us." And she was loving every minute of it. But that wasn't for Sir Eustace to comprehend, poor dear. Veleka had always been difficult.

"Not much to be done about it," Sir Eustace said, shaking his head. "A good cigar and a glass of port dulls the expectation, but then what? Tomorrow always comes, and nothing changes."

Dar got up and wandered to the window. What to say now that didn't sound too false, or reveal how much he knew? He pulled back the curtain and looked out into the curtain of rain.

What would Ducas say? "I wish it were different, sir."

"So does she, my boy. So does she." Sir Eustace pulled a bell and a maid came running. "Take it all away, please. Bring me my port." He looked around at the men. "Anyone care to join me?"

Mid-afternoon though it was, Lanthwaite and Worsley said yes, and Tuttington muttered, "I'll keep company, but this is excessively early for my taste. I'll take tea."

"Don't be a crapehanger, my boy. How can we get buzzed with you perched there like a tiger with your tea?"

"Well, there isn't much else for anyone to do in any event," Lady Lanthwaite fretted. "Blasted rain. I think we'll just get our needlework and join you."

"We should've taken the first train out this morning," Tuttington said. "Bloody weather. Next one left already and now we have to wait till tomorrow . . ."

"Bring the port, bring the tea, bring the embroidery hoops," Sir Eustace cried. "By God, it's a party, even if Veleka isn't here to supervise."

Dar hardly heard him. Port and propriety in the afternoon didn't interest him. The rain was coming down in torrents. He wondered where Veleka had gone. And then, almost as if in answer, there was a movement below, a shadow easing away from the house, cloaked in black, head to foot.

Was he seeing it because he expected to see it? And if it was Veleka. . . ? Where would *she* be going in such a rainstorm?

Hell. "Sir—if you don't mind—"

Sir Eustace held up his port. "No mind, Son."

God, he was gone already, a regular ritual by the look of it. Good.

He could just slip out . . .

"Ducas dear—" The poisonous Lady Worsley. "Where ever could you be off to?"

Shit. And if it was Veleka? He had to know, he had to *know.*

"My lady?" So polite—he wanted to strangle her.

"Are you going somewhere?"

"To my room," he said flatly. "To wait for Alton. Tell . . . Lady Veleka I'll be in my room. For when Alton comes."

Lady Worsley looked uncertain for a moment. Ought she detain him, or let him go? A judgment call at best. Veleka wouldn't want an iota of interference in any event. He was probably just going to have a nap. He looked like he needed one. And God knew there was nothing else to do in this beastly boring house if you weren't playing sex games.

"I'll tell her," she said, waving him away.

Dar heaved a breath, and slipped out of the dining room, and down toward the kitchen and the back entrance to the house.

There were servants everywhere; he flattened himself against walls and moved in the shadows while they silently worked all around him. Through the kitchen, then, as they attended to the cleaning up of the afternoon meal, and into the vegetable garden, now soaking in the rain.

No light anywhere, just the teeming downpour, and the intermittent crack of lightning to show him the way. As he reached the paddock gates, he heard the high-pitched whinny of a reluctant horse as it fought its fear and sought to get away from the thunder and the rain. And then suddenly the thunderous clatter of its hooves as it was driven out into the dark pouring night.

Dar bolted for the horse. The rider's crop came down viciously on his arm, and his face, he slipped in the treacherous mud, and the horse tore off into the wind.

He couldn't move, and lightning danced all around him, and the storm water soaked into his soul, liquefying his bones into the ground, and a long time later, through a distant, darkling haze, as he finally lifted himself from the oozing muck, he heard the distant howl of a wolf.

And then, Alton. Alton hadn't yet returned. Damn it to hell, where was Alton? If ever he needed a buffer between him and Veleka, it was now: he'd had to resort to sneaking into the house, drenched as he was, past those noxious guardians at the gate who had kept Sir Eustace in cups all afternoon.

The damned library doors were ajar too, and they were all six sheets and seven flags over into their snifters.

Thank God, the women had gone upstairs by then; their husbands were so inebriated they would not have known if the Queen herself were coming down the hall.

But Alton . . . on this mysterious errand, and hadn't yet

returned. It was a damned long time to be gone with dinner imminent and still more bridges to cross.

So he was on his own for the moment with all the decisions about whether to appropriate Ducas's clothes to dress for dinner or just plead a headache and keep to his room. So ill-considered to have gone out in that infernal downpour. Now he'd also have to explain the change of clothes. And the welt on his cheek.

And he couldn't even talk it over with Alton.

Damnation. He hadn't appreciated the colonel's choice of Alton nearly enough. The man was a treasure. And Dar St. Onge was a cipher, trying to walk in another man's expensive handmade shoes—and they didn't fit. He didn't fit, and he had been the wrong man for the job from the beginning.

The hell with it. There was a simple explanation. Alton would return soon. He was just waiting out the storm somewhere. The red mark didn't look all that gruesome actually.

And as he expected, Ducas's clothes fit him perfectly. Too perfectly. Tailored to his outer skin. As if they were made for him. For the man he could have been. The man he wished he were.

Veleka presided over the dinner table like a queen. Everything formal, everything beautiful: lace, silver, china, cut flowers, dazzling lights, butler in full formal regalia, the ladies dressed to the teeth and the gentlemen in tuxedos.

Oh, yes, she meant to make it seem as if everything was the way it always had been.

She herself was dressed again in green, watered green silk shot with gold and edged with velvet. Her hair hung long, bundled away from her face, and her sharp gaze didn't miss the instant Dar stepped into the hallway.

She came immediately to greet him. "Don't you look charming. You dressed, I see."

He had the lie all ready on the tip of his tongue. "Alton laid out the clothes for me this morning."

"How thoughtful of him," she murmured. "Well, come. You've seen that Alton has not yet returned from the village. But the rain is so incessant, he's probably decided to spend the night at the inn."

Not likely, Dar thought grimly, so now what? He didn't know what to think. He felt as if he were walking into a den of wolves.

He allowed her to lead him to the dining room where the other guests were already seated, all equally decked out in formal attire.

"So here is Ducas," Veleka said lightly, drawing him to the table, and seating him next to her. "And now we can begin." She clapped her hands and Holmby began the service of the soup.

They talked all around him, but there wasn't a moment that Veleka's gaze was not on him, that unrelenting inexorable gaze that searched and sought for some indication that he remembered who he was.

"Ruddy day," Sir Eustace muttered. "Good for nothing but port in the library and a dozen games of chess. Tuttington was the spoiler, but I beat him at that, didn't I, old chum?"

"Oh you were the games keeper today all right," Tuttington said. He lifted his wine goblet. "A toast to Sir Eustace's prowess at that, at least."

"Hear hear." Everyone toasted and sipped, except Dar, who put a confused look on his face.

"Boring in the country, sometimes. Don't know how you stand it," Worsley said.

"I wouldn't," Sir Eustace said, "but Veleka likes it, and there are *some* compensations."

"We won't discuss that," Veleka said. "Pass the salt?"

"She was damned good," Sir Eustace murmured.

"We don't discuss that," she said again, with steel in her voice.

"Well, at least I sent her home before breakfast; give me some credit for that," Sir Eustace protested.

"A mercy that you did," Veleka said. "I would have killed her."

They all looked startled, and then smiled nervously. She hadn't meant it, of course. It was a joke. But Dar looked into her eyes and he knew—she meant it.

And so they ate, and Dar ate with them, watching with fascination the interplay between Sir Eustace and Veleka, and their guests.

There had been other sport here besides hunting, just as he had surmised. The way they all looked at each other. And the euphemistic conversation. They were all lovers, interchangeable, intermingling, and as frequently as they could manage to get away for a country weekend.

And Veleka was the ringleader. The procuress.

That conclusion must have been reflected in his expression, because Veleka leaned toward him and said, "Don't worry, my sweet. Everything will be as it was, and you will partake as you used to."

His expression went vacant. "I don't understand what you mean."

"I think you do. In some deep part of yourself, I think you do."

Again, she searched his eyes with that intensive needful gaze, looking for something, something very specific, almost willing him to comprehend what it was she was seeking.

He stiffened his expression. She moved away, and motioned to Holmby, stood up and spoke a few words to him, and sat down again, as two maids began removing the first course.

"Mutton tonight," she said. "Cook does a particularly good mutton. And those potatoes *duchesse,* a particular favorite of Sir Eustace. And Ducas, I might add."

"I don't remember," he said, "but the soup was delicious."

"Another small mercy," Veleka murmured. "He still has his appetite."

But she didn't, Dar noticed. She had sipped a little of the soup now and again, and now, after a nice cut of the meat was put on her plate, she sliced off a small sliver and ate it, and another, and a small forkful of the potatoes, all the while directing the conversation so no one noticed whether she was eating or not.

Everyone else had heaped their plates and were devouring the meal with gusto, including Sir Eustace. And himself. He was damned hungry and feeling not a little like Veleka would make him the meal if he made just one small mistake.

There was a lot of food. The mutton was served additionally with vegetable pie, and green beans *a la Lyonnaise,* and removed by a fish course, with side dishes of sweetbreads, cucumbers, and broccoli.

Too much food for the likes of him, so used to meager army rations. He felt like the meal would go on forever. Veleka seemed edgy, but he thought it was only he who noticed.

She slanted a look at him, and he felt that telltale prickling. He blanked out his expression, shoving back hard on every inclination to look at *her.*

She was too sharp, and it was so obvious she orchestrated everything that went on in the house. She missed nothing, and she had adored Ducas beyond all reason. He felt the envy of that down to his bones even as he tried to evade her disquieting gaze. There were things ingrained in a man who had been raised a spoiled child of privilege that became part of his nature, and he wondered how many of those small subtle inherent things he had miscalculated, even in the course of this first day.

He felt intensely uncomfortable with her watching him like that. And weary. All these conflicting emotions. Not what he had expected to feel. Made him uncertain, tentative, not a good stance when you were infiltrating enemy territory.

Walking in Ducas's shoes was a suicide mission on every level. He felt like a ghost, like an out of focus photograph, not quite Ducas, not quite himself, and that the differences could easily become blurred and merge.

Was that what he wanted, really?

"Ducas, my dear—that mark on your cheek—" Veleka again.

"It's nothing—I took a nap with my arm under it." Lies and lies again. As if rumpled wool would cause that kind of bruise.

Nevertheless, she accepted the explanation and went on to another topic. Everything seemed to move in slow motion suddenly as the servants removed the plates and began setting up the dessert course.

Urns were brought in, tea at one end of the table, coffee at the other. Dishes of coffee cream, almond biscuits, blancmange, and meringues were set at intervals along the table. Next, a tray full of fruit tarts and pies, and an ornamental cake which was centered on the table in front of Dar.

"A little celebratory sweet for your return," Veleka murmured.

He said nothing. Her face clouded over again, and she looked at him, hard. The prickling intensified.

A servant over his shoulder. "Coffee, sir, or tea?"

Another unforeseen trap. What *had* been Ducas's preference? Were a man's habits that deep-rooted that even amnesia couldn't wipe them away?

God, he didn't know. A choice had to be made, and he didn't know what to do. He stared the servant until Veleka became exasperated, and snapped, "Coffee for Mr. Ducas."

He looked at her. She stared at him. The servant poured the cup and brought it around to Dar, and bent to serve it over his left shoulder. Just at that moment, Veleka rose up from the table, nudging into the servant's hand.

He couldn't save the cup: it went crashing to the table, spilling and spattering coffee all over Dar, scalding him.

Veleka was at him in the instant with a napkin, murmuring apologies, wiping him all over. He was soaked down the front of his shirt, and the lapels of his dinner jacket.

"I don't know how that happened, I am so so clumsy, Ducas, dear, so sorry." She didn't pause for breath. "Forgive me, I just wasn't looking at where Joseph was . . . and—"

Yes, yes . . . Now what? Damn it, now he didn't know quite what to do next.

Veleka took charge. "We'll remove to the library, everyone. The servants will bring everything in there. Ducas, do go change and join us afterward."

He didn't want to. He needed time to think and plan his moves, and it took every ounce of concentration to respond the way Ducas might, and not as himself.

"I would just like to excuse myself for tonight, if you don't mind," he said finally. "I have no need of dessert."

Again, that deep assessing look that he met with a calm blank stare, and every sense jangling. She looked as if she were about to protest, as if she would come to his room with him and make sure that he changed and rejoined them after.

The feeling was so intense, his every nerve ending quivered. And then the tension eased. She had made a decision.

"Whatever you wish, my dear," she said graciously, edgily. She patted his arm. "Sleep well. We'll see you in the morning."

Oh, dear heaven, Ducas . . . ! He hadn't recognized her, and yet everything about him was the same except—except—he didn't know her.

Angene sat tightly on the edge of his bed, watching the firelight. A fool's errand coming here this night, sneaking in the way she used to, after their encounter in the stables. There was nothing to be gained here. He didn't remember her. Gaetana was right, and she was a fool.

She sat listening to the thunder and the rain, fool that she was, aware that any moment he could come into the room, and everything could change again.

But that had always been the challenge, the only way to deal with a man like Ducas. Never give too much. Always be willing to walk away.

But if a man didn't remember, then what?

You tell him a lie and hope it comes true. . . .

By the saints, what had she done? She had done the one thing Gaetana had never wanted her to do: she had reacted with her heart and not her head. About what she wanted, what was there, and pushing away the reality in favor of the dream. Always the blood, pounding in her soul, demanding her surrender.

And so I sneak into a man's bedroom while my mother rains curses on his head . . . ?

The door opened—her heart jumped, she leaped off the bed and slipped behind the curtain closest to the bed, not ready to confront him yet, a flash of white like a ghost, like a memory.

Ducas . . . striding into the room, tearing off his jacket, his tie, his shirt and tossing them on the bed.

Pacing the room, running his hands through his hair, bedeviled, beguiling, beloved . . .

The firelight playing on his naked back and chest. Everything the same, everything—the hard thick muscles of his arms, the broad shoulders, the childhood scar that looked like a row of three x's just by his heart that was almost obscured by the wiry hair on his chest.

And, oh, she loved those lean hips, and those strong hands, and his insistent mouth; there wasn't anything about him that she didn't yearn for. Still.

How could he not remember her?

She peered out from behind the curtain. The firelight cast shadows all over the room. Ducas stood by the fireplace staring into the flames, a shirt draped over his shoulders.

The door was ajar, and light from the hallway played across the threshold.

And shadows. Movement. Holmby coming to take Mr. Ducas's stained shirt and jacket. Ducas, throwing himself into the chair next to the fireplace. More shadows creeping outside the door, pausing, hovering.

And now she was a shadow—trapped behind the curtain and beyond her dream.

This was what being in limbo was like. Pure nothingness. Worse than the dark and empty night.

No. No—that would never be her fate, never, even if she had to take it into her own hands. All she had to do was move, make real the shadow behind the curtain and see what Ducas would do.

Fate and blood, pounding in her heart, goading her, pushing her . . . how could she not respond . . . ? She slipped out from the behind the curtain and just in his line of sight.

"You . . . !" He jumped out of his chair. "Good God— What the hell are you doing here?"

Not exactly what she expected to hear.

The light was so dim, she couldn't see his expression clearly as he came toward her, but his voice reflected his exasperation. And something else. He was not happy to see her there.

He grabbed her arms. "Where were you this afternoon?"

God, it felt so good to have him touch her. He was so strong, he could overpower her And there was a part of her that wanted it, because it meant his capitulation to her.

But this wasn't lust. He wasn't thinking one thought about her as a woman. He was angry, and the question had a purpose, and she'd be even more of a fool to pretend it didn't.

"I've been . . . around. Why?"

"Around, where? Not outside. . . ?"

"In this storm?"

"Where did you go, after you disappeared from the stable?"

"That's *my* secret, Ducas."

"You didn't take one of the horses out into the storm?"

She sent him a skeptical look. "I haven't left the grounds. But that's all I'll tell you. So," she wriggled against his confining hands, "now that you have me here, why don't you kiss me?"

He stared at her as if she had lost her mind, then he thrust her away and strode to the fireplace. Welcome heat. Not much comfort.

A crazy woman in his bedroom.

His mistress. No, *Ducas's* mistress, but it had not been she racing out into the rain. Alton, perhaps—but he was gone by then, if Veleka were to be believed. And all the guests were accounted for in the library.

So it had been Veleka. But why—?

Angene kept looking at him expectantly. Something about a kiss . . . ?

"I don't think so," he said absently. "I still don't know who you are."

She hated hearing that, hated it, hated him. He was not paying the least attention to her. Which wasn't according to her plan. She leaned seductively against the bedpost. "I'll remind you."

He wheeled on her. "Look, it's too soon for any of this. Whatever you were to . . . me, I don't remember, and I have no good reason get up the enthusiasm you want merely because you say so."

"Come, Ducas. I've been here with you many times, on that very bed."

He didn't want to know what Ducas might have done with her. She was too tempting, really, so beautiful, and so obviously willing, of course Ducas would have had his way with her. Who *was* she anyway? Not that he had all that much time to delve into that.

"Really," he said dryly. "Don't give me a market list of what we did. I don't remember. I don't *want* to remember."

He didn't have to remember: he could conjure up a dozen

things, two dozen positions . . . he felt as if he were in Ducas's mind, seeing what he saw in this beautiful and wily wanton.

"You will," she said confidently, coming up beside him, and reaching for him. She hadn't really expected to do this. It was the blood. It just coursed and pushed and suddenly she was there, pulling him to her, kissing him, a deep searching kiss that hit them both like dynamite, it was so unexpected, and so explosive.

And then soft, she pulled away from his lips, breathless and soft and they stared at each other, stunned, for a long, long moment, and she just had the presence of mind to push away from him while he was still disoriented.

She had to get out, now, and she didn't know why; there was something about the kiss, so different and yet the same, and she knew she had to get out because it was too intense, too overpowering, too inexplicable, and she wasn't ready.

"You will come for me," she murmured with more confidence than she felt. What was it about that kiss? She moved away like a dancer toward the door.

He collected his wits. "Angene . . ."

But it was a moment too late; she melted into shadows and was gone again.

The thrashing rain gave way to a red-streaked sky that looked almost as if some otherworldly hand were spreading a blanket over the earth.

And silence. Again that still dead silence that was as loud as a thunderclap. And the shadows. Skulking, immutable shadows . . .

Dar awoke again with a jolt, that jangling sensation in his gut, in his consciousness. Awoke to the silence and the blackness of the night and the faintly flame-streaked sky, the shadows, and a shrill eerie whistling through the trees—or was it in the trees?

Something detached from the shadows. He felt a presence in the room. Close. A kind of heat emanating from something . . . a tingling in his hands, as if he should know, should be aware somehow of . . . of what? The whistling, unabated, audible through the closed window. And the presence . . . not a sound in the matte still silence of the room, but something was there, still as the air, a drift of smoke, watching, waiting . . .

He knew it, he felt it, it was as instinctual as breathing that he sensed these things, and this sudden knowledge stunned him.

And the fact that he wasn't afraid.

Yet there was something there, a threat, a promise— something . . . he didn't know what . . . He levered himself up on one arm. His hands still tingled. Don't move. Let the light of dawn illuminate the hovering threat.

It was there, he felt it. Watching, waiting. A shadow just beyond the foot of the bed . . .

A faint rustle as Dar maneuvered himself against the headboard.

What did he know about the night and the darkness? He knew something because he sensed what was there. And that tingling would not go away.

The sky lightened, inch by streaking inch. The darkness diminished and disappeared, and when dawn came, there were no more shadows in the room—just the eerie tingling in the palms of his hands.

It was time. He knew to the minute how much time had passed—and from the way his blood was thrumming and the excitement possessed him—he knew—it was time.

It had been hard lying low even this much, keeping himself sentient, subsuming all his natural impulses to the larger focus.

But that was his purpose. That was his life.

But the time was now; he felt it in his blood. The colonel was finally occupied with other matters, the imposter was on his way to Cheshamshire, damn his soul to hell, everyone's attention was elsewhere, and it was time.

All right, then. So things hadn't quite gone the way he had planned. He'd gotten greedy, careless. The colonel was too involved with his men. And the imposter was something he could never have reckoned on.

Mistakes to be sure, but nobody could blame him. You couldn't foresee those impediments. You couldn't plan for them.

But it was time now to rectify those mistakes, to eliminate the imposter before he got any more in the way, and to bring things back to the way they had been.

He would return to battle in another way, under another name, in another regiment, and no one would be the wiser. Things would go on as they had. Nothing would be lost. Nothing would change.

And there were still those here whom he could depend upon to keep on as they always had.

He was the only one who would be branded a traitor. On his shoulders would rest the burden all the sins of commission.

So be it. That was his life, his function, his reason for being. His was the hand that planned, executed, and accepted responsibility.

And now it was time. He had been maneuvering himself into the perfect position for the two days since the imposter had left Dundee.

The time was now.

He punched his fists through the shroud of the shallow grave and reached for the stars.

And in the morning, Constable Croyd came to Sangbourne Manor to tell them that Alton's body had been found.

Chapter 4

"Yes, my lady. Just like the animals. Drained and dead and not a mark on him."

"Where?" Sir Eustace asked. They were all assembled in the parlor, it was early in the morning, too early for his taste—eight o'clock, an ungodly hour for anyone to be calling, even if it was to announce a death.

The ladies were all white and wide-eyed, the men feeling awkward and not knowing quite how to react, not having known Alton above those few hours the previous day, and Ducas sat in a chair by the window, not a nuance of expression on his face.

By God, that made Sir Eustace angry; the man had taken care of Ducas for hundreds of miles on their trip home. And it was as if Ducas didn't remember even that. But he must, by all that was decent, and he must be shocked to his core, and that was why he seemed so withdrawn and emotionless.

They were all shocked. Veleka looked faint. And no one knew quite what to do.

And Croyd still hadn't answered the question.

"On the farmstead road, my lord, just by the woods that skirt the Manor."

"You don't think—" Veleka said.

"I'm just here to tell you, my lady. We've made no determination, but until we do, no one must leave the manor."

"Oh, for God's sake!" Worsley barged right in. "I've got business in town this coming week."

"Send word, my lord," Croyd said, not the least bit intimidated. He looked around. "All of you. This is a mysterious death and we've yet to determine whether it was of natural causes. I will want to question you. I will want to know where everyone was yesterday. I will want to know all about Mr. Alton . . ."

"There is nothing we can tell you," Veleka interrupted him. "Nothing. We know nothing about him, except he accompanied our son home from South Africa. They were with the first infantry brigade, Ducas was injured, and in the course of recovery, he was sent home with Mr. Alton, his aide-de-camp. We know nothing about his background or his family. You might contact the regiment commander, who would have all his particulars."

"Which will take a fair amount of time, my lady, but yes—that will be done. Anyone else?" He looked around. "Mr. Ducas?" And when Dar didn't respond, "My lord— Mr. Ducas?"

Dar shook himself. "My apologies. Constable Croyd, is it?"

"About Mr. Alton," Croyd said apologetically.

Another trap. How much would Ducas have remembered, how much to tell? The news of Alton's death had shaken him to the bone and he was losing all focus.

"I can't tell you much. It is as Lady Veleka has told you—I don't remember anything of my past, and after I was well enough to leave the hospital, the infantry commander assigned Alton to bring me home. We've been here but a day, not enough time to shake loose any memories on my part. We took a brief ride down the drive this morning, he left me by the paddock, and that was the last time I saw him."

He paused and looked at Veleka, whose face was composed. She was not going to mention the errand on which she'd sent Alton—at least not yet. Though it was perfectly clear someone had to have attacked him along the way.

Veleka shot a look at him, and it was almost as if she could read what he was thinking, and that she knew he would tell if she didn't. "Oh, Constable, I remember something else—I sent Mr. Alton on an errand yesterday. Into the village. It was pouring rain. We all thought he might have stayed the night when he didn't return. No one ever dreamed he might have been attacked."

"I see," Croyd said. "So Mr. Alton was out on an errand sometime in the afternoon, after he'd gone riding with Mr. Ducas, is that correct, my lady?"

"Before lunch," she said. "It had just started raining. It was all thunder and lightning. I shudder to think . . ."

And yet she'd been out in the rain, Dar thought. *It had to have been her.*

"Yes, it's dangerous when it's raining like that and you can't hardly see a foot ahead of you. Well, in any event, I will be back, and I expect to fully question everyone before the next couple of days."

"Sooner, I hope," Worsley muttered. "Good God, why did we ever come here this weekend?"

"You know why," Lady Tuttington whispered.

"I beg your pardon, my lady?" Croyd said, his interest piqued.

Veleka looked up sharply. "They came to be indulged for a weekend in the country, Constable. Nothing more, and sometimes a great deal less. Sir Eustace is famous for collecting *friends*, drinking port and playing chess on the weekends when the weather turns bad."

"Of course, my lady."

"Holmby will you see out."

Croyd bowed and Holmby took him in hand.

Everyone else just stared at each other.

"Dead like the animals," Sir Eustace finally said. "Dear God."

Jesus God, now what?

Get out. Kill Ducas again, and get out.

No. That wasn't the answer. He couldn't leave empty-handed in any event. Alton's death should make no difference to the mission. And his first duty was to his orders.

But now there were two mysteries—the murders of the men in the colonel's regiment, and Alton's death.

Odd, odd, odd. But no connection, surely.

Jesus. No—the answer to Alton's death was the most reasonable one: someone killed him as he was on his way to the village. Not uncommon for a solitary traveler to be attacked in the rain. It made everything easier, in fact. Fewer people on the road. No visibility, and the rain a veritable curtain of isolation. The perfect backdrop for an attack.

Croyd would come to that conclusion as well. Sooner than later, one had to hope.

He still didn't quite comprehend it: Alton was dead, his blood drained, and his body left like a carcass on the farmstead road. The thought of it goddamned took his breath away.

He felt the prickling again. His every sense went on alert.

Veleka, stalking him where he'd sought refuge in the library.

"Well, my dear—have you quite wrapped your mind around the fact that Alton is gone?"

Be Ducas—don't say too much. Look perplexed.

He couldn't. "No, I haven't," he said bluntly. "It's an odd death."

"There are always thieves and murderers where you least expect them," Veleka said. "How are you feeling?"

"I don't know how to feel," he said, and much as he tried to suppress it, there was some emotion there. "We traveled a long way together to come here, and if I knew him at all before I was wounded, I don't remember."

"Sometimes not remembering can be the better thing," Veleka said. "But the end result is, we're all stuck here together for the next several days and must make the best of it."

"The sun is out," Dar said, and watched a flash of anger play over her beautiful face.

"I came to tell you breakfast is served," she said abruptly and left him.

He went to the window. There was the front drive just the same as it had been yesterday when he and Alton picked their way on horseback a hundred or two hundred yards away from the house.

Only yesterday?

Alton is dead.

Get out. Get *out.*

Son of a bitch bastard; what the hell is he doing? Already in the trenches, pretending to be me? Like bloody hell. I got here just in time . . . and it cost me all my goddamned regenerative energy to do it. Well, the charade is over—I'll just go in there and . . .

Wait—company's afoot—hellfire. Can't just barge in and announce myself.

Of course, Mother will be in transports when I do. Can't wait too long to do it either; we have work to do.

Let me watch this imposter and see just how accurate his take is on me. I never did see him clearly in the tent.

By God. That is uncanny. The way he walks, the way he gestures. The tone in his voice. What's he saying?

Ha—the memory thing. Very smart. Makes up for all the discrepancies. Not an imbecile, this duplicate of me. Who is he, who looks so like me?

No, no, he doesn't. Not a bit. I'm absolutely astounded Mother was fooled.

Oh, he's righteously clever, that one. Pretending to know nothing. He doesn't know everything, that's for sure. Does he even know what he's looking for? I'd wager not. Not yet.

God, it's like looking in the mirror, watching him. We're not that much alike. Where the hell did the colonel find him?

That throws everything into a cocked hat. I need a plan. I need to get him out of the way.

I'll just kill him.

Tonight.

And then I'll come back home . . .

Something was different. How could a man be that much the same and that much different? But she couldn't define the difference.

Not the face, not the body, not the eyes, not the mouth—and yet, and yet—surely memory wasn't that fickle that if you lost it, you lost everything inborn as well. He would have to know instinctively which hand to use, what food he preferred, how to kiss in that insistent, probing way that Ducas kissed her . . .

Something was different, and she had run from it like a doe, through the lashing rain, paying penance for her brazen blood-pounding initiation, that oh, so disturbing kiss.

Something was different . . . and not, because there, through the downpour, Gaetana had been waiting, framed in shadow in the doorway.

She should have known home would be no refuge; Gaetana knew everything immediately in that mystical way of hers.

And she had not been loath to say so. "So you went against my wishes." She had thrown a woolen blanket around Angene's shoulders. Women were ever fools. Even she, who knew better. "You saw him."

Angene had shivered, and it had not been because she

was cold and drenched. It was Gaetana and how she knew even about the kiss . . .

He knew her not and yet, that kiss . . .

What was so different?

"Women are fools," Gaetana said, drawing Angene into the parlor by the fire. "It is enough. It is time to break the curse of the Sangbournes. We are done with them, all of them. We hate them."

"I don't hate Ducas," Angene said.

"He's the worst of them," Gaetana bit out. "But not for long; I will make sure of that—not for long . . ."

"He's different now . . ."

"His nature is the same—arrogant and cruel—and he suffers the first punishment now. But there is more to come."

"He doesn't remember how he was," Angene had protested even though she knew it was futile. Gaetana had an answer for everything.

"He doesn't need to. It's born in the blood. It's in his heart and his gut. He will never change. And he will be punished."

"You will punish him, you mean."

"I have not seen that far into the future."

"Oh, dear God, Mother—foretelling the future now? If the Earl were to see you like this . . ."

"He hasn't sent word in months about when his next visit might be. All to the good. It gives me time to rectify mistakes that were made, and disavow promises that were believed. All my mistakes, my bad judgments. But no more. There shall be retribution, and justice. The good shall hold sway."

It was almost as if Gaetana were in a trance, looking beyond herself, seeing a picture, a pattern, sensing what was to come.

This aspect of her mother was scary. It was as if the sensual dancing and the banishment from Sangbourne Manor had awakened that eerie prescient part of her that she nor-mally kept tightly reined in.

How else to explain this virulent thirst for the Sangbourne blood?

It was the gypsy blood, the real Gaetana, without the trappings of a fine silk dress, an elegant house and a titled lover, who had no compunction about brewing potions in the fireplace and implementing arcane gypsy magic.

"Wentmore knows what I am. Sir Eustace does not. It is time. The lines are drawn. I see that clearly. Ducas is irrele-vant—" She broke off abruptly, and then, "Unless . . . un-less—no, I can't stop what will happen. You will surrender to your blood, and in spite of every warning, you will do what you will. So be it. These are your choices; know you, I will be working against you, against them, and against your Ducas and all his wickedness."

Her fury was contained, detached, towering. Angene had never seen her like this, didn't know how to protect a Ducas who had no memories to combat Gaetana's wrath. "Even knowing he's different now? Even knowing that I love him. . . ?"

"Love. . . !" Gaetana spat. "Love is the true wickedness, winding its tentacles around you and then squeezing the life out of you and leaving you for dead. You don't love Ducas. You love the *idea* of Ducas—and that doesn't exist any-more."

That, at least was true, Angene had thought after Gaetana had banished her to her bedroom. She was a repository of memories of Ducas, different ones than his family had, things she could tell him about the way they had been together, about how she had . . .

. . . become his mistress . . .

And yet—and yet—she had pulled the curtain away from the bedroom window to look at the impossible teeming rain—Ducas knew everything already, it was all in that kiss, that soul-shaking, earth-jarring kiss . . .

Something was different. She had all she could do to stay where she was when she felt a blood-pounding urgency to go back to him.

Tonight. Now.

Gaetana had spooked her. It was Gaetana's urgency she felt. And the surging need to protect Ducas—and that kiss.

She shouldn't have run from him. This wasn't the other Ducas, the one with whom she'd had to play those wicked games. The one with whom she had had to pretend.

This was a different Ducas, one who was now walking headlong into things he didn't understand.

All that was different now he'd returned, and whatever it was she couldn't define besides. She had to tell him; before anyone else sat him down and filled his head with stories about the way he had been, she had to tell him. About them. *Her* stories, not theirs, woven to fulfill the dream.

She should have stayed.

So much wasted time.

And that kiss. No, she couldn't have stayed. She hadn't been ready.

But in the light of dawn, everything came clear . . . she was no longer afraid, and she had to go.

Croyd was in the dining room, questioning Veleka and Sir Eustace. The lords and ladies libertine had retired to their rooms, overcome with the scent of impropriety attaching itself to the otherwise outwardly upright and uptight Lord and Lady Sangbourne.

No one was watching. He could go anywhere, search anything for as long as he was canny enough to evade the guests, the butler and the stable boy.

Not great odds, but it seemed like even five minutes free of them would be like a release from prison.

It was really time to give up and go.

Except that now he needed to know who killed Alton and why. Alton of all people who knew no one here and could not have made an enemy in the space of a day let alone a lifetime.

Alton, who was battle-hardened, pragmatic, and gentle as a baby's breath, and whose commonsense approach to a complicated quest had been the underpinning Dar depended upon.

A raging success, that: in twenty-four hours, he had infiltrated Sangbourne Manor, infuriated the mother while persuading her he really was her son, lost his trusted accomplice, and discovered that Ducas had had a mistress.

The emotional effort keeping up the charade and juggling all those balls was as stressful as being in battle; but the complication of the mistress was like a bombshell hitting him dead in the gut.

He didn't need it, didn't want it, even in Ducas's persona. She was dangerous to him, she knew too much about him, things his—Ducas's—parents didn't know, things that could trip him up and spell disaster.

God, he just ought to go.

—or, he could use her to find out the things about Ducas he needed to know.

... *Walking straight into a bullet right there. You shouldn't have kissed her. You should have goddamned not kissed her. She could blow you off the battlefield now, because the differences between you have to be so obvious ...*

Shit.

Another goddamned complication, and he refused to even examine his response to that kiss. That was stored in a container in the back of his mind labeled, *bloody damned keep out.*

All signs said, he had to go. Just cut his losses and go. Whatever was going on with Ducas, the colonel would get at it another way. He was too compromised between Alton's death and that kiss.

You don't have to win this one. The fate of nations doesn't hang on your success with this. There are too many variables

*and unexpected circumstances. You'd be better off to just
go . . .*

He'd be better off to think about what he was doing and
to plan a strategy instead of stumbling around like this.

And push to shove, Alton's death changed everything,
and he damned well couldn't leave it alone until he knew
why Alton was killed. Not in conscience, and not in the
context of the mission.

The elusive Angene was his only lead now. And where
the hell would he even find her, if his memory loss logically
would nominally prevent him from even going into the village where he could ask someone about her.

He supposed he could ask Veleka, but she didn't seem
the type of mother to either stuff Ducas's head with bedtime
stories or to be partial to the woman who claimed to be her
cherished son's mistress.

It was like being in a maze—one solution presenting itself, and then something cropping up to block his way.

And someone was always around, watching Ducas,
waiting for a sign.

Even now, Holmby hailed him from the garden door
steps. "Mr. Ducas—Mr. Ducas. Are you aware of where
you're going?"

He turned back and shouted: "Stables. Horses." Holmby
waved him off. Bloody hell. They knew where to find him
now.

Still, he'd have some time alone, even with a hovering
stable boy.

No. Strangely, the stables were quiet and empty, with the
intermittent sounds of flies buzzing and the horses nickering
and cropping at their feed.

"Ducas!" The voice was above him, low, seductive, com-
manding, and then suddenly a figure dived from the hayloft
right into him in a flurry of skirts and they both went top-
pling onto a pile of hay.

"Jesus God—"

She was right on top of him, pressing tightly against him, winding her arms around him, and kissing him all over his face with the exuberance of a child, murmuring, "Ducas, Ducas, Ducas—I couldn't stay away. . . ."

She pulled back abruptly as she realized he wasn't responding to her, that the kiss—that earth-rocking kiss—had made no difference to him, that nothing had changed, and that he was looking at her out of those sharp intelligent eyes she loved, without any reciprocation.

"Ducas?" Her voice went wary even though she was still on top of him, her hips rocking tentatively against his, and propping herself up by pushing against his shoulders so she could see his face.

Dear heaven and hell—to have her fall into his lap like that—after that kiss, and just when he needed her and wanted her . . . oh, fate was just waiting for him to stumble and fall. His rampantly aroused body was just waiting to pull him into the undertow.

He had to go carefully. Ducas's mistress was not someone to trifle with, especially when she was straddling his legs.

"Ducas . . ." There was such anguish in her voice.

Too easy to let that silky vocal caress shoot all his intentions to hell.

"Angene—" Shit . . . he really liked the sound of her name on his tongue. "Angene, you have to help me, and this isn't helping."

"It isn't? We used to meet here too, you know." She slipped off of him gracefully and onto her knees beside him as he levered himself into a sitting position beside her.

"Did we? What else, Angene? I want to know all about Du . . . about me. Everything you know about—me."

She cocked her head and stared at him in the lowering light. Today was no different; nothing had changed. He didn't remember and he was just the same. "I want to help you remember. I came to offer to do just that. There are other memories besides those of your family."

"I know. I need to know them too." They were face to face, sitting on the stable floor. The scent of manure and hay was ripe all around them and there was something too elemental about being where he was with her and the memory of the kiss. It made him want to kiss her again, and do other rank and salacious things with her that Ducas would never have thought to have done.

She was fuddling his brain. There was too much at stake. He could not let himself drown in the memory of that kiss.

He eased to his feet and held out his hand. "We can't talk today. there's been a death, the constable is here asking questions, and I have too many questions for you. We need to meet somewhere later."

She took his hand and let him pull her up. And held on just a moment longer. Ducas's hands. She wanted to press them against her breasts, feel them sliding down her legs, between her legs . . .

She settled for, "All right. I'll come to your room after dinner."

As if it were not an uncommon thing to do. He didn't ask how she knew; he assumed she would. He felt a surge of excitement at the thought. No. Goddamn. Not her. Not now. "Good."

Good—in his room after dinner anything could happen once his questions were answered. Anything . . .

"Till later then. . . ?" She wafted away from him toward the rear of the building and out into the sunlight.

Angene . . . He rolled her name around his mouth as he watched her slip away through the trees, reed-slender, and graceful as the wind.

Angene . . . She was trouble. She was Ducas's mistress, she was lonely and looking for something, and he was the closest to the real Ducas as a man could get, and she probably planned to use him the same way he would use her.

Mutually. No strings. Nothing wanted but what was

freely given. He could get what he needed and give her what she wanted. No altruism here.

He almost believed it.

Angene . . .

"My lord. . . ?" A deep frayed voice behind him, startling him so intensely he almost lunged into an attack. He hadn't heard a thing.

Instantly he felt the prickling and he whirled, every sense at the alert, to find an older man in ragged clothes that smelled of horse and hay blocking his way.

"The host has set the table, my lord."

"What?"

The man turned away and Dar grabbed his arm. "What does that mean, the host has set the table?"

He could just barely see the man's pale eyes. "I'm happy to repeat the message, my lord. Constable Croyd wishes to see you."

"That isn't what you said."

"It is indeed what I told my lord. Just as Mr. Holmby directed me. The constable wishes to see you. Has my lord forgotten the way to the house?"

"No," Dar barked. "Nor have I forgotten what you said."

"It's the memory, my lord. It can play tricks."

This stranger knew about his memory. The prickling intensified. "Who are you?"

"I work in the garden and the stables, my lord. It's sad you don't remember."

"I remember some things," Dar said darkly. "Where is the constable?"

"In the dining room, my lord. Most easily reached going around to the front of the house. If my lord doesn't remember."

"I remember," Dar growled; he didn't move. Every nerve in his body told him not to move.

"My lord?"

There were shadows, waiting . . . Now he sensed he had

to move. And that even if he moved he would have nowhere to go.

He was man of action first and foremost—forward motion was always infinitely preferable to standing still, so he moved, and the shadows took him down.

Chapter 5

"*WHO THE BLOODY FUCKING HELL ARE YOU?*"

Someone was slapping him, back and forth on each cheek, hard, blows that jarred his brain, his memory, his body . . . if the bastard only would let up for minute, if he could just think, if he could just . . . who who who—not prepared, Jesus shit, not prepared, of all the fucking things, never thought—but Alton died, why not him . . . no strategy—that's what happens

—Jesus hell

—move out move out in the box and out . . .

"*Who are you?*"

Thunderous voice way back of beyond . . . can't hear you—better that way—need to go, almost decided to go—women always tripped you up, made you jelly—who am I . . . who am I . . . who who who . . . Ducas Sangbourne—

"D-d-d-ucas S-ang . . ."

Someone's hands lifted and slammed the back of his head against something hard.

"You bloody goddamned aren't. I fucking am."

* * *

So—he had got here not a moment too soon. The imposter hadn't quite taken over yet, and it would be a simple thing to take back his life.

The audacity of it infuriated him. The bastard had no idea, none. Obviously. The code meant nothing to him, thank the moon. But he still could have ruined everything. For all Ducas knew, he had.

But no, if the imposter were pretending a massive loss of memory, he would have discovered nothing, not yet. The worst damage was inflicting such pain on Veleka, making her believe he wasn't whole, didn't remember, wasn't able to carry on.

Hell and hounds. Up close, it was insane: it was a complete duplicate of himself, and he kept noticing things not obvious from his limited surveillance of the creature. Two of him, down to the scar on his chest. It just wasn't possible in this world.

It had to die. The sneaking bastard deserved to die.

No compunction there, although he'd dearly love to find out where it came from and how it knew enough about *him* to have the balls to take his place. No time for that. One day's grace was enough for the son of a bitch. There was too much at stake to waste any more time.

He could kill him now for what he had put Veleka through; he savored the thought for a moment. Ah, but no. He must put Veleka first: she must be reassured that he was himself, and that he was whole, in possession of his faculties and ready to do what must be done.

Damn it to mighty hell—he did not need these complications.

"Ah, there you are, my lord." Holmby, dear fussy Holmby. "We thought you might have lost your way. . . ."

What? Oh, shit, the memory thing . . . he had to reconfigure his thinking. Why was the constable there? Oh, the body . . . the murder.

Think . . . the constable had probably questioned the

memory-impaired Other, so he couldn't just barge in there and be himself . . . blast it all to hell—

". . . the constable is waiting for you in the dining room."

All right now, don't be hasty. Think it through. The imposter must know Holmby's name, So . . . "Thank you, Holmby."

"Indeed, my lord."

And know his way a little around the house and grounds, since he'd been found in the stables. All right. That part made sense. But in order for the imposter to impersonate him, he must have pretended no knowledge of his previous life, because there were things he couldn't know and things he couldn't gloss over . . .

Shit. So he would be operating in the dark, in the persona of the imposter impersonating him.

How the hell had *that* happened?

Where had the goddamned colonel found someone so much his duplicate that he could successfully infiltrate his family?

Not that he himself was not at fault; he'd been careless, a field hospital orderly with an obsession he thought was untouchable.

Reckoned without the colonel who noticed everything. Like too many deaths among the wounded in his charge. Not that that wasn't possible, but he could barely explain away why he was feeding at a dead man's heart the day the colonel caught him, and to allay the colonel's suspicions, he himself had to "die."

So many complications. He'd worked long and hard to foment conflicts that the Empire could reasonably defend. Big ones, little ones, he didn't care as long as he could supply what was necessary for his clan to maintain their luxurious and hedonistic life in the English countryside.

Who would have thought, after all their years of wandering, that their existence would come to this: subsistence by war and a gentrified English lifestyle, the entrée to which had been Veleka's marriage to the scholarly Sir Eustace, whom she had seduced in a snap, and on whom she had foisted him, the bastard child of her liaison with a Serbian expatriate she'd slept with in her native Malaysia, some seven months before the marriage.

But that wasn't to the point now. Now he had to be what he wasn't: a man without a memory—at least until the constable was done.

He entered the dining room and stopped short. Veleka was there, and Sir Eustace, and with them, three couples, friends—no, they had never been friends; sexual diversions at best, and something else to be sidestepped in the course of this interrogation.

And even worse, there was a stenographer, so every word would be recorded and every lie set in stone. More complications.

And the libertines—he should just infer that they too had encountered the amnesia-plagued Other self. It was safer that way, even though it boxed him still further.

Shit. Now what? Now what the goddamned hell what?

"My lord." Well, Croyd still rememberd his place. Inoffensive. Wishing not to overstep his bounds.

Croyd's task was the easy one. His, a veritable quagmire into which he could be sucked at any moment.

How *did* a man act who had lost his memory? He remembered everything, damn it, and now the imposter had taken his memories away from him.

He couldn't know any of them, that was the first thing. And he certainly knew nothing about whatever Croyd's concerns were—barring whatever he had asked the imposter heretofore.

Hell and damnation, let me be able to hedge those answers; let this be fast.

He sat down slowly next to Croyd at the dining room table. Croyd had notes spread out everywhere. Scratchings, really, that no one but he could understand. But something in there that the imposter had probably said that might just throw his impersonation to hell. And if that were discovered, there would a whole new set of consequences.

Shit shit shit—say nothing, let Croyd lead the way. And he was taking a damned long time about it too, reading what he'd written, conferring with the stenographer.

He had to clench his hands around his knees to keep himself still and focused on not making a slip.

All the while, he covertly eyed Veleka, whose expression was stone-hard, Sir Eustace, who looked grave and worried, as did the guests, who had obviously been thoroughly questioned and were a little put out at having to undergo this second interrogation as well.

And now him, the blank page in the lot.

"Well now, sir. So yesterday you said you'd gone riding with Mr. Alton in the morning and he left you at the paddock and that was the last you saw of him."

Credible? A trap? Was Croyd that clever, testing his memory? It hardly mattered. He had no choice but to answer in the affirmative.

"And why exactly did Mr. Alton not continue riding with you?"

Ah, delving deeper and tighter into the what and the where of poor Mr. Alton who had met such a heinous fate.

"I ..." What would the imposter say? "...I ..." Shit hell fuck..."I wanted to continue riding, he didn't." Assinine, contrived even, but Croyd seemed to take that answer seriously.

"And so what might Mr. Alton have done instead?"

He looked at Veleka. No recognition of a difference. She thought he was the imposter Ducas, the one she had taken on faith, the corrosive Other. How could she not know him? How? Because she expected to see what she was seeing, damn it.

She shrugged imperceptibly.

"I don't know," he said, taking the subtle cue.

"And you don't remember anything about Mr. Alton in South Africa, prior to his escorting you back home?"

How helpful of the constable to feed him the answers. Or maybe that was the way of it—to look as if he were formally investigating, get the details over with and close the book.

"Nothing."

"Any idea why Mr. Alton in particular was assigned to be your aide-de-camp?"

Yes and no answers where he could. Everything attributable to lost memory. So convenient, so constraining. "No."

"Did he in the course of your travels together mention anything of his personal life?"

Shit again. That certainly would happen in the natural course of events on such an onerous journey.

But—but—wait, he was the only witness to that, if he was gauging the question correctly. He could tell them anything—or nothing. What was most believable?

Wait—wait, think it through . . .

"I don't believe there was family, sir. He didn't talk about family. . . ."

"But what would they have talked about, the false Ducas and Alton, on a journey of that length and time? His imposter would have had to lie about that too.

So careful here, tricky waters . . . don't say too much.

"Yes?" Croyd prodded gently.

Bloody hell—off the ledge and deep dive into oblivion . . . "He was a lifetime military man . . . the brigade commander would know—"

"Yes, yes, you've said that all already. I'm interested to have some insight into him, whether he might have had enemies . . ."

How goddamned farfetched was that, if Alton's accompanying his impersonator here was his first time ever to Cheshamshire?

"Here?" he said sharply, letting his impatience and anger surge to the fore. *Calm down. You know nothing. You didn't talk about those things on the journey . . .* he hoped.

"Mr. Ducas . . ."

"Yes, Constable?"

"It's your contention you know nothing about this man that could shed any light on why he was so viciously attacked like that."

Let this be the end . . . "Yes, Constable." He looked at the stenographer who was making notations furiously. He looked at Veleka whose face was a blank, Sir Eustace, who looked distressed, and the guests who all were unutterably bored.

"So let me review what we know: No one else knew Mr. Alton prior to his having come to this house except my lord, whose aide-de-camp apparently he was. On the morning of your arrival, he leaves you after a brief ride around the grounds, and comes back to the house."

Croyd stopped and looked up for a moment at Ducas.

"Why *did* my lord go for a ride so soon after arriving on the heels of a long tiring journey?"

Why why why? He skewed a look at Veleka who furrowed her brow and then rushed to say, "I just could not believe Ducas was so lost to us. I just . . . I just wanted to know there was some vestige of him left. I asked Mr. Alton to have him ride, which was one of his great pleasures. I just . . . it was me, I—just wanted to know there was still something of him there . . ."

"I see," Croyd said, and they all wondered what he saw. He bent to his notes again. "To continue: It is not yet raining. Sometime later that morning, my lady Sangbourne has testified that she asked Mr. Alton to perform an errand which would take him into the village. It is raining by that time. Mr. Alton does not return. My lords and ladies assemble for dinner at which time Mr. Alton's presence is missed. The assumption is that the storm has prevented him from returning and he has elected to stay at the inn. However, no one at the inn has seen him. His bloodless body is found in the wee hours of the following morning on the farmstead road. The doctor has examined him and found no external bruises, marks, or bites to explain the loss of blood or cause of death. Now, the Lady Veleka had begged the favor from Mr. Alton that he pick up some medication from the doctor for Sir Eustace, and according to her testimony, had thought he could accomplish that task before the storm broke. We can assume, because the doctor had not seen Mr. Alton nor was the medication given to him, that Mr. Alton was attacked at the height of the storm on the road to the village by persons unknown. I would be inclined to put it down as death by misadventure except for two things: the condition of the body and where it was found, and the fact that no one in Cheshamshire village, and to be fair, anyone at Sangbourne Manor, had any reason to want to kill Mr. Alton. The guests, the lords and ladies Tuttington, Worsley, and Lanthwaite, did not know the gentleman, barring the few minutes of introduction when he arrived; and the Lord and Lady Sangbourne seem effusively grateful that Mr. Alton was good enough to agree to stay and help with Mr. Ducas until he regained some of his footing. I think that's an accurate assessment. Does anyone want to add anything?" He looked around at them. "All right, then, I think that covers it."

"Then we may go?" Worsley demanded.

"Not today," Croyd said serenely, heedless of the flash of belligerance on Worsley's part. He motioned to the stenographer that they could leave, and then as he was about to cross the threshold, he turned and added, "There needs to be some arrangement for burial, my lady."

"Oh . . !" Veleka seemed startled. "Burial. At the church, you mean. But I never go . . . And it wouldn't have to be at the church, would it? We liked him well enough, but he wasn't family, or anything like that . . ."

"I will see to it," Sir Eustace interpolated. "My dear—I know how distressed you are—you need not think about the niceties or worry about a thing . . . I will take care of everything. Thank you, Constable. You can go."

* * *

Slammed down, bruised, bleeding, tied up, dark stinking hole, where the hell was he?

Too groggy still. Can't quite . . . move—think . . .

Thirsty . . . no focus . . . so familiar—he'd been through things like this before—your mind glossed over . . . shut it out—just need time . . .

No time. Wait.

What? . . . wait—Ducas? . . .

Jesus . . . Ducas—*Had* that been Ducas battering him?

No. He was hallucinating. Time . . . clear his head, get it straight—shift into reality . . .

No. *That* was fucking reality. Ducas . . . slamming him in the head—

Jesus Holy God. How? Ducas was dead. Ducas was . . .

He . . . *he* was Ducas . . . That was his Other . . .

He jolted to complete awareness, wrenching at the ropes that bound his body . . . Bloody bloody hell . . . Helpless . . . can't pull free, and Ducas bloody Sangbourne still alive and running loose . . .

He had to get out . . . shit shit shit . . . how?—No time to figure it out . . . Ducas shooting his whole mission to hell . . . got to *get away*—

. . . oh, shit—

. . . *Angene* . . .

"Imagine that man even hinting that Ducas might be responsible for Alton's death," Lady Worsley said indignantly when Croyd finally left the premises. "I can't credit such stupidity—with what poor Ducas has to cope with; and the incivility of him keeping us here, against our wishes, knowing that none of us had been acquainted with that poor man before he came here . . ."

So they weren't yet going to leave. Couldn't leave. Damn and hellfire. Sanctimonious bitches and their pompous puffed up husbands. Thought they knew everything. Why the hell had Veleka ever started up with them?

But he knew—it was her voracious sexuality that Sir Eustace could not handle and which mowed down every man in her path.

That a son should know even that . . .

"Ducas. . . !" And there she was, solicitous, edgy, a little off balance.

He could tell her right now, he could whisper for her ears only, and let her know the truth.

Think! And then what—? Things would get even more convoluted because she would know, and the dynamic would change with that knowledge.

She was better off not knowing. Until they all left. Until Croyd was satisfied that all the pieces fit.

And if he wasn't?

Who else could be blamed but Ducas? He could concoct a scenario or two that would account for Ducas's killing his aide-de-camp. Plus, it was the easiest solution to a murder that seemed to have no solution.

Could things get even more muddled?

Wait—here was a thought—he wouldn't kill the Other yet. He'd wait to see how the investigation went, and if Croyd gave any indication he was considering Ducas as a suspect, why, he would kill the imposter, and hand his dead body over to Croyd—perfect resolution: case closed.

Chapter 6

Things were under control. For the first time since he had captured the imposter, Ducas felt as if things were under control. He had made peace with the fact he couldn't yet tell Veleka he had returned. He decided he could put up with those boring parvenu hedonists for the next couple days until Croyd came to a determination. And he would use that time to reestablish his presence and dominance at the Manor.

He had a plan, and for the first time in weeks, he could be himself.

The host had set the table.

And they had been waiting so long. It would be so easy to just kill those people; they could feed off them for weeks, maybe more . . .

But he was civilized—to a point: you didn't dine on the guests your family chose to copulate with after all, juicy as they might seem to be.

Bah. They were too indulged when you got right down to it. And the murder of the mysterious Alton only compounded all the difficulties. There could be only one reason why he had been killed—the man had got too close to things he should not know, and Veleka had taken the only course open to her.

As would he have, to safeguard all that they had established here.

Preserve and protect at all costs. Live a blameless and luxurious existence deep in the English countryside, and take your hunger outside the realm of the respectable life you had built for yourself. Take it to war, and bleed your sustenance from those already dying, already dead, siphon it out, cork it up, take it back to the Manor so that all who burned for the blood could feed on it, live through it.

It made such sense. It was such a good plan. And then he got greedy. In the heat of one fierce battle, he had craved one long dram of lifeblood from a dying soldier. And the colonel was in the wrong place at the wrong time; and the colonel had seen, but he didn't know quite what the colonel had seen.

He had thought about killing the colonel then and there, but that might have made things worse. Instead he chose to "die" himself. It made things easier; there were never any questions, there was a proper burial, and he lived to kill another day, in another place, another war.

He felt itchy for the kill now. The Other, who had come out of nowhere to wreck his plans, and turn everything topside over, the Other was an impediment he could never have planned for. It meant the colonel *had* seen him feeding, had been suspicious, and wanted to find out everything he could about Ducas Sangbourne.

But how the bloody hell he found a duplicate of him to insinuate into his family was beyond all knowing.

Hell and hounds . . . he would take such pleasure in sipping the bastard to death.

. . . And those tiresome irritating guests . . .

He shook himself. Another day, perhaps two. Get rid of them and the imposter, too. End of the story.

He couldn't wait to shut the door of his bedroom and enclose himself in the silence and take his rest. He had stayed in battle far too long. He was road weary, and drained from the journey and from keeping up this insane impersonation.

But here, for the first time in months, he would sleep on native soil. He needed it badly. His body pined for it. He took strength from it, just a few hours burrowed in his bed, and he would be renewed, reinvigorated and befuddled no more.

There was night-lit fire in the fireplace. Tea and crackers on a tray beside the bed. The room was warm, felt snug, close. The curtains were drawn.

He felt the heat rising in his blood. He had gotten past this first impediment. No one questioned that he wasn't the imposter impersonating *him*.

It was just a matter of Croyd getting past the specifics. If needed, he had a sacrificial lamb. So all was not lost yet—this was not irreparable. Things were not *totally* disrupted...

"Ducas..."

That too well-known musical voice—

His heart dropped to his stomach.

Angene. Shit.

The goddamned imposter had been too goddamned busy by half. He hadn't taken her into account at all. Fucking hell, there wasn't any part of his life the Other hadn't invaded, and it had only been one *day*. It was a clever clever imposter, who even more deserved to die.

He clamped down on his anger and frustration. *Think. Think. Don't rush in. This is tricky. Let her speak.*

She was sitting on the bed, damn it to hell. So no comfort for him there for the rest of the night. She looked like she meant to stay, damn her—she was as brazen as a beaver, sitting there as if she had a gold-plated invitation. From...

...not him. Damn blast it—the Other. Ducas.

The emotion drained away; cold washed over him That son of a bitch—took his place every which where, even with this one, without batting an eye. Convinced her to sneak into his room tonight... catch that... she probably didn't need much convincing—

Fine. Whatever Angene wanted of the false Ducas, he could give her too. Maybe more.

Wait—he couldn't reveal himself to her either. She had dealt with the Ducas of the lost memory, a Ducas who wouldn't have known her. So he, the real Ducas, couldn't be familiar with her. The most the imposter might know was her name. Lies on lies, like a tower of children's blocks, teetering on the brink of falling down.

Names were safe. "Angene."

Good. That didn't shock her, his use of her name.

"So I kept my promise. I'm here and I want to help you."

Ah, a clue. The imposter had won her over too—she believed him, so of course she would want to help him— Ducas—remember . . . things. Things about them? Nothing had progressed far enough for there to be a *them* in his life before the imposter. She wasn't suitable anyway.

He had been toying with her for years, distracting her, keeping her wits tied up in knots by trying to seduce her, keeping his secrets safe by drugging her with kisses and fostering Sir Eustace's infatuation with her mother.

A very good plan and all in a day's work. And all of it by the board now that she'd come to help the false Ducas remember *things*.

"I know," he said, pulling a chair over to the bed where she sat.

"So, ask me your questions."

She was so beautiful, with her lush body and thick dark hair. And she had loved him well, teased him and tormented him, and given him nothing in the end.

For that alone, he should have killed her, too. Everyone around him who was a danger to him, he should have killed long ago.

The simplest solutions were always the best.

But no, he had to be civilized.

And this is what he got—he was like a rat in a maze and now he couldn't quite yet find his way out.

"Questions." What? Oh. Right. The infernal imposter,

seeking to learn about—Ducas. "Ah—questions." And in fact, this ought to be interesting, to hear from Angene's perspective all about himself. "No. You tell me everything I should know about . . . me—and then I'll ask questions."

She smiled, she touched his face. "You are quite wonderful. Kind. Generous. Caring. Devoted to your mother and father. Good to your people . . ."

"Too good to be true," he murmured. Well, why not. She could never love anyone less. Though why the hell Wentmore plopped her and her mother in the middle of Cheshamshire was a cosmic mystery.

"A little reckless," she went on, "a little ruthless sometimes. Impatient and patient both. Impulsive . . . all which are the reasons that I love you, and why I am your mistress . . ."

What? That was a slam to the gut. He had to have imagined it.

But the way she said it—she had told this to the imposter too? . . . hellfire—never never never—and now, *she* had made it so, in spite of his every maneuver to avoid it . . .

Now what was he going to do?

"When?" he asked, too abruptly he knew. His throat was thick, and he could barely get the words past. "When did this happen?"

She gazed at him lovingly. "Just before you left. We were tumbling in the hayloft. We used to meet there all the time, when we couldn't come here. You liked the hayloft. You said there was something so primitive about fucking in the hay. That day, you had your orders, you were leaving me the very next day.

"We couldn't bear to let go. You held me, you kissed me the way only you can. And you were so aroused, so hard, so domineering—you were unstoppable. I couldn't stop you. I didn't want to—but I—couldn't . . . without some . . . assurances—

She looked away for a moment. "But then, you said, you've always known you can't marry me, but if I'd be your mistress and give you everything, you would give it back to me a hundredfold. For that, I said yes. And you mounted me and took me and gave me pleasure a hundredfold over right there and then, and the whole night and into the morning until you had to go . . ."

What?

"But you don't remember, do you, my stallion? No. I see that you don't. Well, that's as it is. It doesn't change things for me. I am still your mistress, whether you remember or not. Can it be enough that I remember and I will never forget that night?"

"In the hayloft," he said faintly.

"In the hay. Drenched with your cream . . ."

"How many times?"

"A half dozen at least."

Such stamina, even for him. Well, he'd take credit for it, even it weren't true.

"I wish I remembered," he said, lacing his voice with regret. "You are so beautiful, who wouldn't want to fuck you?"

"I had hoped you'd still think so. That I'm beautiful, and that any man would want to fuck me. I want you to fuck me."

Blast. Wrong tack. How to mollify her? "Angene . . . I—I know nothing about this, the way I am now."

"Is your penis hard?" she asked helpfully.

He blinked. "I think you could say it has a healthy response to a beautiful woman."

"Hard now, I mean, because of me."

"It's . . . thinking about it . . ."

"Maybe if I . . ."

Hellfire—she was like a runaway mare. He held up his hand. He had to get a handle on this, on her, *now.* "Angene—"

"You could suck my nipples. You used to love to suck my nipples."

She made a gesture as if to start unbuttoning her dress. He stayed her hand. "You have to give me a little time . . ."

"Men don't need time," she said confidently. "Let me give you my nipples . . ."

She really wanted it, his little *mistress*. There wasn't a man alive who could withstand that kind of sexual coercion from a woman as luscious as she. He remembered how avidly he had wanted her body, and how, in all their encounters, she had never had any compunction about pushing him away.

His mistress now . . . ! The irony was delicious. Galling. She would willingly cradle him between her legs now he supposedly had no memory of it?

Oh, there would be a memory made of it now. It was done. She would not get out of this room without submitting to him somehow, some way.

"Did you know you have a long, hot, insistent tongue?"

She was like a little frog, hopping from one thing to the next, seeking to juice him up, all the while she hardened his heart. "My tongue? Tell me more."

"I did so love your kisses. You just fed on my mouth and never let up."

"Did I? Tell me about those kisses."

"We spent hours in the hayloft, and in your bed kissing. My lips were always swollen from you kisses. You lived in my mouth when we were kissing."

Those kisses he remembered. That and subsuming all his hungers into those kisses. Those long, drawn out, lapping, possessive kisses. Distracting purposeful kisses that depleted his energy and were a poor sop for his body's raging need.

"All this talk of sucking and fucking and kissing makes me burn to kiss my mistress," he murmured. "Tell me my mistress would welcome my hot *insistent* kisses."

She held out her arms. "I long for your kisses. Give them to me."

Did she know what she was doing, or was she using the fact he had lost his memory? No matter. He climbed onto the bed, straddled her body and framed her face in his hands. He slanted his mouth over hers, and swooped his tongue deep into her mouth, delving, probing, tasting, hot, wet, purposeful.

She was just the same: sweet as honey, open as a flower, shocked as a nun, her body flowing with her woman juices, and pliant as clay beneath his body. And uncharacteristically willing—as his mistress should be.

His kisses were just the way she remembered, the long reach of his tongue, pushing and probing and taking what he wanted. Drowning in his kisses, utterly submitting to the tyranny of his tongue and anything he wanted of her mouth. Of her. Just the way she wanted, the way she had hoped he would.

Plunging deeper and deeper, the heat of his tongue, feeling her, tasting her, every lap reaching to her vitals.

"My beautiful mistress—" He pulled away from her mouth to nip at her lips, wet them with his tongue; then he forcefully rimmed the long hard tip of it inside her lips until she was breathless. "Look at me. . . . I can't get enough of your mouth and your tongue."

He flicked the whole length of his tongue deep into her mouth again and she gasped as he possessed it with a repressed violence that mirrored his shuddering arousal. He barely pulled out of her hot mouth to whisper, "You see, do you see, what your luscious mistress mouth does to me? I don't need to remember anything to want to feed on you still more."

She felt the thrill of his words to her bones. She had done it, she was his mistress for true now, she couldn't refuse him what she had hoped for, prayed for, and made come true— she opened her mouth and gave him more.

Time—no sense of time, no sense of hour, day, light, dark, just minutes ticking away in his brain as he fought his way to consciousness.

Time . . . no time—he was as good as dead, maybe he was dead—why wasn't he dead?—with the real Ducas by now having blasted his deception to hell—

. . . no, he'd been to hell and back already . . . and survived.

This was just a test of his mettle. So if he could just . . .

But there was no just: he was in what appeared to be a dank rank tunnel with no light, no hope, *near* hell, bound hand and foot, and still in shock from the beating.

But he had collected his wits, and he could parse out a coherent thought now. And he knew that time was ticking away and Ducas the real had to be back in the family bosom and—

Angene . . .

Bloody hell, he couldn't even let himself think about Angene who would be slipping into Ducas's room any hour, any minute now, and there he would be, the real Ducas, with all the real memories, waiting to take his beautiful mistress to bed.

Shit. The wicked got everything in life.

Bloody rotten luck. Bloody rotten life.

A fitting end to that, this.

He sank against the cold rough wall. Cold comfort there.

Time . . .

He was so thirsty—

He wrenched at the ropes, and scraped his arm against the rough tunnel wall. Damn, that was sharp. . . .

Sharp? He scraped against the rock again. Shit, that hurt.

But oh, yes—he felt it: he was still alive, and still fighting. He felt his blood surge, he felt hope, and he wrested his body more tightly against the wall, pressed the rope around his wrists against the rough outcropped rock, and relentlessly began to saw.

She was drugged on his kisses. Just insensate with the heat and voluptuousness of his incessant possession of her mouth and tongue, and the way he sucked her lower lip voraciously or licked and lapped at it between his lush hot kisses.

And the intimate sensual whispering against her lips between kisses.

"My penis is ready for you now, do you feel it—so swollen and heavy like your lips."

"I know." She sighed. He was heavy on her body, sinking into her, cradled against her hips, rocking, probing, seeking her heat.

Her body felt swollen and heavy with lust. She welcomed it, she wanted it, the utter surrender of the most feminine part of her to the purest male part of him. Ached for him to penetrate deep inside her body the way he penetrated her mouth.

Ducas... this was the dream. And everything she had described to him would become the reality. Ducas.

She cupped his cheeks, and stared at his mouth. Beautiful, perfect, firm, sensual mouth.

Ducas...

His long tongue flicked out at her lips. He was tired. It was time.

"Angene..."

He was ready, he shifted his body to part her legs—and she stopped him. Just stopped—everything.

How was this, when she had invited herself into his bed, called herself his mistress, and instigated the intimacy of their kisses and conversation?

"But I came merely to answer your questions," she murmured coyly, wriggling to relieve the intensity of his embrace. Perfect. She had timed it perfectly. Given him just enough. Got him all lathered up, racing toward the finish line. And then stopped him mid-speed.

It was the only way with someone like Ducas.

"And by your kisses, so you have," he said pettishly. "Now it is time to find some other answers. *My* answers."

It sounded as if he was ready to have done with her.

Could she take a chance on that when she was that close to having everything she wanted?

"Ducas . . ."

"Yes, my mistress?" he said lightly, hiding his supreme impatience. It was always the same with her. She would go so far with him and no farther, and yet there was no doubt in his mind, she wanted to submit.

"Not tonight."

"So much for loving my kisses. You are as aroused as ever a woman has been, and yet you deny us both. Is this a mistress? Are you playing with me? Do you know how many women would lie in my bed if I merely snapped my fingers and pointed at them?"

How could she calm him down? "Ah, but the worth of a good mistress is how she builds anticipation and excitement, is it not, Ducas? You have been back at the Manor barely a day. Surely you can wait one night before sinking yourself into me."

"Obviously *you* can." He rolled off her. "In spite of your voluptuous offer to let me suck at your nipples. I could have spent my cream on them at least. I wonder, mistress mine, if you *do* love my long hot tongue as much as you say you do?"

She did, she had to convince him she *did*. "Did I not devour it tonight? I promise—your long strong tongue shall feast on me tomorrow. Even now, I'm imagining where you will insinuate your hot wet tongue into me . . ."

"And the more you talk, the harder I get, and the harder it is to contain myself. When?"

All was not lost yet. "I love hearing that, Ducas. I want you to get hard and hot from my words. It is but another skill I will hone for your pleasure. We'll meet in the hayloft. At dusk. We'll relive that last day just as it was . . . in our own voluptuous little world where no one can interrupt us."

"I hope you mean that, because you have just been

granted the one and only refusal I allow any mistress, ever. From now on, you can never withhold your body, your kisses, or your sex from me. Your mouth, your body, your sex will be available to me whenever I want. I don't remember whether I set out those terms when I proposed that you become my mistress. Perhaps I was too preoccupied? So, tell me now, my mistress-to-be, before I fuck you, *are* those terms acceptable to you?"

"I can never refuse you, I must always be available . . ." she whispered on a shuddery breath. She was almost insensate at the thought. That *was* what she had always wanted. His mistress, and all that entailed. "Those terms are acceptable."

"I knew they would be." He reached out and grasped her arm as she sat across the bed from him. "So if I wanted to fuck you now, you would just lie down for me and spread your legs, isn't that right, mistress?"

"Yes," she whispered, stunned by the reversal. She hadn't considered he could turn the tables on her. This was the dangerous Ducas, the wicked Ducas, the one she was accustomed to dealing with. The death of memory couldn't kill a man's nature, and he wielded that small implacable part of him, that was obviously still inherent, like the flick of a whip.

Perhaps *that* was the real reason for her pushing him like this; she had sensed it was still there, but it was of no moment now. He'd trapped her, and she felt cornered as he watched with smug satisfaction as she pulled the hem of her dress over her thighs, and then slowly lay back and spread her legs.

It was the moment of truth, her deception now her reality, and she didn't know why she felt suddenly as if she were his prey.

He waited, watching, watching, until she comprehended this wasn't all, that he wasn't going to help her. And then she slipped her fingers under the elastic of her drawers and slid them slowly over her hips.

... All my brazen and arousing words ... and this is not what I wanted—not like this, not here, not now ... I never could outsmart him—what have I done, what have I done? All my lies ... how can I explain them?

In a minute, he would discover the whole deception, penetrating the curtain of words and flesh and find nothing more substantial than her illusory and wavering desire to have a one great love of her life—at any cost. And the cost would be dear. When that barrier was breached, she alone would be the one to pay.

And there was no way out.

All her fine, bold, wanton mistress words, as if words could give him the pleasure of her body.

Naïve of her to think so, to believe she could gloss over the moment and come out ahead.

She kicked away her undergarments. Now she was naked, spread, and vulnerable to his gaze, to his lust. His eyes kindled as he examined her.

"Oh, I know just where I want to lick, mistress mine, just what I want to taste ..."

Her body twinged—she was not immune to his suggestive words, or his lust; it was the blood, after all, pounding like the ocean in her veins, and wild carnal yearnings she had never been able to subdue.

It was just ... he slipped off the bed and knelt between her legs ... just—parting them just that little wider so he could see her cleft perfectly, nuzzle it, perfectly ... swipe it perfectly with his tongue ...

Crash! A shattering sound like a boulder tossed through a window, and then a shower of raining glass ...

"What the fuck—?" He scrambled to his feet as she jolted to a sitting positon. "Damn and hellfire, what the—"

"Ducas—*Ducas...!*" Veleka, shrieking at the top of her lungs.

"—goddamned hell was that—?" He jumped for the door before Veleka could get to it, and popped out in the hallway. "What ... what?"

"The hallway chandelier—hurry . . . look—"

He raced to the landing and peered over the banister to see shards from what had been an enormous, elegant, expensive, imported crystal chandelier strewn all over the hallway below.

And he had to remember that he had no memory of where it had come from and what it had meant to Veleka, and he had to compose his expression, goddamn it, and he had to control his rampaging lust, blast her capricious soul to hell, and he had to wonder if there was any chance in the universe that Angene's luscious muff would even be waiting for him when he could finally get back in his room.

Perfect. Sneak attack and make it the unexpected. Couldn't have been more perfect or well timed, even with his raw bleeding wrists and battered body. This was such a victory, sound and sweet.

A victory for him and for Angene; he couldn't let him have her, and now she was gone, because he had made certain that Ducas the real would be busy with his family and guests for hours to come over this disaster.

Served him right. The bastard deserved nothing less, after everything Dar had overheard skulking in the shadows outside the room.

And his pretending the memory loss with Angene was unconscionable.

Hell, he shouldn't care. But Alton's death had made that impossible. And Ducas's return made it imperative.

There was something going on here, and he needed to find out what.

He felt revitalized by the thought. He needed a wash and a bite to eat, both which he could get in Ducas's room, and then he would implement sneak attack number two—take Ducas the real prisoner again, and assess the damage done.

Something was so different. She couldn't exactly define what it was, but something was not the same. And some things were—his kisses, the way he made her feel, and that pitiless inflexibility that he flicked so effortlessly.

She had made her bed. She had kept him dangling as long as she could, she had made him chase her.

But in that turn-back moment last night—something had changed and the excitement had seeped out of everything.

Nevertheless, she'd have to meet him as promised, because otherwise, she was certain he would come for her. Come to the house and mortify her in front of Gaetana. He'd do it deliberately too, he was that displeased with her. He'd tell Gaetana that she'd accepted his terms, and that she was well and truly his mistress.

He'd demand her body and her kisses. And those kisses—the memory of those kisses set her body pulsating, her blood pounding, and made her afraid, and consumed her with a shuddering excitement and wanting more.

But something was different. Even though his kisses, the way he treated her were the same. What did that matter? She had made gypsy magic, she had made herself his mistress and he would become her lover forever, at dusk, in the hayloft, today.

Ducas had not revealed himself. He had pretended otherwise with Angene, but as far as Dar could tell, he had not told anyone he was the real Ducas. So everyone was still tiptoeing around him and his lost memory.

And that was the last thing Dar had expected and at that, it was just plain bloody damn luck. Or maybe not: maybe it was just the wily Ducas, protecting the deception in service of preventing suspicion settling on him in the matter of Alton's murder.

The irony was stunning. Both of them pretending amnesia, Ducas impersonating him and he impersonating Ducas, now that Ducas was his captive, and safely put away.

He wouldn't take a wager on how long. Maybe just long enough to discover who killed Alton. But he wouldn't take a bet on that either. There was not a shred of evidence lead-ing anywhere conclusive. Alton had died for nothing. For this. For him.

For what?

And not a clue to Ducas's secret life anywhere either.

Hell of an operative he was. Or else he was missing what was right in front of his nose.

This was his third day on this carousel, with those pumping horses, with nowhere to go but in a circle, chasing his tail.

The guests were restive, desperate to leave. Worsley was ready to trot out on the early morning train, and he didn't care what Croyd would say or do. Even if he would issue a warrant for his arrest. He didn't care—the enforced inactivity was getting to him, and it could not even be assuaged by their usual fun and games.

"I should think *not,*" Veleka said stringently. She'd set up a late afternoon tea just to give them all something to do between lunch and dinner. "The last thing I want is . . . that, now. How could you even get it up with all this hanging over our heads?"

"I can get it up all right," Worsley said staunchly, "if you'll go down."

"Bah. Fine. Go upstairs and fuck like bunnies. Eustace and I will keep Ducas company right here."

Which was the last thing Dar wanted after another dull, tense afternoon among these sexual playmates who were already snapping and pouncing on each other because they had nothing else in common.

"I'd much prefer to go to my room until dinner."

"Maybe this is a good time to . . . talk about things," Veleka said. "You know—the past, your life, what things were like before you went off to the battlefield . . . we haven't begun to try to shake out your memories—maybe . . ."

"Don't push the boy," Sir Eustace said.

"Another time," Dar said, pushing back his chair. "I

don't want to keep distressing you, but so far, there's nothing there." He looked around at the guests. "You will excuse me?" He didn't wait to hear them say yes.

"You ought to build a tennis court," he heard Worsley say as he took the stairs two at a time.

"We could get up a game of badminton. Or croquet."

"I'm sick of croquet. How many games did we play yesterday?"

"All afternoon, it seemed like—"

Their squabbly voices diminished as he reached the top of the stairs. Alone again. Finally. He thrust open the door; the room was, as always, dark and shrouded, the curtains invariably drawn against the sun.

He pulled them open and stared at the view. It was nearing five o'clock; getting toward dusk, toward the time that Ducas was to meet his mistress in the hayloft, and he was still debating whether to go.

Why not go? Why not salve your soul in her kisses and her love, why not? She won't ever know if it was Ducas or it was you.

The image of her lying on that bed, naked and open to Ducas last night was like a photograph in his mind. All he had seen them do, all he had heard them say.

He had wanted her at that instant as much she had seemed to want Ducas. And yet, she had pulled away. Why?

He didn't want to speculate. He turned abruptly away from the window and leaned against the sill. At that angle, just a ray of dying sun crept in over his shoulder. Just at the angle, when he wasn't even looking for anything, he saw it. A discoloration right beside the bed, that, even if he had been looking for it, he might never have seen it.

He knelt down to take a closer look. Whatever it was, it had dried, and it was about the size of a coin. He rubbed it with his fingers. Dry as a bone. Dry as a scone—odd, nevertheless.

Right by the bed. Why by the bed?

Forget it: it was something from a long time before, nothing to think about now.

But, still—he moved back, and squinted at it in that little flaring ray of sun—still . . . it was reddish and stiff and dry and . . .

He could almost swear it looked like a drop of blood.

Chapter 7

It was the waiting that escalated everything to a fever pitch. She was accustomed to waiting for Ducas. It was just the way things were, and today, it was no different. She waited, high up in the hayloft, over the heads of the horses in their stalls, almost to heaven, she thought, as she spread a thick quilt over the layer of hay she had forked from the bale at the far end.

Soon, to heaven. Everything ready for the evanescent moment of surrender. The bed placed deep in a shadowy corner and hidden behind a stack of bales, a carafe of water to slake a different thirst. Another quilt to spread over their sins. The fire in the stove below radiating a different kind of heat. The sounds and the scents of the forbidden wafting in the air.

She waited.

She dressed in the usual simple dress and minimal undergarments she always wore for an assignation with Ducas. He had made that very plain in their previous times together: everything must be easy to remove, every part of her visible. He wanted to be able to see and touch all of herself she would give him.

He taunted her, and he punished her for her clinging to her virginity, but he never stopped wanting her. It was a strange power to have. This incredible sophisticated aristocrat choosing her when he could have had any well-born woman a hundred miles around.

But it was her he could not send away. It was her surging gypsy blood that he could not give up. It was the kisses, and her restless body, it was the way she handled and fondled him and made him frenzied with lust. The way she submitted to everything he demanded except his penetration.

Not today. Today she would become in all ways his mistress; today, she would enfold his penis in her sheath, and pretend that barrier between them had never existed.

She waited. She could just see out the stable door, see the sun withdrawing inch by inch by inch as the dark came over.

Any minute now.

Ducas . . .

Her body felt molten, liquid, ready to receive him, primed to feel the hard forceful thrust of him pervading her very core. Her nipples stiffened as she imagined it, and a telltale wetness secreted like thick honey between her bared legs.

Ducas, come . . .

The light was lowering. It couldn't be that he had changed his mind.

Perhaps he had; it wasn't unusual for him to change his mind. To want to penalize her for leaving him adrift like that last night.

So like Ducas. Some things were just honed in the bone.

She drew a shuddery breath. No, he would come. Even with his intriguing loss of memory, there was *something* in the blood that called to him. She felt it and she knew he did too.

She was so hot for him now, he had to come for her. And then she would make everything right.

* * *

He shouldn't have eavesdropped. It colored everything, his feelings, his memory of that kiss, how he saw her now, what he wanted to do, what he had to do.

He felt like Ducas. He felt Ducas's expectations seeping into his soul, and he wanted her, he wanted her kisses and he wanted to ream her as hot and tight as he could, and he wrestled with it for hours, but in the end, he knew he would willingly go to her, and be Ducas's body, and take Ducas's place.

She was a drift of white in the lowering light of the hayloft. He stood watching her until she became aware of him—aware of Ducas—aware of the charged air between them.

It took but that: Ducas alone with her in the same space, and the air instantly thickened with lust and desire. How could she have denied him last night, when, at this moment, she felt as if she could melt into his arms.

Dar read all in her beautiful face. Regret, desire, lust, fear. He moved toward her, slowly, the way Ducas might have done. Her breathing was shallow, shuddery with a violent tension.

He could see the rounded shape of her breasts and her tight hard protruding nipples under the bodice of her thin dress. The nipples that Ducas loved to suck.

He had heard way too much last night. He felt a potent craving to suck them, to pull and tug at the stiff hard tips, and watch her melt, and become pliant in his hands. *His* hands . . .

Time for that. Time for everything he could conceive to do to her and with her as darkness came down like a blanket over the earth.

"So," he said finally. "She who would be my mistress is here." *My . . . ? Mistress? Ducas's mistress. Ducas . . .* "After the way you kissed me last night, and led me on with your suggestive words and the temptation of your body, and then denied me what I wanted, and rejected my penis . . ."

What? Where had this come from? What was he doing?

In a blink he comprehended it: he was doing what Ducas would have done, instinctively saying what Ducas would have said, because taking Ducas's place meant assuming his attitude, his thinly concealed malice, and his overwelming lust-driven appetite for her.

He didn't want her to know he *was not Ducas.*

". . . I wonder why I'm even here."

"Then leave." As consumed as she was, she wasn't going to beg. That wasn't her way; she still had the pride and blood of the gypsy gushing inside her.

"Fine." He turned on his heel, and Angene whispered, "Stay—"

Of course. They must have played these games a hundred times. Even last night. All a game. He felt a little prick of anger on Ducas's behalf. She was holding her sex over him to tantalize him, to make him—Ducas—beg.

He turned back to her. "I'm sorry, what was that?"

"Stay—if you want to."

"Is there any reason to? Or am I wasting my kisses, my tallow, and my time?"

"Ducas—I feel like you're punishing me . . ."

"No, you punished *me* last night." He could almost feel it as if he had lived it, the hot hard gnawing thrusting pressure in his—Ducas's—penis—when she denied it surcease.

He didn't know why—Ducas didn't know why—he had come tonight. No, he knew: he wanted her still. And he had come solely to fuck her, and exert his mastery over her. To finally and forcefully take what she had so often denied him.

Nothing more, nothing less.

"Come to my bed and let me—"

"Let you—what? Repudiate my penis? Refuse my sex? No. A man doesn't tolerate that but once, if that." Oh, God, what was this? Would Ducas be this angry, this hostile?

He would. Dar felt it, he *knew* it. "There are too many other willing women in this world. And I don't need to know them personally, either. I've given in to you too much in my hunger to possess you. You don't understand that being a mistress means everything you do is subject to the will and whim of your protector. You don't ever reject the man who owns you. You are his property in every way."

Oh, yes, would Ducas feel that way. He owned her. *He* felt that way about this woman. He wanted to corral her, hide her away to keep her from inciting this streaming lust in any other man; he wanted make her *his* mistress—and he did not know where all this surging obsessive possessiveness was coming from.

"So—this is what you might not have understood last night: *if* I choose to go to your bed now—*if*—your body must be wholly and completely mine. You'll give me anything I want, any time, anywhere. You have no say, no opinion, no desires of your own when we are together. That is what a mistress is, what a mistress does. Whatever your lover and protector wants you to be, you become: he molds and perfects you for himself alone. You are always at his—my—beck and call, and nothing less than your complete and utter submission is expected, *and* your total immersion in my wants and desires. *That* is the bargain you agreed to last night. And those are the only terms which will bring me back to your bed."

She was shaking with a violent and repressed sensual excitement. His words aroused her, made her want everything he said, made her want *him,* and to be perfect for him, her body open and wet and willing, her legs spread for him all the time.

"I want that too," she whispered.

He knew it. *Ducas* knew it, and still—there were lessons she must learn—*Ducas's* lessons—before he allowed himself to burrow into her. And it was going to be damned hard to withhold it too.

"I'm sorry—did you say you wanted me back in your bed. . . ?"

Her eyes flashed. "I said, I want you back in my bed. I

said I will be the mistress you described in every way, and that fucking you will be my sole thought and desire from now on. I said, my body is yours to do with whatever you wish."

"Is it?" he murmured. "If being my mistress is your real and true desire, then why aren't you naked for me?"

"I have only just agreed to the terms," she muttered, pulling at her gown, lifting it over her shoulders and letting it drop to the floor. "There." She was naked underneath, the dim light shadowing the curves and hollows of her body in a most enticing way. Her breasts were heavy with desire, the nipples peaked, thrusting and hard. Between her long shapely legs, he could just see the most luscious muff of pubic hair that made his hands itch to touch her.

What Ducas saw last night; what Ducas nuzzled and licked, and had fully intended to plumb . . . where *he*—Dar—would root his already iron-rod penis in Ducas's stead . . .

"Get on the bed."

She moved to the quilt and sank down on it gracefully. *No will, no desires but his* . . . she had to forcibly restrain herself from lifting her arms to him.

"Lie back—"

She arched her back and propped herself on her elbows. "Come to me, Ducas."

This was the crux of Ducas's obsession with her, this mind of her own. This willfulness he could not control. There wasn't a man who wouldn't want to tame it and make her subsume everything to him. "You heed no one's wishes but your own in complete violation of what we just agreed."

"I cannot express my desire for you?"

"No. Everything is predicated on my desire for *you*—which is waning in the face of this small infraction of an agreement we made not five minutes ago."

This was not him talking, not him. Never. *This was*

Ducas. . . . Ducas's cupidity, Ducas's pitilessness . . . and he couldn't seem to get it under control—

—and yet, there was something so seductive about isolating her for his sole complete pleasure.

"I am not to talk?"

And he was falling headlong into the temptation of being her master. He almost couldn't help himself. "I thought I spelled out what I want very clearly, but I'll tell you again. I want your complete submission to *me,* my wants, my needs, my desires, my whims. Not yours." No, Ducas's wants, Ducas's needs . . . he felt like he was on a runaway train, heading off the rails.

Her eyes glittered in the dim light, but she said nothing.

"Good." He loomed over her, and sank to his knees. "Let me amplify: a man doesn't come to a mistress to be bedeviled. He comes to her for surcease from the everyday world. She creates a pleasure palace for him alone; she is the naked pleasure hole into which he sinks himself and pours his lust.

"He doesn't come for conversation." He reached for her right leg and began stroking it.

"He doesn't come for sustenance." He burrowed his head between her legs and tasted her hair.

"He comes to fuck she whom he chose to be his naked refuge." He licked his way from her mound to her belly. . .

"He comes for her tongue . . ." up to the underside of her breast.

". . . her nipples . . ." He covered one nipple with his mouth and pulled at it tightly; her body jolted and she arched that breast more tightly into his mouth.

". . . and her nest," he growled into the saliva-soaked nipple. He sucked it into the hot wet of his mouth again. He swirled his tongue around it, he licked it and lapped it and squeezed it between his lips, all the while she sinuously writhed and shimmied, seeking his hand.

She couldn't get away from it—the insistent flicking and

sucking of his long probing tongue, pulling and tugging and soaking her taut hard nipple in his hot saliva, never letting up, feasting on her tit, until she was bucking wildly against the feel of his tongue.

He never touched her, never, except for the succulent pull and tug on her nipple that sent molten gold streaming down between her legs. Her body jolted with every hard tug at her nipple. She needed something hard—really hot and hard—between her legs. She needed to grind down on it, she needed to explode all over it. She needed something, anything, his hand—

She grabbed his free hand and forced it between her legs. He tugged the nipple again, and her hips bore down on his hand, and he pulled at it, and sucked the very tip of the tit, and the explosion hit right between her legs, right there, and broke like a firecracker on his hand thrust hard between her legs.

He wouldn't relinquish her nipple. She couldn't say a word. She had never—they had never . . . and yet, now—her body was his, and the pleasure was unspeakable, like nothing they had ever shared before in all their grapplings in the hayloft.

It seemed like hours went by; the orgasm still resonated in her body. He still held her nipple tight in his mouth, but he had moved his hand from between her legs.

The air felt thick. Everything felt heightened. Fragile. It was fully dark now, the time when all forbidden things happened in secret. She wanted to say his name. She chose not to speak. This was enough. This fleeting bombshell of pleasure that had inundated her and pulled her into the undertow.

These were the things a mistress knew. These were the things a man would never do with his wife. This was a mistress's reward for her total submission to her lover.

This was what she was made for. This, and Ducas . . .

She felt a waft of air cross her sensitized breast. She felt his hand feeling and stroking the underside of her breast, her hip, her leg. She felt him move closer, more tightly against her body. She felt his tongue lick her cheek. She turned her head toward him, and his tongue grazed her lips, parted her lips, and slipped within.

She caught her breath—this was the kiss, the stunning, overpowering kiss that she had so missed last night. That was what was different. The kiss. She turned her body to his, into that kiss, into the sensual world that he created for them with that kiss.

Nothing was forbidden to him with that kiss. She unfurled for him with that kiss, and when he reached for her bottom, she shifted to ease his way as he began rubbing the soft rounded shape of her buttocks and stroking it slowly, patiently, deliciously, until the shocking moment he insinuated his long questing fingers into her crease.

She had thought his sucking her nipples had been an unspeakable pleasure. But this—this was unimaginable pleasure, the way he expertly fingered her crease, slowly slowly, with the utmost patience, seducing her, making her need that caress more and more—and then suddenly that anal erotic jolt as he inserted one—two fingers—and, as she made a rapturous little erotic sound, possessed her there.

She canted her bottom out toward him, writhing and wriggling almost involuntarily to invite his fingers to probe even deeper, the pleasure was that intense.

"Do I know my mistress?" he murmured, delving back into her mouth. "I knew you yearned to be fucked there, even if you didn't." He slipped his tongue between her lips and caught her tongue. "I know all your secret desires." He flicked his tongue all over hers. "All your obscene cravings." And took her tongue between his teeth and tugged on it, all the while pushing and probing deeper into her crack. "I will satiate every single one." Back into her mouth, with deep, dark, delicious kisses with that long insistent tongue she so adored.

"This luscious little intimacy comes first," he whispered against her lips. He pulled at her lower lip as she rode his fingers with a violent urgency. "Oh, my mistress does like the secret erotic things a lover would never do with a wife. This pleasure, my naked mistress, is reserved solely for you . . ." as he sucked at her lower lip, and then lost himself again in her hot sweet mouth.

Just like that . . . devouring her, holding and stroking her buttocks, and pumping her . . . subtle volatile movements in concert with his deep probing kisses . . . a haze of carnal pleasure peaking suddenly, and unexpectedly, from behind.

"*Stop . . .*" Did she say it, whisper it, breathe it, think it? She felt faint from the soft eddying sensations that flowed like molasses through her veins. Never had she experienced anything like this with him before.

He had never done this to her before. Never in all their times together. It was a revelation. It was one of the deliciously forbidden pleasures only a mistress could know, and now she was his mistress and deserving of the pleasure.

He eased his fingers from her, and caressed her there. He kept his tongue deep in her mouth, probing her everywhere. He kept that one hand tight on her bottom as he kissed her. Slow slow slow. All the time he needed now. He would take her so slowly she would melt in his arms.

Slowly, he stroked her crease and worked the fingers of his other hand down, down, down between her legs to her desire-swollen cleft. Stroking her there, feeling the luscious muff hair concealing her most feminine secrets.

She writhed against him, spreading her legs to ease his way. Luscious little intimacies as he slipped and pushed his fingers into the hot honey of her cleft.

She loved that. His thick questing fingers pushing into the depths of the most secret succulent place in her body. Deepening the caress, pushing—pushing, feeling . . . deeper, deeper . . . ah . . . !

"What is this?" he pulled his mouth from hers, leaving her bereft. He was furious for Ducas's sake; really shakingly furious. The virgin bitch lied.

To both of them.

Deliberately she had lied, taking advantage of Ducas's impaired memory. Taking what she could get without giving anything in return. Just like a woman.

He pushed her harder and she winced. The barrier. The secret of secrets now revealed.

"Well, now—" He felt the pure fury that Ducas would have felt. All those detailed descriptions of their fucking. Her love for Ducas's tongue, and the way he sucked her nipples. Lying that she was his mistress—telling him what he wanted to hear. "My mistress, are you?"

"In every way but one," she whispered.

"And you just love my long insistent tongue, do you?"

"Ducas—"

"Be quiet. All your promises of complete and utter submission—what did you think I meant? *I want that too, Ducas ... Fucking you is my sole desire from now on ...* Did you think I wouldn't remember every sweet sticky word?"

The fury he felt was overpowering, potent: the disappointment that he couldn't just root his throbbing penis into her honey pot at the instant, Ducas's roaring displeasure, and his, all tangled up together ... he couldn't get over his disillusionment. Everything now came clear: she had rejected Ducas's penis last night because of this, and now her obstructive virginity would prevent his immediate satiation while he wasted a damn lot of fucking time initiating her into her womanhood.

He could almost hate her except he was already so obsessed with her. Ducas would have wanted to kill her.

And now he had to be her teacher in Ducas's stead.

"Spread your legs, you lying bitch," he growled as he tore at his clothes and his penis jutted skyward. Oh, he was going to pour himself into her when he got past that barrier. He was going to fuck her all night and into the morning. And Ducas was going to punish her for the lie. Give *her* pleasure and then make her wait and beg for his penis ...

... insolent bitch, she had conception of the games adult

men and women played ... "if indeed you meant any of those lies ..."

"I want it," she whispered. "Everything. All you can give me. I meant my promises ... I hunger for your penis ..."

"Good, because you're going to get it ..." He rolled between her legs, pushing them farther apart, and then up on his knees so he could angle his penis just at her cleft.

Just there, pushing the tip of his penis tightly against her pleasure point, just within her tight hot sheath. She gasped at the restrained power of his penis, pushing, pushing just that little much and no farther, until her body enfolded just his bulbous throbbing penis head.

And in the dark, in the roaring furnace of his displeasure, where there was no other stimulation but her agonized expectations, she went utterly breathless at the naked and potent feel of his penis prodding at her.

She had hefted that penis, held it in her hand, rained kisses all over it, but there was nothing to compare with the sensation of its head poised at the juncture of breaching her womanhood and knowing what lay ahead.

She braced herself for the ultimate thrust.

And instead she felt him rimming her cleft with his penis head, moving it up and down her labia, pushing just the thick ridge of him against them, and pulling it out, in and out, in and out just the ridge of his penis head, just at the rim of her cleft.

Another unspeakable sensation. Her hips lifted to take him farther inside her, but farther he would not go. Just to the ridge, and he knew just how to hold the power of his penis right there, with his ridged tip inserted just inside her cleft.

She undulated frantically, and he would not give her more of his penis in her cleft than just the bulbous ridge because she had denied them even this much pleasure in the past ... last night ... he couldn't guess how many times.

And he had the power, the restraint, the fury and desire, to keep himself inserted just at the rim of her labia—all night if necessary. And just flicking the ridged tip in and out, in and out, rubbing the inner rim of her cleft in and out, pinning her to the makeshift bed by virtue of that subtle movement alone.

"*Ducas* . . ." her agonized whisper, heavy with lust-laden yearning.

"No." In and out, in and out . . .

"Please—"

Dar comprehended perfectly why Ducas wouldn't fuck her—because she had withheld her most secret place from him, because she rejected his penis, and in doing so, repudiated this intense and bone melting pleasure that only his penis head could give her. *And* she had pretended otherwise. Pretended everything. Made up fairy tales that had so aroused him, they made him avid to possess her nakedness for his own.

Ducas would have been in a rage at this monumental deception. Neither would he have given in to the temptation of her willing body so quickly. He would take his pound of flesh for all the humiliation she had dealt him, preying on his weakness.

Well, there was one part of him that was supple, strong, and bringing her to the begging point right between her legs, and he was reveling in it, and he wanted her to know it, all the while he had been thrusting his penis head just into her slit.

"Feel it, my deceptive lying mistress. This might be all of my penis you get tonight."

"*. . . Ducas* . . ." It was barely a whisper, fraught with need and a frantic desire she couldn't voice. She was floating on a haze of pure voluptuous sensation with no peaking point, no hard-rock penis to break over and give her culmination.

He was punishing her, she knew it, even in this slide of dark satiny pleasure, he was disciplining her, in his way, showing her what she could have had all this time, with him, without the lie.

In and out, the round ridge flicking her labia each time, in and out . . . her breath coming faster, her excitement ballooning out of control—in and out . . .

She licked her lips. " . . . *Ducas* . . . "

"*Tell me* . . . " Was that his voice, so raw and tight?

"I—*need*—your penis . . . "

"Your sex belongs to me . . . "

"My sex . . . yours . . . "

"If you ever lie to me again . . . "

"*Ducas* . . . "

"Women lie, mistress mine, all the time. A woman needs a penis only when she wants something from a man. So it remains to be seen what my not so trustworthy mistress wants from *my* penis." He grasped her legs and shifted them against his chest so that her body was at a slant against him.

"Give me your hand."

She gave him her hand and he pulled her to a sitting position, still with his penis head inserted in the rim of her cleft. "Feel my penis, feel how stone hard I am for you. All the time, my mistress, that is how hard my penis is for you. And I will cram every thick long inch of it into you—and I will make you . . . " He let go of her hand, and she eased onto her back, and he shifted her body closer to his. " . . . beg for it . . . " And he contracted his stomach, and he reared back, and he took her, just plowed all the focused force of his heat, his anger, his need into that sweet hot part of her that could give him peace.

Her body caved as her maidenhead gave way, and the pain sliced through her; but there was no stopping him. He thrust again, embedding himself still deeper into her core, finally still and at rest, certain finally that for this one pure pulsating moment, she was wholly and completely his.

The Other was with Angene—Ducas felt it, he knew it. *She* didn't know it, not yet. That coruscating bastard, alone with her, doing the things with her that he had done. Other things. Intensely erotic things that made her writhe and moan with pleasure. Things he perhaps had never thought to do. Naked things.

He knew it. He felt it in his blood.

And now his penis would never be the first to penetrate her heat and pound her honeyed woman flesh into submission.

He felt the rage stoking inside him like a furnace. Oh, he couldn't wait to get hold of the Other again. Death was too good for him. He would make his life a living death. He would take him, sip by sip, drop by drop so he would feel the incremental pain of his lifeblood seeping, oozing away, slowly, oh so slowly.

Chains couldn't hold him, walls couldn't contain him; nothing would keep him away from the duplicate, the Other, and his inevitable fate.

It was just a matter of loosening his bonds, which to do that, he must drain all his psychic strength. He had hoped he wouldn't have to do that, when he sapped so much of it to make the journey home.

But hours of heaving and straining had not weakened the links or pulled the hasps from the wall.

And time was running short.

And now Angene—that bastard had gotten to Angene, was pretending to be *him* with Angene. Was going to pole himself into her tight hot virgin hole where *he* should have been cradled—last night.

. . . last night . . . another disaster in a long string of them—he had not been able to excuse himself from all the postmortems about the chandelier. What was it but a thousand pieces of intricately cut glass—who the hell cared?

Obviously, Veleka did, but then the central debate of the evening was, how had it happened? They had seen no one, they had all heard the crash, and they had all rushed to the hallway.

No one was there.

Well, he had had enough time in this benighted dungeon

to parse out a possible scenario: it could have been no one else but the duplicate, the Other. A drastic tactic to divert him from reaming Angene, blast his soul to hell. He must have heard everything. He must have coveted what he, Ducas, was about to forcefully possess.

And so, the diversion, the capture, and all the information the Other needed to know exactly how to proceed with her, blast him to hell.

Bloody shit. He wrenched at the chains. The Other, kissing Angene, fondling Angene, sucking her nipples, licking her between her legs, forcing his hot hard penis deep past all obstacles into her sweet hot hole. . . .

He roared with frustration and fury, pulling frantically at the chains, feeling everything the Other was feeling, right to the succulent heat of Angene's honey pot as the Other embedded his rock of a penis deep within.

It was done . . . He was wasting the vigor and energy he needed for other things. The Other had triumphed, the Other possessed her now, and he was going to drain him to within an inch of his life . . . and then utterly destroy him. Give him to feed. Let the body fall where it might.

It was almost time to give everything up and go anyway. This whole episode had been one disaster after another. One more mistake and everything would come to the surface and it would be end of this life, sliced right to the quick, and precipitate the quest for the next one.

And damn it to hell, he did *not* want to start over again, he did not want to have to reestablish the host in another place and begin at the beginning. It would take so much time, so much distance, and endurance, perseverance, and a certain amount of luck to forge that new life and find new feeding grounds.

It was too much to give this up. Everything was in place. Everyone knew what to do and when to do it.

There had to be a way to save this situation, to convince Croyd that Alton's death was caused by some stray animal in the forest, to get those smug assinine guests out of his hair and out of his life, to rid the world of the duplicate of him . . . to feed the host—that was the worst. He hadn't returned with any sustenance. They'd taken it elsewhere, getting careless in the process.

Another goddamned catastrophe in the making.

Shit. Thinking about that . . . and the duplicate with his hands and mouth all over Angene and taking from her naked body everything that should have been his—every animal instinct snarled and reared up inside him . . .

He had to get out . . . by whatever means possible. He'd siphon off his own blood if it would help, but the answer would be the same: all he had to do was concentrate every atom of his being and dissolve his corporeal body into mist, and very slowly drift away to freedom.

And it always took longer than he thought it would. Inch by inch, his body melted into a swirl of vaporous air to the point he was able to propel himself through fissures, cracks, holes out of his dungeon, and then float into his bedroom through his cracked-open window, where he settled on one of the chairs.

He had no life force left after that. It had taken too much out of him, and he wondered about that, but he didn't even have the energy to examine the reasons why.

And anyway, he couldn't attack a kitten, let alone the duplicate, at this point. He was so tired; he couldn't even push himself to reanimate just then.

So the bloody duplicate would just be free to roam, deep in his pretense, the first to fuck Angene in the final moments before he met his fate. He would pay dearly for that alone. The morning was soon enough to wreak revenge on the bastard. All he wanted to do was rest, and reconstitute his physical form.

He needed his bed. And he needed at least his hands to get to his bed. It was a matter of concentration and will.

Give me my hands.

It was too much after the effort of breaking out of the dungeon.

Hands . . .

Nothing was too much for an Iscariot.

Hands. . . !

He could just just . . . just feel them taking shape, feel them becoming fleshly, earthly. He just needed his hands, just for a few minutes, and just enough strength to twist the bedposts, there and there.

The mattress immediately swung up from the footboard and he propelled his mist-self inside, spreading out in the coffin beneath the mattress and feeling every atom of his being dissolve into the bed of his native soil.

Now came the hardest part—getting the mattress back into place.

Done.

And the galling part—knowing that the duplicate would be sleeping above him on that very mattress tonight.

Dar was wrung out to his very core. In those few short hours with her, Angene had wrested the very life force from him and squeezed him—squeezed *Ducas*—dry.

Ducas who had possessed him, Ducas whose personality had ruled the whole fiery encounter with Angene tonight.

But he could not have approached her any way else, after what he'd seen the previous evening. Ducas was what he was, and any deviation from that remorseless malice that seemed inherent in him would have raised her suspicions too.

It was too, too easy to slip into Ducas's personality. Which meant there was a secret part of him that reveled in exerting his own power over a woman's sensual flesh.

And he already wanted to lock her in chains and keep her for himself.

Jesus. He was weaving himself into one tangled web.

And he hadn't checked on Ducas, probably a major mistake; but he was so enervated, she had taken so much out of him. He'd stumbled back to the house and up to the bedroom and just fell on the bed.

He needed his bed, he needed to rest, and he needed desperately to get Ducas out of his head and mind and out of the hayloft with him and Angene.

He wanted to fuck her again, now, his penis rock hard, rampant and at the ready just thinking about sinking into her lush sinuous body. He wanted to just embed himself inside her and live there . . . forever.

God, he was getting in too deep with Angene—

Angene . . . everything was now even more screwed up because he had fucked Angene—

Who thought he was Ducas . . .

Who had pretended to be him—

While he impersonated Ducas.

God, what a mess.

He couldn't think straight, and sleep was impossible; Angene kept getting in the way.

He felt edgy and restive, *prickly,* like there was something he'd missed, something he hadn't taken into account.

The spot on the carpet. The murder of Alton. The resurrection of Ducas. The dead animals. *The host has set the table.* The random murders of the dying on the battlefield.

Three days at Sangbourne Manor, and the ensuing utter chaos with Ducas's return.

But Ducas had been on his deathbed. When I walked into that tent, he was nearly dead. How is this possible . . . and how did he escape accounting to a military tribunal for all those other deaths?

How? He knew the answer: it was war; casualties were dying in droves, were nearly dead. Ducas would say he had done nothing but offer what medicines he could, what comfort he could summon in the worst of situations.

Dar could almost hear him—he could almost have written the script.

Too many dead—in a war on a battlefield? Did the colonel count the losses, keep charts, records, have comparisons of how many died on what battlefield in which war, to be able to say the losses were greater, more concentrated, in Ducas Sangbourne's care?

How could the colonel be so certain Ducas was a murderer, taking out his own men on his own side? No one could be sure of anything on a battlefield.

Or was it that the colonel was looking for a scapegoat to cover his ineptitude in battle? Perhaps it was the colonel who should be questioned about his leadership as opposed to an orderly whose sole assignment was to help wounded men die.

Perhaps the colonel overstated the case, given the exigencies of war.

A case that could never be proved, never be won by either side.

And somehow, Ducas had survived.

Something about that . . .

. . . and that little spot of blood . . .

—it was blood—

. . . Angene—

The prickling intensified . . .

. . . something wasn't right—*always trust your instincts . . .*

He started to get out of bed, but he couldn't . . .

. . . he felt himself suddenly swirling away . . .

—and he slept.

So. Angene had done it. She had taken him—Ducas—as her lover. Gaetana felt an anguish so deep it reached right down to the soles of her feet.

She could not have prevented it, she couldn't have. But she would never ever be sure that there wasn't one thing she could have said or done that would have dissuaded Angene.

She sat stolidly before the fire, a table before her, and cards in her hand. It was time to read the cards, to see the future, to plan her defense. Everything had been set inexorably in motion, perhaps since the time she had first been enchanted by Sir Eustace and Angene had been a child.

Her fault, then, all of it. She should have seen, should have known. But now it was clear that the purpose of Sir Eustace's devotion was that she shouldn't see. That his intention was solely to deflect her attention from things she wasn't to know.

She wondered if *he* knew.

And if he knew—did he condone any of it, all of it? After all these years?

What did it matter now? All of it had never been more than mirrors and smoke to distract her, and refract the reality of things as they were.

It was she who had let herself be fuddled by the fog of passion, the distorted reflection of desire.

She, who should have known better, had fallen deep into the trap. And so deep, she could not protect her daughter, and save her from the exact same fate.

She had become too much a proper Englishwoman, having turned herself inside out for her own lover Wentmore, to be everything that she was not, so she would be everything he wanted.

And where was he now? Up to London with his fine noblewoman wife and his aristocratic children, leaving her to the serpents and the wolves.

Never trust a man's promises. Never believe a man's lies.

She would have been so much better off in the gypsy camps, living with her own kind.

She heard the howl of a wolf, the clock striking one.

She felt the cold damp of the incessant fog outside. She felt the darkness steeping in her, brewing in her, straight to the boiling point, warming her like no fire ever could.

She had lost her fire, but not her flaming need for retaliation. This would be done. How and where, she didn't know.

Yet.

It could very well be in the cards. Had she not warned Angene? She would do whatever needed to be done in the face of any choices Angene might make.

And now it was done, she had become her daughter's adversary, and Ducas's enemy.

He had not changed. And he would use every trick at his

disposal to combat her. Anything, and anyone. Including Angene.

And now with this one foolish move, Angene had put herself right in the forefront of the battle.

Dear heavenly saints, what *was* she going to do?

Angene was in the way.

Chapter 8

"Ducas . . . !"

He shook himself in the matte dark confines of his coffin. Someone was calling him, impatient, imprudent, and no response from the Other outside.

"*Ducas* . . . are you sleeping?" Veleka—shit.

Was he . . . no, wait—it was all about the imposter's amnesia. If she was at his bedroom door, it meant the imposter had come to his bedroom at some point during the day. It meant she thought he was here, because where else would he go, since he remembered nothing?

And if she got no answer, she would break down the door.

Hell and hounds . . . he had to at least answer her.

Bah. He flexed himself—found his hands still in corporeal form, and his body partially reconstituted, thank the moon for small favors—

"*Ducas!*"

—and pulled the levers that lifted the mattress before he answered with a calculated grogginess in his voice: "I'm here. Who's there?"

"I'm coming in." Determined Veleka, needing to know every detail.

There was only one puny response to that. "Don't, please. I'm not dressed. I fell asleep." Who would believe *that* claptrap except an overeager mother with a memory impaired son, who was leery of making a move that would scare him?

There was a long pause.

He spat at the door in his impatience.

"Dinner will be served in twenty minutes." Her voice low, servile, for her. Scared to the bone about the coming days with Ducas . . . and no idea how to cope. What to say.

"I'll see you then."

Another long pause, and then the soft sound of her footsteps receding.

Trapped again. Where the hell was the Other? *He* should be juggling his family and his lies, and instead, Ducas was caught again—and if he wanted to keep this merry-go-round going, he had to impersonate the imposter yet again.

What? Did he? Wasn't it time to tell Veleka the truth?

But then what? The Other was still on the loose; Croyd had made no determination about the cause of Alton's death, and those awful gossipmongering guests would get an earful to take back to London.

Bloody well *not*.

All right. One more night of this insanity. And there was nothing to say the imposter wouldn't walk in the door at dinnertime anyway. And at that point every consideration would go out the window.

Shit. More complications to fray his nerves.

Where the hell was the Other?

He froze. He knew. Angene . . . doing all the things that Ducas had vowed to do. He knew it, he felt it.

Shit shit shit. The whole fucking night . . . ?

The bloody nerve of him, the balls of him. To come in

and just take over everything without a memory; without a life. It was time—way past time—to end the charade and take out that bloody bastard once and for all.

She stretched. Slowly, languidly, sinuously, she tautened every inch of her bare body, just to feel her nakedness, just to revel in the still-reverberating pleasures of the long and strenuous night.

Darkness enclosed her, enchanted her. Everywhere she could feel his long questing fingers exploring her, opening her, invading her, fondling her body in places she never knew she wanted to be touched, and then his penis—long, strong, rock rigid with his passion for her—spending all his lust in her . . .

His mistress did not refuse his penis this night . . .

So exactly the right tack to take with Ducas.

Mistress.

She was is all ways his mistress now, and it was worth everything to have achieved that, even his displeasure at discovering her deception.

But he had gotten over that disappointment the way Ducas would: by forcefully showing her what she had denied both of them in the wake of her egregious lies.

All that time, all that pleasure wasted, he had been so right about that; after, his taking her maidenhead had not been that hard to bear.

One long powerful thrust and it was done, quickly, simply, and with so little pain, and he had been so titillated, so enthralled by having been the first to breach her virginity, that it had been worth the wait for her as well.

She was made to be naked for him, open to him, mistress to him. That was the lesson he taught her tonight: her body belonged to him, he owned her, but she went willingly in his thrall.

This was the time to tell him, to whisper that she regretted all the nights she refused his penis that she could have serviced him, that she wanted nothing more than to be naked for him all the time.

But perhaps it was too late for that. The way he had used his penis, had tantalized and teased her slit, showed her more than his anger could ever tell her about all the naked and intimate pleasures she so willfully tossed away.

He didn't want to hear it. He had wasted too much time tonight. All he wanted was her body, her tongue, her sex. All the pretty promises and vows could wait. He didn't need the words. Just her body, sleek, pliant, and wide open to take his penis deep into her tight hot hole.

He couldn't get enough of her, her nakedness, her nipples, the deep rich honey enfolding his penis.

Over and over he plumbed her, burrowing deep deep inside her; hip to hip, thigh to thigh, mouth to mouth, he fucked her over and over the way she had imagined he had in that arousing sexual fairy tale she had fabricated for him.

Again and again, he took her, pounded her and filled her with his seed.

He showed her all the things a mistress needed to learn that she should have already known—not least her capacity for pleasure. All those intimate furtive little points of pleasure that he knew and taught her this night. Pleasure from his long, hot, unrelenting tongue, and his supple lips, sucking at her nipples, her cleft, her crease. Pleasure from his hot jutting penis, pressing against the pleasure point of her clit.

And that kiss. She drowned in that kiss over and over, as he pumped her and drove into her and blasted his semen into her tight shuddering core.

All this naked pleasure she could have had with him so long ago. But oh, it was worth the wait.

He lay with her side to side, his penis filling her, rock hard and thick, his right leg possessively draped over her thigh. He was playing with her nipple, squeezing it between his fingers, snaking his tongue in and out of her mouth, and rocking his penis relentlessly deeper in her hole.

It was the moment for intimate talk between a man and his mistress.

He pulled out of her mouth to suck her lips. "Now, my mistress, when I'm just barely satiated, and there are so many hours to go—now . . . tell me those regrets—"

She heard him in a fog of molten sensation, but she knew what he wanted to hear. "I regret I refused your penis," she managed to whisper. "I wish I hadn't wasted so much time . . ."

He twisted her nipple gently and she convulsed. "And all the time I wasted in discipline and teaching you. But—" he slipped his tongue between her lips, and whispered against them so she could barely hear him, "—it was ravishing that mine was the first penis to penetrate you. The pleasure of that reaming was beyond anything I've experienced with anyone. For giving me that voluptuous gratification, I forgive you . . ."

"You forgive me for wanting to be what I should have been to you all these months?"

"Because my penis was the first penis to penetrate your sex, yes. And there is no price that can be put on that." He pulled her closer, and pushed deeper into her mouth. Deeper into her sheath. Surrounded her taut turgid nipple with his fingers, and drove himself home.

And he wasn't done then either. It was as if the realization that his was the first penis to burrow into her hole was uncontrollably arousing in and of itself. His penis was a continual stone hard jut between her legs, pulsing and pounding between each paroxysm of pleasure.

She was panting as he spewed his seed into her. He rolled her onto her right side so he could pleasure her left nipple, and he avidly rooted for her tongue. His leg claimed her again.

The dark surrounded them—the rich earthy scent of the stable, the wafting night air, the subtle sounds—she swallowed the sounds, the scents, his tongue, felt his spurting seed where he was still poled into her, felt that dreamy creamy sensation of his fingers working her nipple into a tighter harder peak.

Her body felt insatiable. There was no end to the pleasures her body could bear. This never needed to end. They could fuck in the hayloft forever. They could have been fucking in the hayloft for months before this . . . but he never would have been this relentless to possess her.

These were the things mistresses knew. Her instincts were utterly right, now she was initiated into those intimate secrets too.

His tongue worked in her mouth, and he took her, rode her to a lathering explosive climax. Held her. Kissed her. Rooted deeper into her. Didn't want to go.

And left her, sometime in the early hours of the morning. Left her naked, sated, and sleeping and suddenly it was barely dawn, it wasn't enough and she was hungry for more.

But her wishes were of no moment here. She could put up with that. All those voluptuous private intimacies—*mistresses must wait* . . . but then mistresses were rewarded with the most obscene of forbidden pleasures.

And he would remember every lustful thing he had done to her tonight. Tonight was the bedrock of the future she had dreamed of with him.

And when he came back to fuck her tonight, she would be naked, willing, and waiting.

So he had dressed and gone down to dinner, and put up with Veleka's ceaseless reminiscing about everything he already knew, and kept his face a careful blank while he planned the long drawn-out demise of his brazen impersonator who was fucking Angene as he sat there stewing.

But hell, the Other wasn't a machine: he would have to come back to the house at some point. He would know Veleka would be looking for him, her idiot son, and he would have no idea that he, Ducas, had taken his place tonight.

No—that he, Ducas, was being Ducas, minus his memory.

He couldn't wait to get his hands on that bastard. He couldn't count the ways and reasons he had to exsanguinate the bastard. Soon. Back to the house, to the room—and he'd catch him there and he'd . . .

". . . do you remember anything at all about that incident, Ducas? Anything?" Veleka, at him again, reaching too hard, trying too much.

He was that close to telling her he hadn't forgotten a thing, and that there was an imposter roaming the grounds.

Caught himself just in time, looking at Lady Worsley's avid face. Oh, they were loving this, those imbecile friends. Just couldn't wait to take it all back to the social circles in the town houses and whisper behind Veleka's back.

Clods . . . peasants—little did they know . . .

They could never know—he was veering off the point. First things first. A small list of imperatives, really.

Get through the dinner. Find the imposter and kill him. Get rid of the tedious Croyd and the tiresome guests, cover his tracks, and then he could finally come home.

Now the next tricky thing—and Dar was leery of just what he might be walking into as he made his way to the dining room the next morning.

Leaving Angene had been well nigh impossible this morning; his whole body was utterly sapped, from sex and from all those conflicting emotions about Ducas, almost as if he were split in two.

But that was the hallmark of going into battle: nothing ever went according to plan. Strategies changed in a heartbeat. The ending was always a surprise, and every decision made always influenced the outcome, and usually not for the better.

His choice to stay rooted in Angene's potent, seductive body already had its consequences in his absence from dinner, and he had no idea what he would face as he warily came down the stairs.

It was one of those mornings, a bright light day, which was curtained from the breakfast table and sideboard. The aroma of eggs, ham, fresh baked brioche, hot chocolate, and coffee permeated the entrance hall.

He heard the murmur of voices—the guests, Sir Eustace, the rattle of a newspaper, Holmby's fluty voice asking who wished tea. It was warm and close, there was a fire in the fireplace, and, for one suspended moment before he joined them, he had the curious sense of coming home.

This was how it always should have been. The house, the quiet elegance, the mother, the father, the butler. The food steaming on the sideboard, good friends drinking morning tea, warm greetings as he entered the room.

What Ducas had always known.

What Dar hadn't known he yearned for.

And he waited for Veleka to leap on him about his absence from dinner last night.

Not a word. Strange. Everyone occupied with the morning paper or food, Veleka conferring with Holmby at a small table near the fireplace. Desultory conversation about nothing in particular, and some pointed comments from the gentlemen guests about the boredom of being cooped up in the Manor house, and speculation as to whether Croyd might finish with his investigation in time for Lord Worsley to save the Empire financially.

Odd.

And then—"Oh, you look so rested this morning," from Lady Worsley. "You looked absolutely bloodshot at dinner last night."

He froze. Last night . . . ?

Only one answer—Ducas. *At dinner . . . !*

He was absolutely rooted to the spot for one thunderous minute. And then he moved. He forced himself to move and lift a plate and take some eggs and kedgeree, toast, a cup of—coffee—it was coffee Ducas preferred, he remembered, and he made himself sit down at the table and take a fork-ful of food and put it in his mouth.

The ambush. The thing least expected with the least pre-dictable ramifications.

Ducas had got loose. Ducas had come to dinner. They never knew it wasn't *him*. Bloody hell. Everything shot to oblivion, and Ducas somewhere on the prowl.

"I slept well," he murmured at her still inquiring gaze.

He felt Veleka's attention veer toward him. He felt the prickling. Every sense of spurious peace evaporated.

"Hmmm—it must be a function of your condition then," Lady Worsley mused. "You sleep a lot, it seems, but per-haps that's your memory trying to knit itself whole."

Ducas hadn't revealed himself.

Veleka was looking at him strangely. Did she look a little pale this morning? There was nothing but tea beside her at the table, and Holmby writing down instructions, and her intense pale gaze burning him.

"I hope so," he said, in response to Lady Worsley.

"The human body is an unknowable mystery," Lady Worsley said. "Anything can happen when one sleeps."

"We need not to be so impatient," Sir Eustace put in. "We need to give Ducas time to adjust to being home. We've got to get past this ridiculous investigation Croyd is conducting over nothing. Then things will start to get back to normal."

Ducas had not told them the truth yet . . .

Dar turned that over in his mind while he forced himself to eat. Why? Last night would have been the best opportu-nity. He could have just told Veleka. But he hadn't. *He had-n't.* He had just taken Dar's place while Dar was being seduced by the siren call of Angene's body.

More and more complicated. Where was Ducas now? The prickling intensified. He could be anywhere.

He could be with Angene . . .

Holy damn hell, and he couldn't leave, he couldn't move. And Ducas . . . Jesus God—where *was* Ducas now?

*   *   *

He knew where to find her. And if there was one thing he was avid to do this day besides capturing his duplicate, it was to find Angene and take back what was his own.

Damn and blast the duplicate. No other man was ever to have touched her; even though he didn't love her, and he had his reasons for pursuing her, he had never found it an onerous chore to kiss and fondle such a willing and luscious wench.

Gypsy bitch. She was just like all those half-breed wantons, thinking of herself as more than just a diversionary spread of the legs for the lord of the manor. Wanted . . . what had she said? Assurances. Bitch.

They always wanted something. The only thing he had planned to assure her of was that he'd fuck her whenever *he* wanted. And now his impersonator had robbed him even of that one long anticipated pleasure.

She should have known it wasn't him. She knew him well enough. Had touched and fondled every part of him, bitch, without giving anything up. He didn't understand why she didn't know—even though all last night she and his duplicate had been in this dark hole-in-the-wall hayloft.

With her eyes closed in ecstasy . . .

Not fucked by him . . .

He felt the rage gathering in him.

Veleka hadn't even known it wasn't him either.

Shit. His own mother. It was the damned amnesia. Bloody blasted brilliant ploy, that was, manufacturing the perfect excuse for him being not who he was.

Well, let the Other play dress up this morning with his parents. He was going to dress down one gypsy bitch.

Time to put on the mask. Almost there . . .

And she was waiting, as he knew she would be, now that she had discovered fucking and the walloping pleasure of orgasms. She was just starting to pull on her dress when she saw him climbing the ladder to the hayloft.

Immediately she let the garment slip from her fingers and pool at her feet.

"Ducas . . ." His name was a breath on her tongue. "I knew you'd come back."

"I couldn't stay away," he murmured, with an irony that amused only him, playing for time, eying her critically. But there was nothing different about her, nothing to show that another man had so thoroughly possessed her with his penis the night before.

She gave him the same compliant and deferential welcome he had taught her. But now they could skip all the coy little games.

He had already tutored her in all the basic pleasures. He knew her body. They'd spent hours kissing and caressing right in this hayloft. He'd inserted his fingers between her legs; he'd thumbed and played with and sucked her nipples. Fondled every inch of her body. Plundered her mouth.

He had done every lascivious thing to her but the one thing that was a man's triumph: reaming her cunt. And now it was too late. At this point, when he could fuck her all he wanted, he would be damned if he poled his penis where another man's penis had rooted.

Hellacious duplicate. Now goddamned what? She was sitting on her rounded haunches as patiently as a geisha, waiting to be the receptacle for whatever her lover wanted to do.

He wanted, all right. He felt it welling up inside him, spurting his penis to life, galvanizing his desire. He wanted. Not the Other's takings, no—he would let her take him in the one hot wet place where she would have to suck away her sins.

"Ducas . . ." Her tone was absolutely reverent. He felt his hackles rise. How fucking good *was* this bloody imposter anyway? Enough to turn the resistant Angene into melted wax, obviously.

Well, he'd get the benefit of it now. At least he'd foregone all her mewling whimpering at the pain of his taking her virginity.

He got down on his knees before her, as he stripped

away his clothes. His penis angled up at her, massive, throbbing, eager for her sex.

"Did you love it last night?" he asked softly through gritted teeth.

"*Everything* you did to me," she whispered, obediently reaching out and taking his hard massive length into her hands and sending his already heated imagination soaring. "Last night wasn't enough, today won't be enough."

"Today won't be but a few stolen moments," he lied, trying to keep an even tone. "But I needed to see you." He needed something, and she was the one to give it to him to assuage his ballooning fury. His voice sounded too flat. He had to curb his anger.

"I am your mistress," she murmured as her stroking and caressing of his penis intensified with her growing excitement. She felt moved to rain kisses all over his shaft. To pump the ridged tip. "Oh, did I love that, when you taught me with this luscious part of you what pleasures I had denied us both." She looked up at him as she rolled her tongue around his penis head, and gently thrust the tip into the sperm slit as she enfolded the whole of it into her hot succulent mouth.

Taught her? *Taught her* . . . the son of a bitch *taught* her?

Fine. Fine. He couldn't think straight suddenly with her avid eager mouth sucking and pulling at his penis head, her tongue rooting all around it, licking the pearling drops of ejaculate that seeped past his control.

She could have been the mistress who made him lose control, he thought in a sensual fog. He could have set her up in a house, made her the sole source of his pleasure.

But the fact she hadn't noticed any differences, any inconsistencies between him and the imposter was galling.

No matter. He would take her. Her nakedness was his for the moment, her kisses, her cunt, her nipples.

He felt his excitement escalate with her arousal: her kisses and caresses grew urgent, her sucking purposeful.

He thrust deep, testing her, and she took his pulsating

length willingly, as a mistress should. Willingly and with a galvanizing greediness of her own.

He braced himself against her shoulders as she bent to accommodate him, her posture submissive and aggressive both.

His body went heavy, languid, he felt his juices thicken, congeal, his blood boiling with the need to mark her with his scent, to coat her nakedness with his seed.

Spend his cream on her breasts, coat her nipples with his thick spunk.

He reached for her naked nipples as his body gathered force. Pebble hard tits, all the time, begging for a man's mouth, or the coating of a man's cream.

She pulled his penis head hellaciously hard, just at the tip. Yes—he felt himself coming, slowly, sinuously, a flood of rich semen to spew on her breasts . . . right . . . *now*. He wrenched himself from her mouth, and grasped his shaft as he spurted onto her body, there, there, there—he rubbed the creaming tip of his penis against her nipples, one and the other, smearing his semen on each hard tip, back and forth, wet, thick, luscious, coating them with his cream.

And then he swooped into her mouth, his tongue ruthless in her, abrasive in her, sucking at her, thrusting deep into her mouth where his penis had been.

He was in a frenzy to possess her; he sucked at her neck, scraping the tender skin with his rough, persistent tongue. Fed at her mouth, her ears, her chest, scraping what felt like his teeth against her breast.

Her nipples were creamy with his come, and he still couldn't possess her. Couldn't get the thought, the taste, the knowledge that the Other had fucked her out of his blood.

He felt his excitement drain away like water. The Other had ruined it for him, ruined her, and taken his pride of possession from him in the process.

He thrust her away. "I have to go."

"Ducas . . . not yet . . ."

She should beg. She should be on her knees, prostrate,

obedient, begging for his sex, his forbearance, grateful that he even came.

"I don't have time to fuck you now," he said coldly. "You should be thrilled I found some time to let you taste my penis this morning."

"I treasure all the time we've spent together, Ducas." She didn't say, after last night. He might have done something drastic if she had. To have to compete with the imposter's sexual proficiency enraged him beyond words.

"I told you the terms," he went on, yanking his clothes on. "This is not a love story, Angene. You're the instrument of *my* pleasure. At my convenience, at my behest. And you're perfectly free to seek another lover elsewhere if servicing me has suddenly become onerous for you."

"No—not that. I just want even more of your penis . . ."

"Then I'll have to find a way to come back to you today, won't I?"

"Let *me* come to you later."

He considered it for a moment, all the inherent dangers, all the possibilities if she were caught, if the imposter was still on the loose.

"Please, Ducas."

He liked that aching little thread of desperation in her plea. Maybe it was for the better she couldn't tell the difference between him and the imposter, because if he stuffed himself into her tonight, he would make it a ramming she would remember forever.

"Maybe so. Yes. Come to my room . . . and I'll be happy to give you the fucking we both richly deserve."

Chapter 9

And then Croyd arrived, unannounced and unanticipated, following Holmby into the breakfast room with the air of a man who knew he was an interloper, but doggedly determined nonetheless.

"Good morning, Constable," Veleka said in rather frozen tones. She looked at Dar; Dar looked back at her. Her face went drawn, and she pushed away from the table and stood almost as if she thought she could be a barrier between this intruder and her family. "What is it now?"

"I'm releasing Mr. Alton's body, mum."

"I see." She sat down again. "Holmby, some tea for the constable, please." She waited until Croyd was served, motioning him to sit at the table opposite her. He sat. "So, have you come to some kind of resolution about Mr. Alton's death?"

"Yes—that it can't be resolved, mum. There are no clues, there's no evidence, no witnesses. Just the state of the body and the fact no one in Cheshamshire could possibly have a motive for wanting to kill that poor man. But I'm certain Sir Eustace will still want to do right by him, seeing as how it's been this long since he died, and no family to claim him, and he performed such a signal service to Mr. Ducas."

"Yes, yes, Sir Eustace has agreed to assume the burden of the burial. Is there anything else, Constable?"

"It should be soon, mum."

"We'll arrange it for late this afternoon," Sir Eustace said instantly, "before our guests leave. We'll send the poor blighter off well. Let me write a note for the vicar." He motioned to Holmby who immediately provided him with some stationery and a pen.

"Then that's that," Croyd said. He hadn't touched his tea. He was watching Ducas, and Lady Veleka, and Dar was very aware of his scrutiny, and watching Veleka utterly ignore Croyd altogether.

"If the vicar can accommodate us, let us say three-thirty this afternoon," Sir Eustace added, as he scribbled his note. "It only wants for a grave be dug; I'll have a coffin put together before then. This works out perfectly: our guests can then leave directly after."

A brief murmuring of approval met that statement.

"I will be in attendance," Croyd said. "I'll relay your instructions to the vicar." He took Sir Eustace's note.

"Thank you, Constable," Veleka said pointedly.

"Good morning then, mum, Sir Eustace, my lords and ladies." He had to withdraw then. There was no choice. He supposed he ought to be glad that Sir Eustace had spoken for the body; no use putting another unknown in the pauper's graveyard, but still—that drained and dry body, it plagued him, because of the animals. But there was nothing more he could do, nothing more to go on; every last supposition, lead, and surmise followed and discarded—he had to let it go.

And he had to go—off the premises, off the grounds.

"*I* will not be in attendance," he heard Veleka say just as Holmby showed him the door.

"My dear," Sir Eustace protested, "we must show all due respect."

"Not I," Veleka said adamantly. "I'm grateful he returned Ducas to us, I'm sorry he died, I fully agree with burial for him here, given the circumstances, and that is the extent of my compassion toward a man I did not know."

"Ducas—" Sir Eustace appealed to Dar "—convince your mother."

"It's not necessary," Dar said. "I will stand with the vicar." A silence fell at his words. "No one else need come. He was my aide, my responsibility. I remember that much at least."

He felt a sense of relief flood the atmosphere. But not Veleka. Her expression was frozen, her eyes tight on his face as he added, "I will take care of him."

"Excellent sentiments, my boy, but I will stand with you," Sir Eustace said. "That's proper. You're absolutely right. Anything else would probably be excessive. We'll just assume that Croyd has notified the relevant authorities. Otherwise, and if Mr. Alton has any family that wishes to claim him, why . . . we'll . . ." he petered off.

"We'll do everything we can to make that happen," Veleka said stiffly. "Ducas, are you sure? You barely knew this man, you said."

What? There was something in her tone. Something she wanted him to be aware of, but couldn't tell him. Her gaze was so intense. Every one of his senses tingled. The prickling started up again. Awareness, of tension escalating, of Angene distracting him, of secrets, of things he might have missed . . .

One wrong step now—but still, it was Alton . . . he could not in good conscience leave him now. "He brought me home," he said. "I will bring him to his final rest."

"As you wish," Veleka said, and there was something dire in her tone; it struck Dar suddenly that whatever it was that Veleka was desperate for him to comprehend, Ducas of course would have lost all knowledge of it.

Or was it something inherent, visceral? Something that was not solely of the memory, something born in the bone?

She was obviously visibly upset at his decision. The prickling felt like little daggers digging into his skin. Something he missed, something he should have deduced. . . ?

Something . . .

"Well, let us begin the process," Sir Eustace said into the silence. "If you'll excuse me . . . Ducas?"

He was startled for an instant, but of course Sir Eustace would expect him to have a hand now. "Yes, sir."

"Veleka?"

"I think I will just go to my room," she said, her voice still tight. "You all will have to entertain yourselves this morning."

"I know we can find a way to do that," Lord Worsley said, eying Lady Tuttington across the table. "A little do-si-do in the morning never hurt a soul. Get rid of this abysmally morbid atmosphere in any event. I don't suppose you'd care to join us?"

How like them, how perfect.

Ducas moved restively in the shadows as he eavesdropped on them. Impossible to reveal himself. Of course, Veleka was utterly stunned by the imposter's decision to attend the funeral. And he couldn't go to her. But she knew. Or—she believed Ducas the imposter didn't remember and she couldn't tell him, couldn't risk what might happen if she did.

He didn't know what to do. Maybe he should tell her . . . ? Or kill the imposter now? While the guests were still here? And then what—explain his volte-face?

No, he had to let the Other play out the mourning scene.

In the churchyard, surrounded by the one thing that should sap his life energy and in the ordinary course of events, bring him down: a cemetery full of religious symbols and crosses, his thorny crown.

Something was different—and yet everything was the same. Just as she expected with Ducas. That forcefulness, that touch of pettishness, that complete surrender to her potent femininity, as she wielded the power of his lust for her naked body to finally bring him to point.

What was it? His kisses? Stunning her one day, plundering her like a pirate the next? Did it matter? Ducas was hers in every possible way now, for as long as she could sustain his interest. That part was easy too—all she had to do was subjugate herself to his will and his desires all the time.

She had always known this. He had never pretended anything else. He had made it plain and clear over and above that before she even became his mistress. Love didn't enter into it on his part, and on hers—she loved him; being his mistress was all she'd ever wanted, she couldn't have given herself to him that way otherwise.

She loved him, but she couldn't help thinking something was different.

Thrilling, in a way. Dangerous. On the edge of pure volatility every time she was naked with him. But that was the seduction of it, the amazing thing she had learned: the more he fucked her, the more she wanted to be fucked.

She was aching to be fucked right now, and there were still hours to go before she could sneak into his room and surrender her nakedness to him yet again to do with what he would.

She was beset already with lascivious fantasies of how she wanted to be with him, what she wanted him to do to her. She had never appreciated the length and breadth of his penis until this morning, as she swallowed it in the aftermath of his taking her maidenhead.

And there was more to come. What *was* he doing now, when he could be fucking her? She didn't care. She must do as her mother had done with the Earl all these years: as long as he was still fascinated with her, she didn't want to know.

In the shadows, always in the shadows. Ducas followed and watched from beyond the cemetery gate as the plain pine coffin was carried to the grave site that had been chiseled out of the cold hard ground on the hill above the church. Strangers, carrying a stranger to his rest. A curious circularity that seemed almost right.

And then Sir Eustace, and the imposter.

Here, he got another good look at the One who would be him. And the resemblance was even more staggering. He was looking at himself, a pure, seemingly undiluted duplicate in every way: height, stance, body, gestures, planes of the face, timbre of the voice . . .

The Other *was* him, and the danger to him and his clan was incalculable while a duplicate of him was still alive. He thought it through with lightning speed as the vicar recited an abbreviated service that sounded like a buzzing in his ears from that distance.

He couldn't take the chance of getting closer. And all those stone crosses. And statues of saints. And crucifixes. He'd go down like a rabid dog, foaming all over his body.

It made no matter—the Other, Sir Eustace, and the constable were the only important ones there.

And the minute that Alton's body was consigned to the earth, it would be over. And then the guests would go, the charades would be over, and he could finally reclaim everything that was his.

Alton's burial was the beginning of the end: no more complications, and no more reasons for the Other not to die.

Now. Soon.

Mother, don't despair . . .

But Veleka looked absolutely shocked to see him after the funeral when they gathered for tea. She grabbed hold of the table as Dar entered the room, worked to steady herself with that intense iron will that he had always sensed she had.

"Ducas." Her voice was like rust.

"We had the service for Alton," Dar said, for want of anything to say in the face of her stunned expression. And why? The prickling started.

"And the vicar kindly provided tea for the pallbearers, the constable, and ourselves," Sir Eustace put in. "Very decent of him. And I'm sure Mr. Alton was a decent man and a good soldier. And we buried him as such. With all due precautions, as the vicar was careful to do. And now—I need a drink."

Dar thought Veleka needed a drink, she looked almost faint at Sir Eustace's words, but she never took anything stronger than tea. He wondered peripherally if he had ever seen her finish anything on her plate or in her cup.

"Then that's over," Veleka said, and there was still that rusty quality to her tone. "And it went smoothly?" directing her question to Dar, but Sir Eustace answered, "The vicar said a brief service, Ducas said a few words, they lowered the coffin, and the vicar sprinkled some holy water, and . . ."

Veleka sat down abruptly

". . . they laid on the thorns, the crucifix, and . . ."

"Then it's done," she said faintly.

"It's done. The investigation is over. We're free to move about. And Ducas is returned to us. It has been less than a week, my dear. There is nothing to be upset about, really."

"Of course. Nothing. Really." She stared at Dar. He stared back.

Something something something . . . the prickling . . .

"Just that Ducas doesn't know us, doesn't remember his home, his life before he went to that forsaken country, doesn't remember anything—still. Nothing, really—just . . . nothing . . ."

But there *was* something—the prickling danced up and down his body. All his senses suddenly went on alert as Veleka composed herself and rang for Holmby.

"Tell Cook—we'll have tea now."

"Of course, my lady."

Of course. Everything as normal as possible, in spite of the fact she was exerting master control over her emotions. A streak of color finally came back to her cheeks. She ushered them into the library.

No one else noticed anything amiss. The lord and lady guests were conversing among themselves about train schedules and how much packing still needed to be done. They had an hour, maybe more. They were no more happy to leave than Veleka was overjoyed to have them go. But they pretended otherwise.

Sir Eustace poured some wine. Veleka refused it, looked at Dar uncertainly, then turned away.

Shadows moved as the lowering light faded away. Servants entered, carrying trays of scones and sandwiches, urns of tea.

Everything was suddenly calm and serene.

But there was something—in the shadows . . .

Ducas in the shadows, and watching, always watching, cursing and damning the Other, waiting, waiting for the moment . . . Close now . . .

Soon—so soon—everything will be as it was . . .

They tried to seem as if they were not hurrying through tea. They really tried to make conversation, and drink slowly, and enjoy the sandwich triangles and sweets, but it was impossible with Veleka's haunted expression and the specter of Alton's funeral like another entity in the room.

They really just wanted to leave.

Ducas, in the shadows, willed them to leave.

"I'll have Cook wrap all these delicious sandwiches for you to take on the train," Veleka said. She tugged the bellpull beside the window. Holmby appeared. "Prepare the food for traveling. Our guests will need sustenance for the trip."

There was a five-thirty train. They raced up the stairs to their rooms to make sure they had packed everything. Servants began hauling their trunks down to the entrance hall.

Holmby summoned the coach and driver. It would be a tight squeeze, but they didn't care. They had a basket of tidbits, a bottle of wine, and they piled themselves, and every inch of the coach with their belongings.

"Good-bye, good-bye, thank you for everything, thank you..."

They meant it, they supposed. The first night had been decent fun. The gypsy dancer, the frotting and trotting in the aftermath. Sir Eustace, looking utterly besotted, taking the gypsy off into the shadows.

Juicy gossip that could never be told unless they wanted their own excesses touted in the *Times*. But lots of delicious conversation for the train ride home.

No, if it hadn't been for the son's unexpected return, and that heinous death, it would have been an excellent country house weekend. Veleka knew how to provide just what a guest needed.

Sir Eustace was a fool, they all agreed. If he weren't around, what wouldn't Veleka try?

It was amusing to speculate. And lord, they were hungry. They tore open the basket, napkins and waxed paper, with crumbs flying everywhere.

The host has set the table.

Shadows moved. The coach was swallowed in the darkness.

And now, the obnoxious guests were gone, his one and only purpose was to kill the Other. The stupid, ignorant Other, who would have no idea why he had sacrificed his life.

Then, everything would be as it was.

They were still clustered around the door, watching the coach barrel off down the drive. Veleka seemed rooted in place, and even Sir Eustace's awkward pats on her shoulder offered her no comfort.

In the shadows, Ducas watched, wondering. Did she know?

She knew—she had to know. What could explain the Other's imperviousness to everything that should have destroyed him?

She had to know... it would make things easier if he

could believe she did, because he couldn't stop to tell her now. The minute his duplicate moved out of that room, out of her sight, away from any witnesses, he would attack and feed.

The imposter would die so the Iscariot could live.

So he watched, and waited.

Veleka turned from the door. "They are finally gone. I am exhausted. Nothing has changed." She looked pointedly at Dar.

"My dear, we've been so numbed by all that's happened in the last week," Sir Eustace said, trying to comfort her. "You can't expect everything to fall in place all at once."

"No, why should I? Murders and intolerable guests, and my son a mere husk of what he was—everything falling into place now would be some kind of miracle, and I never believed in them."

"You ought to go to church, my dear."

She shuddered. "In all the years we have been together— you've never stopped trying get me on my knees."

"Nor shall I. With you, or with *you*, my boy." He turned to Dar reassuringly. "Stop trying, I mean to say. We can get doctors, we can . . . talk to you, show you your history, find some new medical thing or technique that might work. We'll do everything in our power . . ."

It was a too kind old man, Dar thought. The kind of father *he* could have loved. Such a good heart—a little fuzzy sometimes, liked his port a little much, and perhaps needed to blot out the fact he was getting old and Veleka was so much younger.

And Veleka's intensity had to be wearing.

"Anything you think is best, sir."

"Sir, Sir, Sir!" Veleka snapped. "He's going to *sir* you to death . . . he's gone—it's so clear—I don't know what I'm going to do . . ." Her voice broke.

Watching, Ducas felt his impulses split in two. He couldn't go to her . . . he watched the Other go to her . . . cursed the Other for going to her, would kill the Other for going to her . . .

"I'll try," Dar said to her. "I'll try to remember." What the hell, he thought, he could play it through—it cost him nothing. He felt her anguish. He felt Ducas hovering around him. He felt danger, as real as pain.

The prickling shimmered all over his body. Ducas, close as a breath. Something else—something he'd missed . . .

"Will you?" Veleka asked, her voice raw.

He felt hot and tight, the prickles like darts piercing his skin. He flexed his hands. There was something about hands . . .

"I want to remember as much as you want me to," he said unsteadily. God, he had the most unnerving feeling that Ducas was around—that Ducas was listening to every false and artificial word he said.

Veleka stared at him, her fierce eyes searching, always searching, something in her gaze uncertain, wary. "I hope so," she muttered. "I need to go upstairs now. I won't want dinner—you two may fend for yourselves."

They watched her ascend the stairs. "I should go to her," Sir Eustace murmured.

He had to find Ducas. "I should rest," Dar said. He felt the urgency pulsing in him. Something had come to a head. The guests were gone, the pretense was over.

Ducas was ready to reveal himself.

They walked up the stairs together.

Two doors slammed, one after the other.

Ducas emerged from the shadows. How perfect, how utterly familial of them. How pathetic. He would give his noxious Other about five minutes to feel sorry for that stupid old man before he brought him down. A generous five minutes because of what Veleka's marriage to Sir Eustace had given his clan.

Four—three—two—

He slipped back into the shadow and moved up the

stairs. Quiet in the house in the early night hour. All to the good. Never many servants around. Too dangerous. And the ones that were here . . . well, they were here.

He heard the wail of the train whistle in the distance. Praise the moon, the insufferable guests would be miles away within the hour.

And now the Other . . . He savored the anticipation. It had been a hellacious few days, but now, there would be blood and retribution . . .

He was at the door, turning the knob—voices within . . . damn it to hell, that little tut Angene . . . couldn't keep away, not that he blamed her, but almighty hell, you give a woman a foot of penis and she devours the damn thing whole . . . and demands more, not hours later?

Thinking it was *him*—? Shit, he should wring her neck, kill her too, why not—she was still virginal in spite of the fact she'd been plowed; her blood was still fresh, dewy, shimmering with light and discovery—

He could almost taste it, had almost made up his mind to take them both . . . take Angene first to fuse himself with her sexual vigor—

And then a deep frayed voice behind him interrupted his thoughts.

"The host has set the table."

No no no—not now . . .

He whirled to find the old man in ragged clothes who smelled of horse and hay. *No no no . . .* He grabbed the man by his shirt. "*What do you mean?*"

"The host is feeding at the table," the man whispered.

"*No . . . !* They didn't—hell and hounds. Shit shit shit . . ." Ducas thrust him away, waved his hands, and the man disappeared.

"Blast and hell, the fools couldn't wait, couldn't see . . . *shit*—"

He was five feet away from his prey. Not five feet away from reclaiming his life, and from gorging and avenging his own.

And he couldn't even open the door because of Angene. Bloody slutty Angene and her insatiable appetites that *he* had unleashed and now the Other was fucking her in *his* bloody bed where *he* should have been, taking advantage of him priming the bloody pump.

He couldn't begin to find the end of his rage.

And now this.

Dammit all to bloody hell.

The host had attacked the coach.

They were feeding on the guests.

Another fucking disaster . . .

The bloody Other would have to wait.

Chapter 10

He waited until he heard Sir Eustace close the door. It was dead quiet in the hallway, no one was about, there was no sound except the faint howling of wind. No sensation but the everlasting prickling up and down his body.

His hand was on the knob, but Dar couldn't quite bring himself to open the door to his—no, Ducas's—room.

He could feel Ducas swirling in the air all around him, inside him, become him . . . Ducas was close . . . hovering in the shadows, on the attack.

He had always known it was a matter of time. Ducas would subdue him or he would subdue Ducas. He wondered if it mattered, really.

What mattered, really. . . ?

He pushed open the door to find—Angene on his bed, her naked body sculpted and hollowed by the firelight.

He had expected to find Ducas, to do battle with Ducas; the last thing he expected was Angene, pale and luscious and the essence of sensuality.

Lord almighty—not now . . .

Angene, looking up at him with those beautiful eyes, and

patting the bed beside her, murmuring, "I was waiting for you to come."

Angene—not Ducas—he had to shake himself to make the switch, had to instantly shift the intensity of his focus to her—not Ducas, not mystery, not shadows, not death, but Angene—everything that was light and life and radiant.

Angene. Her one leg angled so that she was open to him, inviting him to come to her. Angene—he couldn't afford to give himself over to Angene—not now, not *now*.

He pushed everything else out of his mind.

Maybe now . . .

"Ducas . . ." All her longing for him was in that one word, as she made one agile movement and levered herself upright.

No man could resist her. Not the way she looked, perched on her knees, her bottom rounded so enticingly, and begging him to come to her.

He stripped as he strode to the bed. All sense of Ducas diminished. The prickles eddied away.

Angene. She wanted him on the bed seated behind her. She wanted to drape her legs over his thighs, so that she was wholly open to him. She wanted to sip and suck his kisses, and feel his hands sliding all over her, squeezing her nipples, caressing her breasts, teasing and finger-kissing her slit; she knew what she wanted, his mistress Angene, and he saw no reason not to give it to her. This time.

Her skin was milky soft, her nipples hard at the tip as he fondled them and tugged them and made her convulse. His hands felt her everywhere, tormenting her nakedness every way he knew how, as she writhed and her body jolted against his straining thrusting penis. She rode her buttocks tight against his shaft, her arched body demanding his expert heated touch the one place he would take her.

No, he preferred to torture her, cupping and feeling her mound, stroking her slit, inserting a finger and removing it, stroking, inserting, stroking, inserting, and tugging her nipples in concert with the stroking so that she almost screamed with frustration.

And when he finally parted her labia, and began stroking her there, brushing her clit, and stroking, brushing and stroking, squeezing her nipple, and finally allowing her to ride his fingers to a shattering culmination, he felt her fracture in his hands.

There couldn't be more, she thought in a haze, she didn't know she could take anymore. But there was, he insisted on it. And now he was in control, it was for his whim and his desire that she stay parted for him.

He wasn't nearly finished with her there. He had not fully penetrated her there, and he wanted her there, with every finger he could thrust into her, he wanted her there.

Never forgetting she thought he was Ducas, and that Ducas had initiated her, that she believed Ducas had deflowered her. He felt like Ducas, he *was* Ducas, mastering her, enthralling her, making her his slave.

"My mistress has interesting ideas," he whispered in her ear. "I like having you spread out over me like a feast. Every delicacy for me to touch and try and taste. And it is my turn to feast." He moved his hand, the hand that had pleasured her, and stroked the nipple of her other breast.

Her body quivered. He squeezed the nipple, and she groaned. He held it between his fingers, just so she felt it being compressed, and her body jolted. Perfect.

He held her nipple, and ravaged her mouth and she writhed and undulated and shimmied trying to get away from his fingers that held her nipple tip so lightly, so intimately, so commandingly, and his savage mouth.

It was a soul searing kiss, stunning, in concert with the erotic way he held and compressed her nipple, and nothing else. She needed nothing else. Every nerve in her body was focused on what he was doing to her nipple, to her mouth. To her body. The tight swirling molten feeling skeining from her nipple right down between her legs.

And she couldn't close her legs; they were spread wide apart, angled adamantly over his. All that hot gold was his if he wanted it. He had only to dip his fingers into it and she would dissolve.

But he wasn't ready yet. Her kisses were too luscious, her nipple too enticing to give it release. His body swelled, his blood poured through his veins, and his already distended penis elongated still further.

"*Du-cas-s-s—*" Agonized whisper. Body throbbing, her hands seeking his penis as she canted her hips forward to lift herself just so she could get at his penis and maneuver it under her sinuously twisting body.

If she could just have it there, between her legs where she could cushion herself against its thick hardness, if she could just seize it and hold it in concert with his expert manipulation of her . . . his masterful stroking, his fingers dipping and sliding . . . elusive and hard both, she couldn't quite catch the breaking point, couldn't quite bear down on the pleasure.

So it hovered, sending her into a thick swoon, both of his hands now invading her cleft and playing with her clit, probing her every which way he could think of as she hung onto his penis and rubbed and squeezed the tip.

And suddenly she felt it blooming, gathering, the feeling mounding, thick, rich, hot, hot as the semen that oozed from his penis head, as she languorously massaged it into his skin, the feeling split like lightning right between her legs.

She pounded against his shaft, every crackling pulse convulsing her tight, tight, tighter onto his shaft.

And then suddenly, in the midst of this tidal wave of sensation, he shifted her forward, pushing her into the mattress and drove into her from behind.

Her head popped up. What was this? This obverse position, this feeling as if she were connected to her world solely by the length and strength of his penis?

It was nearly sublime—he could reach almost any part of her, she couldn't touch him. She was at his mercy, and yet the anticipation of being at his mercy was exactly where she wanted to be.

He held her buttocks tightly because he was that close to letting go, too close, her bottom too enticing, her orgasm too explosive; a man's penis could only take so much, and the way she was wriggling and wiggling to pull him more deeply into her . . . all he wanted to do was drench her with his seed. He pulled out, pulled back and forcefully drove himself home, again, and again, and again, pulling her with him, so out of control to possess her that he didn't know where she began and he ended.

And then he ended, in a final, soul drenching spume of ejaculate that wrenched him to the core. Boneless, he draped himself over her, covering her naked body completely.

She was as utterly drained as he. There were no words for this, not for her, not for him.

He was hot on her, elongating hard against her, enveloping her, head to foot.

She undulated under him, soft sinuous movements of contentment, little humming sounds of contentment at the back her throat that increased his sense of satisfaction.

Except that she thought he was Ducas, she believed he was Ducas, and when he allowed himself to remember that, he felt the evanescent moment of gratification begin to drain away.

No. He wouldn't let Ducas do that to him. She was his in every way possible, he had taken her in all ways . . . she belonged to him, and he would never relinquish his claim on her.

He pushed a stray hair away from her ear and blew on it. She shuddered and shimmied her body against him, and he felt himself awakening again.

Slow this time. All night this time.

He stroked her hair. She had bound it into a tight bun, the better to give him access to the long sweet line of her neck.

It was what Ducas would want her to do so that he could suck on that tender flesh; that was what Ducas would do, he felt it, felt the urge suddenly and powerfully to lick it, just swoop out his tongue and gently scrape it . . .

Scrape?

He felt Ducas at him insistently—scrape her, mark her . . .

How?

He fought the urge. He kissed her neck just under her ear, then up to her ear where he took her lobe gently between his teeth and shook it.

. . . scrape her . . .

He swiped her neck with his tongue.

. . . mark her . . .

He jolted back almost involuntarily. The drive to do it was so relentless, it took every ounce of his will to restrain himself, to pull back, to lift himself up, panting and growling, while every muscle in his body strained to get at her . . .

She turned onto her back and opened herself to him.

. . . Take her . . .

. . . Mark her . . .

He jacked himself off the bed, but it was not enough. He wanted to leap right back onto her body, to feel and lick and scrape every inch of her soft silky skin with his tongue—

What?

He stood there, his hands on his hips, his body shaking with the effort to suppress the need. *Goddamned Ducas . . .* it had to be Ducas . . . the force of the urge was so overwhelming, almost overpowering. Ducas was near, goading him, taunting him.

"Angene—"

"Yes, Ducas?" she murmured sleepily, and he felt like slamming his fist through the wall. All that lush flesh. All

that naked need. Not his, never his; she had always belonged to Ducas.

She still did.

He edged away from the bed. He had to get away from
her *now*. Ducas was too much in his consciousness, too
much on his mind.

Darkness fell—Ducas was near . . .

She held out her arms, she spread her legs, no words
needed. She wanted it again, wanted him, wanted Ducas.
Wanted.

And Ducas would take her, now, and ride her, rough,
hard, hot.

Take her . . . mark her—

The impulse was irresistible, her body was a temptation beyond anything he could withstand. Ducas wouldn't even try.

He climbed onto the bed, he mounted her, he poled himself between her legs, and he rode her, rough, hot, hard.
And he marked her, rough, hard, nipping her neck, her
chest with his teeth, with his lips, sucking, biting, this way,
that way, tasting her scent, her mouth, her skin, lunging,
thrusting, driving himself home.

Gaetana sat brooding in her parlor, her head swathed,
her heart heavy.

Death was in the air. She felt it. She knew it. It was all
around her. It saturated her bones.

Outside, the fog grew dense, obscuring an orange moon.
A dog howled. Bat wings fluttered. A silence blanketed the
earth like death.

Before her, on the hearth, she had made an altar, laying
out her best silk shawl, her copper tray on which there were
thick candles that would burn the entire night. Her trea-
sured crucifix. A vial of holy water. A silver dagger. A bra-
zier of incense in a ring of thorns.

She had such a feeling of unreality. She had come so far,
and she was sinking to this . . .

All of it so clear now. Too clear, and there was nothing she could do to save Angene. Nothing. The way no one could have saved her, Gaetana, had she not been so rudely thrust from her fantasy.

"I thank the Lord for His mercy," she murmured. Because she might never have known, never have emerged from the fog and seen what was truly before her eyes.

Now she knew. Now her every sense was honed on the truth, but still, there was so little she could do.

Even this small gesture seemed futile, when the air swirled with the sense of death.

They were on the prowl, she sensed it, she knew it, and had her mind not been corrupted by lust and sex, she would have known it long before this.

And yet, what could she have done to prevent it?

She brushed the silk shrouded altar with one hand. Beside her, on a small table, she had put everything necessary to work her spells. Soil from the graveyard. A wooden spoon made of hawthorn. Holy water. Rusted nails to contain the evil and pin it in place. A candle, to shine light on the evil, and a small piece of mirror to reflect it onto the sinners.

The ritual was simple.

She threw a handful of dirt onto the altar.

"Let the earth and every creature repudiate thee."

She took the wooden spoon and tipped some of the holy water into it, and poured it onto the dirt.

"Let thy corrupted body turn to wood."

She pushed a handful of rusted nails into the soft wax of the candle.

"Let the black earth take hold of thee that thou be stayed in thine evil flight."

She took a small mirror and shone it upon the crucifix.

"And let thou remain corrupted that thy sins might be reflected and contained."

It was enough.

It was not nearly enough.

"Let thy corporeal body repent and let the earth yet spew thee out. Let not the earth consume thee, nor the heavens accept thee into divine rest . . ."

She felt frantic suddenly, as if divine goodness could never win the battle against the deathless and corrupt. "Let thy God repudiate thee wholly for thy sins. Let the earth swallow thee into eternity . . . let every creature of the night reject thee . . . let the earth and thy sins corrupt thy body . . . let the worms eat thee and rot thy soul . . ."

And on and on she prayed and rendered judgment, as dogs howled and the rolling fog covered the countryside, deep, deep into the night.

She awakened in his arms, pinned to the bed by his body, with his penis embedded to the hilt inside her. She could feel it so intensely—just an amazing length of hard rock. It was a marvel, his penis, it was so unrelentingly *there*. And his stamina . . . it did not bear thinking about, or she would feel more exhausted than she was already.

And yet, and yet—he was everything she had ever imagined, everything she had hoped and dreamed. He was the lover of her fantasies. A little rough—she could still feel the rawness on her neck and chest, a little tender, and wholly perfect in the way he fondled and fucked her. He knew her. He knew everything about her now, after he had expertly explored every inch of her inside and out.

The thought made her breathless. Her body twinged with memories of its own, coming awake, unfurling, seeking him on its own.

He felt it, he jolted to awareness, his penis instantly elongated, and he eased himself onto his elbows and cupped her head between his hands.

She was so beautiful in the dying firelight, with her hair so tightly bound, her long neck showing the faint pinkish scrape of his passionate nips, her swollen lips and pleasure-hazed eyes, and the faint shimmy of her hips as she stretched against the hard rock of his penis in her body.

"So," he murmured, smoothing her hair, "here is my naked mistress barely awake and she took all of two minutes to make me hard and hot to fuck her."

"Your mistress would love it," she whispered.

"Good. Because I don't think she has a choice," he whispered back, and claimed her mouth. Deep deep inside her mouth, inside her body he went.

She was hot, she was like honey inside and out, and he used his penis like a piston, taking her in short, hard, hot rhythmic strokes, riding her, driving her body into a thick rich surrender.

And when it came, so quick, so hard, it was like molasses, pouring all over every inch of her body with pleasure that pooled and eddied away deep between her legs.

"I think," he whispered against her aching lips, "I think I will keep my orgasm for a while. I want breakfast . . ."

She was panting, still feeling the thick swirl of her orgasm coursing through her. "And what would breakfast be, my lord?"

"Nipples. I want your succulent nipples for breakfast, my mistress."

She caught her breath. Her nipples hardened still more. He rolled onto his back, taking her with him so that he was still enfolded in her heat. But now she was above him, her breasts swinging free, her nipples hot, tight, hard for him, and his mistress bending forward to give him the easiest access to them.

Just the nipples. He surrounded each nipple with his fingers and held her there. Her body creamed, heated, moved restively against his rooted penis as she felt the subtle pressure of his fingers on the hard tips.

Her hips gyrated, shimmied, writhed as she sought to get away from the pressure. It was such a pleasure point, her hard nipple tips. She almost couldn't bear it, the feel of his fingers possessing them just there, lightly lightly holding them, just that way.

Every which way she moved, he held her, never relinquishing his touch. Never squeezing. Never tugging. Just firmly and relentlessly there.

"Oh, please . . ." She hung onto his hips, she wriggled and moaned and pushed against him, his fingers, his penis, his body. She rode him, she swallowed him the way he swallowed her nipples with his hands.

"This . . . this isn't—breakfast . . ."

"This is the . . . appetizer . . ."

"Don't stop—no, stop . . ." She could barely breathe the words, she was so swamped with sensation coursing through her from his manipulation of her nipples. "Yes—yes . . . please—" Now it was threading through her like gold, thick molten gold, moving hot and slow through her veins. Now, soon . . . a skein of gold, bright as light, furling voluptuously through her body to envelop his penis with her convulsive heat.

And still he didn't come. He covered her breasts with his hands and held her there, gazing deeply into her eyes that were so fogged with pleasure she could barely see straight.

That was fine. That was her purpose. To give him all the pleasure she could handle. And he knew her now, knew every flash point on her body. Knew just how to make her squirm and writhe.

And he wasn't quite ready to spew his seed. It was rather amusing to keep fucking her and not explode. But he was as pent up as a volcano. He wanted her still more. He wanted her under him, undulating, pumping, begging . . .

He rolled her onto her back. "And now, the main course . . . mistress mine." He went back deep into her mouth, deep into her honey, a kiss as long as tomorrow, as deep as the future.

Her jangling body arched against his, reaching for those kisses and what they signified. *Everything she ever wanted, everything her mother ever had . . .*

And more . . . ? For as long as she fascinated him, more . . . More . . . more . . . and more . . .

As he drove into her mindlessly, again and again. More. And more still . . . Was it that she couldn't get enough of his penis, or what her being his mistress meant?

What did it mean?

In the heat of the moment, why was she thinking this way? He would expect her to find her pleasure, and she suddenly felt rubbed out. She wanted him done, over, and a man's mistress never ever thought that way.

She canted her hips upward, lifting herself so that he took her at a high hard angle that would position his penis in more direct contact with her pleasure point. Things a mistress knew.

Things to juice things up when they were drying out. Immediately she felt a crackle of pleasure. She got wet. She felt supple, sinuous, strong.

Her nipples peaked. Her hips undulated, enticing him. She sought his kisses. Everything a mistress in desperation would try to do.

He had lost her, and he knew it.

Almost immediately everything stopped, and he withdrew from her, his penis swollen and slick with her honey and heat and desire.

Nothing needed to be said. She tried anyway.

"Ducas—I . . ."

Ducas . . . He rolled onto his back, his hand over his forehead, his penis a jutting granite shadow in the firelight. The hell with Ducas. Ducas wasn't in the bed with her—and her lies.

But he felt Ducas in the room with them. He felt Ducas's keen irritation that she hadn't given him what he wanted. What she had convinced him it was her pleasure to do.

And he knew what Ducas would do, what Ducas would say. He felt Ducas's hot-blooded displeasure course through him. Lies should be punished. Mistresses shouldn't be trusted. He felt Ducas's blooming anger that she had wasted him like that.

"So, mistress, you reject my penis again."

"Ducas—no, no—" She reached out to touch his penis, and he brushed her hand away.

"Don't be condescending, Angene. You didn't want my penis yet another time. And one rejection is all you get."

He could almost feel her heart stop. "What do you mean?"

"I mean this is the second rejection of me and of my penis, and what else can I mean? If I own your body, if as my mistress everything you do is in service of pleasuring me, then you've failed. I'm hardly pleased that my penis can't plow you to another peak this morning."

"Ducas," she begged in a broken voice, "please . . ."

"Please what? You accepted my terms, and now . . . you make your own rules. You retreat from your orgasm. You reject my penis. You still want to be my mistress. You claim to want my penis, but how is that possible after this? How can I ever be confident that you're wholly and fully mine? I thought you were. I believed you were, and that you and your luscious naked body were completely dedicated to my pleasure. Only *I* haven't had my pleasure this morning, but you've surely had yours while you were spurning my penis."

"Ducas . . ."

"I told you what I expected of my mistress. I don't think there's any more to say."

"I want you. I never haven't wanted you."

"Not this morning."

"It just . . ."

"No . . . you removed yourself. You rejected my penis."

"I'm ready now," she whispered. How had this ricocheted into this nightmare? "I want everything your penis can give me."

He flexed his penis. "Yes—it looks so tempting in the firelight, doesn't it? So hard and indomitable. And yet, ten minutes ago, when I was fucking you, you didn't want any of it."

"Ducas, don't do this . . . don't—you know I love being

your mistress, you know I love how you fuck me. Don't *do* this."

He contemplated his penis for another minute. "How many chances does a man give a mistress, Angene? Tell me. Three? Ten? A hundred? How much abuse should his penis take, that which is the professed instrument of his mistress's pleasure? When is a man ever sure of his mistress under those circumstances? Perhaps this is a sign you're looking elsewhere for your pleasure—*is* there another penis, Angene? Is that why you got lost this morning when I was fucking you?"

"I swear to you, there isn't anyone else. How could there be anyone else? Ducas . . ."

Ducas . . . the name echoed in his head, reverberating down to his soles. He knew what Ducas would think, would feel, how he would act, what he would do. How was this possible? And yet, he knew. Ducas would give in, this time, because he was a volcano of semen ready to erupt. Because he liked to wield this control.

And he had Angene at his mercy, just the way Ducas would want.

"I hear you, Angene."

"I'm your mistress. I will never be anyone else's mistress. You are the one I dreamed about and longed to be naked with. You. Let me touch your penis. Let me fondle it and suck it . . ."

"No. Women are too facile, women lie. But nevertheless, I have decided to take your offer anyway. I need a good fuck this morning, whatever way I can get it. My way. Get on your knees."

She pushed herself onto her knees, bracing herself with her hands on the mattress. Anything, anything, so that he would take her back.

"Hold onto the bedpost."

She crawled forward and grasped the post. The minute her fingers curled around it, he grasped her hips and forcefully drove into her from behind.

Her body rocketed forward and then she pushed backward against the thrust as he began his pounding possession of her. All she could feel was the hard rock length of his penis, and his hands hot on her bottom as he pushed her and pulled her the way he wanted, the way he decreed.

Connected to him only by his penis, by his hands, hot everything, hot, hard, raw . . . his fingers sliding in her crease, pushing there, possessing there . . . she hung onto the bedpost as he ravished her, on and on and on, in iron control, until the very last moment, as his fingers fully penetrated her, reamed her, claimed her, and he blasted into her body, gyrating wildly, totally out of control

And then everything stopped and there was silence. Dense silence, with her body aching and straining against his hand.

And then slowly and silently he eased himself from her, and she fell onto the mattress

He stared at her coldly—*Ducas* stared at her coldly. "I *will* admit you're a good fuck. I'd be a fool to give up a such willing cunt. But that's all you are to me now. A hot, juicy, available cunt. These are my terms now: I'll summon you *if* I want you. *Now,* get out of my bed."

Chapter 11

Perfect. He had gotten her away from the Other, no small task considering that he was deep in bloodlust with the host. Bloody moon, he had to do *everything* around here.

But she was gone from his room, and the Other was alone and ripe for the taking. Soon it would happen, soon, after he gorged and feasted with the host. It had been too long, and it would be longer still before he could mount a body to go back on the battlefield.

He didn't even want to think about it; the complications were enormous. Things had to be put right here.

One thing at a time . . .

So this was the time to nourish himself and reinvigorate his powers, there was that much to go around, an abundance to be ingested this first night.

The host had waited too long, too long, and he was unusually patient about letting them feed their fill.

But there must be caution, too, and a husbanding of resources until they could get back into the field. He was the practical one after all. Someone had to think about these things. After they fed, he would set the host to work.

And then, tonight, he would take the Other—and, with that, everything would go back the way it had been.

And he would even take back Angene, even though he was not predisposed to wallow his penis in another man's leavings; he would have her nonetheless, *just* because the Other had fucked her—in his name, *and* because it would be vastly amusing to see whether she even noticed the difference.

And if she didn't? He felt a flurry of anger that he tamped down. Trust him to turn his thought immediately to the negative point.

She'd notice, notice he was better, bigger, longer, stronger, more powerful, and if she didn't—well, he'd bloody well kill her for *not* noticing.

But—for now . . . now that she was nicely plowed and furrowed, he'd fuck her until she saw stars. And Veleka would hand Sir Eustace back to the gypsy whore he was so fascinated with, and things would go on just the same from there.

It was all a matter of taking care of the little details, and then the crisis would be over, their haven would be secured, and Veleka would be happy again.

". . . let the earth turn thee black and spit thee out . . ."

She had to get him back, she had to. She felt frantic as she fled through the grounds of Sangbourne Manor in the early morning fog. It was cold, but he was cold, and she pulled her cloak more tightly to her body.

She had to get him back. All her plans and the rest of her life depended on it.

She was still stunned at how he had been able to tell when she was not soaring with him. How? She had to know how and to rectify it. It was too humiliating to be demoted from mistress to . . . melting pot—a place to discharge his semen, and nothing more.

No no no—there would be more. She didn't know how,

she didn't know when, but she had invested too much time in wanting him, and in planning how to become Ducas's mistress to let him do this to her.

It was just—he had come into her again too soon. She had been rubbed raw. Exhausted, in the best way, and deep in gratitude at this turn her life had taken. There were *reasons* why she had not been quite concentrating on *him*.

Except, all her thoughts at that moment when she'd lost focus had involved him.

Exactly. And that was what she must make him understand. She'd been thinking about him, reveling in the fact she was naked in bed with him, that she was finally and in all ways his mistress, that her cherished fantasy had become a reality.

Whatever she had to say, whatever he wanted her to do—she wiped away the tears streaming down her face—that was the nature of being a mistress, that was the nature of Ducas.

She knew that about him, that vein of cruelty in him that reveled in bringing her to her knees. He was too pettish in some ways, and obdurate about getting his own way.

But he would never find a hot, wet, responsive body like hers, or another woman who craved for his fucking as much as she did. She knew it, she was counting on it.

He could take a milkmaid or tweeny from the village anytime he wanted, but they weren't her. They'd lie on their backs, they'd barely spread their legs, and they would expect a rich reward for their compliance in the morning.

No. Ducas wouldn't give her body up that easily. He loved rooting his penis in her honey pot way too much. And where would he find nipples like hers to feast on?

The answer was, he wouldn't—not here in Cheshamshire. Not even close to here. Perhaps not even in London, were he to go.

She thought not.

It was reassuring in a way. He had put her through this song and dance to punish them both, even while he was rigidly hot to fuck her in spite of her insubordination. She had left him with his penis still standing, rock hard and angled to plow.

She *could* play it his way, she thought. But then, that would mean her waiting for him, his whim, his desire, which, being Ducas, he would withhold as long as he could stand it. But she didn't want to. It was time for him to stop the games, now that she *was* his mistress.

He hadn't meant a thing he'd said. And if he had, then he'd just have to throw her out of his room again. She didn't care. She wanted his penis between her legs, *now*.

Dar lay on Ducas's bed, exhausted, emotionally and physically. He felt drained, sapped, lethargic.

What the hell just happened here?

He stared at his rigid penis. He couldn't be more hot and primed to burrow into Angene, and he'd gone and banished her from his bed. What the hell had he been thinking?

No, not him—Ducas . . .

Everything was about Ducas. Ducas in his head, Ducas his duplicate, Ducas in the bedroom with him . . . Ducas with Angene—

Don't even think about that . . .

His penis thickened even more. Was there ever a cunt as hot and tight and honey soaked as Angene's? She was his, his—she had surrendered everything to him, not Ducas, to *him*, and goddamned Ducas was not going to get into his head and take that away.

No, he just invaded your mind and made you *send her away.*

Shit.

He could be feeding on her pliant naked nipples right now. He could be sliding his fingers up between her legs, probing her heat, penetrating harder and deeper inside her.

Inside the place so hot with honey, so deep he could bury himself to the hilt and fill her with his thick spewing semen.

That hole he chosen *not* to fuck. No, he'd saved his semen and sent her away.

Time to pull back. Much as he enjoyed fucking her, it didn't mitigate the fact she belonged to Ducas, she believed he was Ducas, and that she was giving her naked body to Ducas in service of being his mistress.

He was the one taking another man's leavings.

All in good cause.

Fool.

If she came back now . . . ?

I'd be a bigger fool not to take her.

His penis spurted. Shit. *Think about fucking her and you lose control.*

He knew better than to get that involved when he was on a mission, *ever.*

But my penis kissed her cunt first . . .

Fucking hard to let go of that. But Ducas had fixed it for him; he owed Ducas a damned debt of gratitude for that. Don't give an inch of penis when a punishment will do. Clean break. Send for her when you most need to fuck her.

I need her now . . .

Damn it to hell, if I goddamned knew where she was, I'd be deep inside her now. . . .

"Ducas." Her soft voice from just behind the door as she cracked it open.

Something in him leaped, and then he felt that rising vexation, Ducas's vexation, with her.

Ducas again . . . how could she not know . . . ?

He felt Ducas's frustration insinuating itself into his mind. He felt Ducas's pique, Ducas's displeasure. He couldn't seem to push it away. Ducas was there, Ducas was angry.

Let her see what she's done. Let her see that not everyone has taken his pleasure. Let her regret what she turned down.

He maneuvered himself so he was facing the door, his

rampant penis stiff and thrusting, turgid with a man's un-fulfilled need.

"What could you possibly want?"

She came around the door, and she was naked. She dropped her cloak, her clothes, and she closed the door. "I want what a mistress wants."

"I didn't summon you."

"I summoned myself, Ducas. I couldn't go home without slaking your desire, as a good mistress should. I couldn't leave you like that, with your penis hard and demanding a good hot fuck. That's my responsibility, isn't it? To put your desires first. To give my naked body in service of your plea-sure. To be owned by you and used by you whenever you will. I didn't forget, Ducas, and in that lost moment that an-gered you so much, I was reveling in that fact. I *am* your mistress. It's all I ever wanted to be."

Fine words—gloss-over words... Honeyed words, gushing from her lips, hot and thick.

At the moment, he didn't care. He wasn't even listening. He just wanted to get at her honey hole and sink his penis into her and find surcease.

The rest would come later, and he would make certain it did. No woman ever ignored him or denied his penis. Ever.

"So when are you going to demonstrate this utter sub-mission in service of my pleasure?" he asked—no, *Ducas* asked, snidely.

"If I prove that is my only desire—will you take back your mistress?"

The insolence...! Ducas recoiled. "I'm not seeing sub-mission, Angene. I'm not seeing anything that has to do with *my* pleasure."

She drew in a deep breath. He was hard in more ways than one, still. Determined to make her work for the plea-sure of having him fuck her. She wasn't quite sure what he wanted now. Her inclination was to climb on the bed and take his penis in her mouth and devour him.

But only he knew what he wanted of her, and she could only guess.

"Can I come to you?" she whispered.

"Do you really want to, Angene?"

"I really want your penis, Ducas."

"On your hands and knees then, you can come to me. If you want my penis that much."

She bit her lips. It wasn't that far from the doorway to the bed. He had levered himself upright, supporting his body with one arm, while he draped the other over his angled leg. His penis jutted upward, rigid, thick, throbbing, luscious, bursting with cream.

She got down on her hands and knees and crawled, slowly, painstakingly to the bed.

Ducas loved it. Loved seeing her craving his come so much she would crawl for it. Loved seeing her crawl, loved pulling her down . . . loved the rhythm of her bottom as she moved across the floor; it was so naked and lush and rounded. And only he knew all the delights to be felt and fondled deep in her crease.

"Well, well, well, what won't you do for my cream?" he murmured, *Ducas murmured,* as she reached the bed rail.

"Take me back, Ducas," she whispered.

He swung his legs around and straddled her shoulders so that when she looked straight up, all she saw was his tight taut scrotum and his towering erection.

"Maybe I will."

"I'll be whatever you need me to be," she breathed. "Take me back, Ducas."

"Maybe."

"You know you want me."

"I want you crawling to me. I like that a lot, Angene."

"What else do you want, Ducas?"

"I don't know. I can't seem to think of anything—"

"*Duuucccasss . . .*"

God, he hated Ducas. *Hated* him. Son of a bitch, doing

this to her. But he couldn't seem to stop, didn't want to stop, loved exerting this sexual power over her.

No, Ducas loved the power, the excitement of mastery over a woman. Ducas loved it, Ducas . . .

He was getting lost in Ducas—falling into Ducas's need, Ducas's whims.

Ducas was in the air again, the full dark sense of him swirling around, and sinuously seeping into his thoughts, his mind, his head, his heart.

Ducas—he was going to kill Ducas . . .

Ducas—she would never think of him as anyone else . . .

He couldn't break away from him. Ducas wanted her to lick his balls, to suck his cock, and not what *he* wanted, what *Dar* wanted, Ducas would have her on her hands and knees; he couldn't break away, and Ducas's will held sway.

Bastard was with her now. Bastard doing everything he would have done—just what he commanded—but it just wasn't any fun at one remove. It wasn't him, Ducas, pounding Angene to the ground. It was the Other, infused with his will, and his desires.

He snorted. You tried to keep track of your worst enemy and he becomes your worst nightmare. And that blasted trollop Angene. You would think she would have discovered the truth by now. But no—the son of a bitch had her in such a sensual fog, she didn't know which way was up . . . witness her on her hands and knees, with her ass in the air, and willing to pay whatever price the bastard demanded.

He demanded. Of course—

On the other hand, he could sympathize with that. That was absolutely where he would want her too, if he were there. Would have had her there long before this if it wasn't for the Other.

He felt all of the Other's warring emotions, but the bastard wasn't strong enough to fuck Angene and take him on too.

That was about to end. All impediments had been removed but one. The Other. The duplicate. He who deserved to die just for deflowering Angene.

Damn and blast, what a mess. And worse, he still had to deal with the question of his bloody amnesia after it was all over. Couldn't just waltz back into the house and announce he was fully recovered when everyone in the village knew about him and had bought the story that his memory was gone.

Just for that, he would kill the Other five times over. Leave him to the host, the wolves, the bats, the night.

Not a stairwell away from retribution and he had been foiled again. Didn't expect bloody Angene to go crawling back into the Other's arms. Thought the quickest way to send her running was to humiliate her, but apparently the flaming bitch didn't care how much she had to debase herself, as long as the bleeding Other finally fucked her.

And he was going to have to compete with that?

Bloody hell. These two fools were *not* going to bring down the Iscariot.

Or him, even though it was sapping a boatload of psychic energy to weave his thoughts into the Other's mind.

He couldn't attack unless he was ready to kill Angene.

He had to think, to plan. At least the host was bedded down, satiated and calm.

He could wait until Angene was gone. Dawn was rising, it wouldn't be long, they couldn't risk Veleka finding her with *Ducas*. She'd just have to go home . . . and then—he licked his lips—

The Other is mine . . .

"*. . . May the host of angels smite thee where thou standest . . .*"

Sun was flooding the room as she awakened and moved restively in Ducas's arms. She touched his face, his nose, his lips. He nipped at her fingers.

"Tell me," she whispered.

"Maybe," he whispered back. His head was clear, Ducas was gone. He felt like himself suddenly, like an oppressive fog had been lifted from his mind.

The room was bright, and reeked of the scent of sex. Endless, reaching sex that when he even thought about everything they had done last night, he immediately ached for more.

She had utterly subjugated herself to him. Willingly surrendered all her will and desire to whatever Ducas wanted, Ducas demanded.

To *Ducas. God, why couldn't he forget that?*

Deep in his mind, Ducas controlled everything that Dar demanded of her. And the thing that scared him in the cool light of morning was that he had loved it too. And hated the way he loved it. Hated Ducas. Loved what he did to her, and everything *Ducas* made her do.

He would do it again.

No! Ducas *would do it again.*

He had to stop this. He had to find the bastard and kill him because otherwise, Ducas would own his soul.

"I need to know," she whispered.

"Maybe." No games; Ducas played games, and Ducas was still in control, in spite of his feeling Ducas had gone from his consciousness, and Dar couldn't seem to force out any other words but what Ducas wanted him to say.

And what would she say, when she looked in the mirror and saw the way he had nipped and marked her body? He touched her neck, the brutal little crosshatched X's that he had nipped into her skin. And on her arms, her chest, in a frenzy of possession.

"Maybe," he said again, capturing her mouth. He had to kill Ducas, he had to get free. He couldn't think of anything else as he savaged her mouth. There was nothing else, just the heat and her pliant body and his raging need to embed his penis in her, and he drove himself between her legs, and just rooted there, rocking, pushing, reaching deeper and deeper as her hips undulated under his like a belly dancer.

"Better and better," he murmured against her mouth, as he licked her lips, as he nipped them, and swirled his tongue in and out of her mouth.

She loved this Ducas, and these ineffable moments when he could be tender, and not so capricious and sulky. She loved the way his penis nested so deeply inside her, and the way he just let her feel it there, snug, tight, thick.

She could feel it throbbing, feel his body seizing up as he tried to keep control of his cream. At this moment, when he was so soft, so gentle with her, she wanted dearly to be the only one in the world to make him lose control.

This was the Ducas she loved, the one with whom she wanted to make a home and a life, even if it was an illicit one, just like her mother had with the Earl. Ducas would have to marry someday, would have to have children, would have to live a separate life. She knew that, she was prepared for it.

But at times like these, she felt as if she could endure anything he must in conscience do, if she could have shimmering moments like these to treasure forever.

Her body shimmered, seeking his hardness. She felt his body ripple with tension, surge, swell, and begin to move ever so slowly. He didn't want it to end, neither did she, but it was the nature of a man to drive to his culmination, whatever he otherwise desired.

This was the endgame, where every part of his body gathered, and slowly and deliciously worked her pleasure point until she was dizzy with sensation, sliding, rolling, tumbling into the lustful backwash of his explosive ejaculation.

And then silence. Pure harmonic silence. She never wanted to move, she just wanted to live in his arms, connected to his desire. It was enough, it really was enough—for now.

No words, not yet. The sun was creeping into the room. Early yet, but still, too late. There were other things to consider. Her mother's worry. Veleka coming in on them . . . Sir Eustace—

No. "I have to go," she whispered.

"You should go."

"Ducas . . ."

She wanted assurance still. *Just like a woman,* he thought—*Ducas* thought. Not enough to be fucked thoroughly and soundly. No, she had to be assured he would take her back.

Shit—Ducas *would take her back . . .*

Any man would. Turn down a willing honey-drenched hole like hers? Not bloody likely. And let her believe what she wanted to.

"Don't look in the mirror," he said lazily from the bed as he watched her slip into her serviceable dress, watched his penis respond to the way her hands moved and her body wriggled as she smoothed and adjusted her clothes, her hair, so she wouldn't look like she'd been fucking all morning.

She looked like she'd been fucking all morning.

"I got carried away last night." It wasn't an apology, but still, it was a little shocking to see just how far he'd gone with the love bites.

He got even harder remembering how her body had twisted sinuously under his as he nipped her. And he was thick as a tree trunk to begin with; he wanted her all over again, but she was just about ready to walk out that door. Damn damn damn and damn.

She looked at him blankly. "There are no mirrors in this room, Ducas."

Something flashed. He shook himself. "What?"

"No mirrors. But I promise I won't look anyway. I'd rather feel them, and remember everything you did to me last night."

No mirrors.

She paused at the door. "Ducas . . . ?"

A little note of pleading? Oh, Ducas loved that.

"Maybe," he said, his mind elsewhere, something crackling in his brain. *No mirrors?*

"Ducas—please . . . ?"

He looked at her, finally. There was no denying she aroused him—aroused *Ducas*—almost beyond sanity. He could have plowed her again three times over, the way his penis was jutting and throbbing and reaching for her.

He found—*Ducas found*—immense satisfaction in the vision of her taking that image away with her this morning, and then reveling in it, and dreaming about it. Yearning for it.

It would excite her, and incite her passion and her need for him, for it, his sex, his penis, for Ducas—

He—*No!*—*Ducas*—didn't have to be any more hard-hearted than he had been already. She instinctively comprehended that the more she pacified him, the more deeply and intensively she bound herself to him. She wanted it, she had deliberately sought it, she was willing to do anything for it.

So he—*Ducas*—had no qualms about how he treated her, or what he demanded of her. And at this point, she could call herself whatever she wanted.

But *Ducas* knew—she was already his slave.

Chapter 12

"Ducas . . . ?"

Still soft, still waiting, always waiting. Make her wait more. Make her cream with anticipation. Make her . . .

This was insane. *This wasn't him!*

He jacked himself out of bed and swiped up his trousers. "This afternoon. I'll find a few minutes." *Shit—that wasn't him talking, it wasn't.*

"I'll come," she whispered, and slipped out of the room. *Oh, she would come all right . . .*

Bloody hell. He ripped into his trousers and a shirt, shoved his feet into his boots.

Ducas was near—the sense of him was palpable—black as night, evil as sin . . .

Prowling, waiting, watching . . .

Nonsense. The day had barely begun. He'd have to join Veleka and Sir Eustace for breakfast. He'd have to start thinking about this mission that had gone over the wall and off to sea.

What the hell was he thinking? He had never ever let himself get sidetracked like this. A mission was a mission.

You went in, made a quick strike, obtained your information, destroyed your enemy, and got out before maximum damage could be effected.

This whole amnesia strategy had been an unmitigated disaster. He wasn't one step closer to finding out anything about Ducas. And now, Ducas, who was supposed to be dead, was alive and on the loose in his head as well as in the house; there were animals killed and sucked dry; Alton dead and bloodless, and buried with all due precautions; the host had set the table, but the guests had finally gone; Veleka acting strangely, and there were no mirrors in the room.

What an odd disparate list of . . . what? The prickling started, slow at first, on his neck, on his shoulders.

No mirrors.

He turned around. No mirrors.

No mirrors anywhere he had been in the house that he could recollect.

All those mysterious deaths on the battlefield. A man alive who was supposed to be dead. *The host has set the table.* . . . All due precautions—no mirrors . . .

The prickling intensified. He knew the answer—he didn't want to know the answer.

. . . *Blood on the carpet, one telling drop of blood on the floor the day Alton went missing—*

He felt his own blood congeal, the prickling cascading head to toe.

No. That was a thought beyond imagining.

What did it mean, the host has set the table? The odd older man who had disappeared and him remembering nothing after that until Ducas had punched him awake.

And now Ducas was deep in his head.

Ducas was pounding in his blood—

Where *was* that spot? By the bed. On the window side, just by the foot of the bed. He knelt down to look, but there was nothing there. Nothing. Not a spot, not a stain, not a stiffness in the nap of the carpet.

Nothing. Just Alton, dead and sucked dry, buried *with all due precautions.*

He felt his head exploding in ten different directions. he had to stay calm and rational, even if the situation didn't seem rational. It was the only way. And to believe that anything was possible, even probable, and not let Ducas get to him.

But Ducas was near, toying with him.

The prickles were like little darts, pricking him.

No mirrors. He felt Ducas breathing, pulsating, evil, raw.

All those bites all over Angene's body . . .

Not him. Not *him.*

They don't bite . . .

Did he think it, or did Ducas insinuate the thought into his mind?

Jesus . . . all those deaths; who would have noticed in the midst of a bloody war? They were coming in by the hundreds, dead, dying, bleeding, horrible bloody messes, arms and legs blasted off, wounded in the chest, the head, the back. . . . Ducas had attended them in the wagon house . . .

. . . *feeding . . .*

. . . so many deaths . . .

And the colonel noticed.

No mirrors . . . all those bites—

An unconquerable enemy—

It explained so much. And nothing at all.

But they don't bite . . .

That was the sticking point—

And Ducas was near—too near . . .

He felt his senses stretching, believing . . . why? Why him? How?

He needed answers . . . and he wouldn't get them here. . . .

"Ducas!"

He whirled, just at the point of opening the door to his

room, just at the instant when he would have pounced on his enemy and drained him dead.

Veleka. Oh, shit, what now?

What to say? He could tell her anything now, he could tell her he was him, even, now that the guests were gone, but she still looked distraught and faintly suspicious. And he wanted to present the Other to her, exsanguinated and dead, so that no explanations would be needed, and everything would be made right.

"Good morning," he said finally, making the decision. "Are you on your way to breakfast?"

"This early?"

"If you wish."

Mother—it's me . . . !

How do I know? How do I know who you are when the Other made such a fool of me—

No, he couldn't tell her, not yet, not before he knew what and who the Other was, and why he had come to the Manor in the first place.

And then, and then—oh, he would feed and suck the bastard until he was a husk of a body and his soul was consigned to hell . . .

Veleka was wasting his time now. He felt a searing impatience with her. The Other was waiting, knew he was coming . . .

"I'll come down . . . soon."

Veleka stared at him, her gaze dark and wary.

It's me!

Stupid Other, tramping all over the graveyard with all the damned crosses and saints—and that vicar with his vial of holy water; no wonder she was skeptical of Ducas. Ducas the real couldn't have survived it—if he had even come in the presence of any cross in any way, he would have gone blind. And the holy water would have scalded him, made him a living skeleton.

She was looking for signs that he had been marred in any

way. He should have been, if it had been him standing beside the vicar, under the cross, holding a crucifix. He should be blind. He should be burned to bone.

She couldn't understand it, and he didn't have time to explain.

"I'll join you—soon." He couldn't contain his vexation. Every minute counted.

She took a step toward him, lifted her hand as if she wanted to touch him to see if there was substance to his body, and then she dropped it.

"Very well." She turned away, she floated down the steps, almost as if she had no energy to walk.

He had no time to sympathize—his enemy awaited. He thrust open the door.

". . . let the the corrupted soul rot in its place; let the suppurating evil sink into the ground and be consumed into eternity—"

Ducas was near, was right outside the bedroom door, Dar could feel him, every sense prickling, telling him now what he should have known all along. The danger was real. And every one of his finely honed senses had been warning him, while he let himself get distracted by Angene.

There had to be another way out. He heard Veleka's voice—he had a moment's respite, maybe two or three. Through the dressing room? No, closed off there, nowhere to go. Except out the window. He ducked behind a curtain, and sized up his chances. Second floor. Not too bad. Maybe into a bush . . .

Too quiet out there . . . and he hadn't even given Veleka a thought—no time now—he rolled open the casement window. The opening was barely big enough for him to squeeze through. There was a narrow stone sill, a tree too far from the window to be of use, a bush that might just break his fall . . .

That, or confront Ducas now—

No choice—one, two, three—up—and out. Tuck his head, into the bush, down on the ground—pain, hellish pain in his arm where an errant branch caught him . . . his leg twisted . . .

He rolled to the side, into the roots of the bush, and held tight for a long moment. He heard Ducas cursing. He sensed him looking out the window, seeking *him*. He could feel it.

God, what Ducas couldn't do in aid of pursuing him . . .

Silence. Then the creak of the window being rolled back in place.

Dar moved then, leg not too bad, arm feeling like a knife was embedded in it, crawling under the bushes until he could cut across to the back of the house to the stables. Quickest way—grab a mount, no saddle, just *get out of there . . . !*

They tried to stop him. There were three of them, and the ineffectual stable boy, questioning him, pulling at him, trying to detain him.

He threw them off, had no idea where he got the strength or the power to fend them off with those injuries, but he did; he chose a stall, he jumped on the horse, he beat them off again, and in a pounding of hooves, he streaked out of the stables and was gone.

"*. . . let their sins be burned upon their souls, and mercy denied them everlasting . . .*"

Dead boring breakfast. He had to make plans and the tedious Sir Eustace just wouldn't let him go. Questioning how he slept, whether he was comfortable, wasn't it better with the guests gone—*yes, dear Sir Eustace, immeasurably nutritiously better*—and now they really would commence to try to reclaim his memory.

Oh, that old thing, Ducas almost told them then. Almost. But there was the Other to contend with. And now the bastard had gone into the village, which presented another small complication: his visit to the vicar.

So nice to have a vicar to explain the eternal mysteries. People always believed the most incredible things when they heard it from a cleric.

The vicar would tell the Other what he wanted to know, what he knew already. Only right. The Other ought to have confirmed what he was up against, after all. In concrete terms. Except he probably did know, and he was making this vicar visit just to annoy *him*.

Well, he was annoyed. Everything was shot to hell, and listening to Sir Eustace rambling on and on made him want to crown the old rooster.

Well, of course—his instincts were impeccable as always: it was exactly what he had to do—and about time, too.

Sir Eustace had to die.

Too bad. Shriveled old gherkin. Accommodating old jack-rabbit. Outlived your usefulness, you old lob louse. Veleka should've fed on you long ago. She hasn't needed your protection for years. And at this point, you're too damned desiccated to be much good for food either. Or anything else.

So that was decided. Easy.

The last thing to be taken care of was the Other. Let him think he had some control. That way, his inevitable death would be that much more rewarding, his blood that much more sweet.

He looked Veleka. She looked at him.

It's me . . . !

No recognition in her eyes . . .

Damn her eyes—she should have known. She really should have known . . .

The vicar was a village-bred man ministering to a village community deep in the wilds of a northern shire. He was fighting so many other things than just lack of faith. There was poverty, lack of education, ignorance, superstition, and just plain stubborn stupidity. And the notion that, when generations of a family had lived in one place, it was written in stone that a man could not try to raise his station or seek a future elsewhere.

There were many frustrations attendant to herding his village flock. He tried all the time to better them, educate them, provide for them. To give advice and comfort, and aid and a boost now again when someone had lost hope.

Even he himself hadn't given up hope on one family—Sir Eustace's family, and the stubborn Lady Veleka who never came to church, not once since she'd come to Cheshamshire. And now, with the miraculous return of her son, you would think she ought to be asking for the Lord's mercy, but instead she was even more emphatically pushing Him away.

So be it. He prayed for Ducas whether the lady wished it or not; Sir Eustace would want him to, even though Ducas was not of his seed. Ducas was the son he never had, a foolhardy son admittedly, to go off to war when he had no obligation to, but a son to Sir Eustace nonetheless.

And a good son since his return, seeing that the stranger was buried well, with a proper service and all the precautions.

You had to take precautions. There was just no other way, no matter what he, personally, felt. People would believe what they wanted to believe.

So if you were a priest, you would accommodate that—no grand gestures: no chopping off heads and burying them at the foot of the grave; no interment at a crossroads; or burning the body, or nailing it in place, or stuffing it with incense or garlic.

Nonsense, all of it.

But he was willing to do the subtle things that made people feel secure that the corpse would not rise: wrapping it in a nice tight shroud, for example, and strewing the body with hawthorn and ash.

The little things, so easy to do. A Bible and some holy water at the end, and the ritual was complete, and everyone rested easier.

And thus had he done with poor Mr. Alton who had traveled hundreds of miles only to meet such an untimely death. But, it *had* been rather odd that his body was so bereft of blood.

But then, that wasn't his purview. And there *were* murderous animals prowling in the woods and hills, and attacking farm animals. It was the way of nature, the only explanation, really. The constable was satisfied, and Sir Eustace, bless his bountiful soul, had provided for the funeral, so he had no business at all ruminating on any probable cause.

Still, there was just that little niggling thought in the back of his head. A thought that he dismissed a hundred times as improbable and ridiculous. In spite of *all due precautions*.

That was Croyd's idea anyway. Because Croyd knew his people. And the vicar was so rational and sane.

So he was surprised to see Mr. Ducas riding up to the church the very day after Mr. Alton's funeral service. From what he understood, Mr. Ducas had no memory of anything of his life at Sangbourne Manor, not Sir Eustace, or his mother, or even not attending church, for that matter.

Though yesterday, at the interment with Sir Eustace, he had seemed himself enough.

He came out of his office to greet Ducas. "My lord . . ."

The title still jolted him. "Vicar—" And now he was here, Dar wasn't exactly sure what he should say, or what he wanted to know. No, he knew what he wanted to know. "I wanted to express my appreciation for your kindness yesterday for poor Mr. Alton."

The vicar raised his eyebrows. So unlike Mr. Ducas to say thank you for anything. Perhaps the new Mr. Ducas, the one without the old memories, would be an improvement.

"What can I do for you, my lord? That cannot be the sole reason you came barreling up here at such a gallop. Come inside."

He led Dar through the vestibule of the small stone church, and into his little office. "Please—sit."

Dar sat. Looked around. It was small square room with one window, a long table strewn with books, bibles, writing paper, ink, candlelight.

"The next sermon, of course," the vicar said, following his gaze. "Always difficult. You can never quite put your finger on what your community needs to hear on any given Sunday. And there are so few messages they will really listen to. But that's not why you're here. Tell me how I can help you."

Dar levered himself out of his chair. He felt him—*Ducas . . . Ducas knew exactly where he was, and why he was here—shit . . .*

"Croyd—what he said about precautions . . . how you prepared Mr. Alton's body—"

Ducas was waiting, patiently, calmly, with certainty, savoring the inevitable moment of confrontation . . .

"How interesting you mention it. I was just thinking about that. It's the undead, you know. The people believe in it. Any little thing goes wrong—the chickens die for no reason, the cows don't give milk. A child is born with a caul. Or it isn't baptized. Or someone dies violently, like Mr. Alton. Or he has different color eyes or hair, or religion. For all those reasons and more, people in the countryside believe that the dead will rise up and transform themselves after they are buried."

"Transform themselves—how?" But he knew, *he knew . . .*

"Into the living dead, my lord. Vampires. Even though there has never been any real evidence that any such monsters are preying and feeding here. Nevertheless, it is always necessary to take some steps to reassure people, as we did with Mr. Alton. There are any number of preventives. As you saw, we chose to wrap the body tightly, to lay it on a crucifix, and lay another one over it. The seeds—well, this is passed down through folklore—the undead are said to be fascinated by seeds, and will always stop to count them, which would delay it in its hunt for victims. We could have done many more things, including dismemberment, but why? The villagers are satisfied with these minimal precautions."

"And the sheep that was found earlier this week?"

"The same, my lord. Any living being can be turned under the right circumstances, at least, so it is said."

"And no other proof of any other bloodletting in Cheshamshire, barring the sheep—and, what was it, did Croyd say, chickens?"

"Exactly, my lord. So the sheep was buried with *precautions*—different from Mr. Alton, I grant you, but adequate for the purpose nonetheless. Though the amount of blood drained from the bodies, in each case, still troubles me a little. But if Constable Croyd is satisfied, then there's nothing more to be said."

"And there's been no other unexplained human death due to excessive blood loss, other than Mr. Alton?"

"Not in my memory, and I've ministered here many years, which of course you don't recall. So, it must be an aberration, my lord. I would prefer to think that in any event. So we do what we must and hope for the best."

Exactly—he had learned his lesson well: cater to ignorant superstitions and hope the darkness diminished. But the darkness had come anyway, in the person of Ducas Sangbourne, for reasons that seemed senseless, and even though Cheshamshire didn't seem to be where he hunted his prey.

No, he murdered the wounded, the maimed, and the marginally alive on the battlefield, and that was his feeding ground. That was the cause, the reason, the explanation. The thing Dar had been charged to investigate. Well, he had that answer all right, but it didn't explain why Ducas wound up *here*, in Cheshamshire. It didn't explain Alton's death. Or the blood-drained bodies of the dead animals. Or his preternatural resemblance to him.

Or Angene . . .

God in heaven, it didn't nearly explain Angene . . .

"Is there anything else?" the vicar asked gently.

He shook himself. "How would you account for the fact that, if there were vampires, they are not hunting victims here?"

The vicar stared at him. "But my son, that's the very reason why I *know* they really aren't here."

". . . may the night claim you, destroy you, and never give you peace . . ."

Gaetana was rooted in the parlor before the hearth, where she had laid out what looked like an altar.

From the kitchen, where she had covertly entered the house, Angene could just see the flicker of a candle, could hear Gaetana murmuring prayers or curses, she couldn't tell which.

Surely Gaetana wasn't praying for her . . . ?

What to do? Gaetana knew as surely as the sun was up just where she had been and what she'd been doing. Gaetana knew everything, she had done it all herself. So she couldn't castigate her own daughter for following the call of her blood, for wanting the very thing her mother had coveted.

It was time to talk to Gaetana, to make her understand.

She tiptoed into the parlor.

". . . may the black earth eat thine eyes . . . may the light of divinity consume thee . . . may the earthworms root in thy feet . . ."

An invocation—now she could see clearly the weapons and symbols piled on the altar, the silver dagger, the dirt, the nails, the mirror. . . . Gaetana sensed her, and turned to look up at her with burning eyes.

"So you've finally come."

"Mother . . ."

"No, no—I know what I know, I see what I see. He is wicked and he never changes. *Mullo* . . ." she spat. "Enough."

"He has taken me as his mistress."

Gaetana's blood turned cold. "He will ride you to ground, and never think twice about destroying you."

Angene froze. "So much hate, when you know him not at all, and you sit here chanting incantations as if that will solve anything."

"It is what I can do."

"Mother, don't."

"It is too late. He is in your blood. He will infect you and kill you."

"What are you talking about?"

"Look at your neck. Even from here, even with your wrapping yourself to hide the vestiges of his bites, they can too easily be seen. The mark of the sinful and the wicked. The one who gets into your blood. Look at you—*look* . . . *!*"

She thrust the small gold-framed mirror into Angene's hands. Angene lifted her hair, and pushed her shawl away from her neck.

No mirrors. She caught her breath. The pattern of teeth marks was clear, a series of small X's, tracking right down her neck toward her breasts.

"Where else has he infected you with his unholy lust?"

"Everywhere," she whispered.

"That one is so clever," Gaetana muttered. "May his teeth rot and his mouth swell with sores."

"I love him."

"Bah—it is what women do best—destroy themselves in service of loving a man. Listen to me. This is not a man."

"Oh, it's very much a man, Mother."

"I don't doubt he is well fixed where a man should be. But have you noticed nothing about him out of the ordinary?"

"You talk in riddles. I won't listen. I am going to see him again this afternoon."

"You go to open your body to his possession. Don't be a fool, Angene. Don't lose yourself in lust for him as I did with the father. Blinded by my desire for Sir Eustace. Utterly distracted from what I was never supposed to see. They knew, they did it deliberately. They have used both of us, Angene, and you must must must be aware of what they are and what they are doing."

"Who? Who is doing . . . what *are* they? You talk in riddles . . . and you can't dissuade me from freely giving my body to Ducas. That is the one immutable thing. I will have him, as long as he lusts for me."

Gaetana stared at her a very long time. There was no telling the truth to her, no convincing her. Angene wouldn't believe it anyway, she was too besotted with Ducas, too in love with his sex, too willing to be his slave.

Gaetana barely believed it herself.

But there was that finely honed, bred-in-the-bone gypsy second sight. The one that Sir Eustace blinded with all his sexual attentions over all these years. And Ducas's determined pursuit of Angene and her determination to wrest from him what her mother had settled for in her liaison with Wentmore.

The patterns of family deceit. They dug deep and they always came back to haunt you, hiding the evil, disguising the clues with lust and love and everything a woman hungered for.

"Let good smite evil, right fight might . . ." she murmured under her breath. "Give me strength . . ." She took a big shaky breath. "When next do you go to him?"

"Not many more hours from now. And you can't stop me."

"I wouldn't try. I ask only one thing of you, Angene. Do this for me. If there is any affection in your heart for your mother, you will do this for me. Take the mirror."

Angene looked at the small palm-size mirror in her hand. "And do what with it?"

"You—look at him reflected in the mirror, and see what you will see."

"That's it?"

"That is all I ask."

"Is this some kind of crystal ball?" Angene turned the mirror in her hand.

"You are not far from the truth in that. It will show you your future," Gaetana said, "right in your hand."

Chapter 13

Vampires . . .

He felt explosive, his consciousness expanding to encompass the reality. He felt Ducas close to him, watching him, mocking him, but he felt something else as well—a power of his own as the sentient prickling seemed to coalesce into a certain knowledge that his sense of Ducas was more than just Ducas's thoughts saturating his mind.

He felt dizzy suddenly, as if his entire body were weighted with this awareness, absorbing it, and repudiating it as beyond sanity, beyond what was real, and accepting it at the same time.

He staggered slightly as he and the vicar emerged into the sunlight. The clear, glaring sunlight that limned everything in a bright golden glow, burning off the morning fog, burning the truth into his mind.

And that was the thing: it *was* real. That was the anomaly of it: that which shouldn't exist did, and deep in the English countryside, living as, pretending to be, gentry, while it foraged for survival on foreign battlefields.

A killer without qualm. But then what? Back to the privileged life in an English country house?

"My lord," the vicar murmured, putting out his hand. "It's too much for you to be riding around like this so soon."

So soon—The words startled him. So soon? Had it even been a week since he and Alton walked in the front door of Sangbourne Manor?

Maybe less.

Vampires.

Which, because there was no record of them feeding off the peasants in the surrounding countryside, of course they did not exist.

How naïve of the vicar.

He thought it, Ducas thought it, almost in concert with him. Ducas was close, Ducas was waiting.

In the space of that moment, the game had changed.

Get out now . . .

Dar stared across the narrow road through the village center. The inn was across the way, the blacksmith shop, the doctor's office, the village seamstress, the cemetery, up on a hill.

Idyllic. Golden. And a vampire in its midst.

He had completed his mission; he had all the answers for the colonel. He could just ride out down that road and away. Leave them all to Ducas—Sir Eusace, Veleka, Angene—all of them . . . They knew what he was. They had to—

Angene . . . ?

Do they . . . ? It defied belief. . . .

Ducas, mocking him, knowing he wouldn't take the chance.

I'm waiting . . .

Dar knew it. He was shocked at how wholly and thoroughly he sensed Ducas now. It was as if a door had opened, just a crack, and he could see inside a room, but not every detail.

Just enough to know it wasn't a place he wanted to be. It was dark, dank, and dangerous. A place of traps and snares and deadfall. Of seething hunger and murderous impulses. Of bloodlust and a throbbing burning evil.

But he didn't have to stay. That was the thing: his work was done. All he had to do was climb onto that stallion and ride out toward the sun.

Come to me, don't run away . . .

Ducas, stalking him in his thoughts . . .

Sir Eusance and Veleka, alone with him within the confines of the Manor. Angene, so blindly in lust with him. The vicar—Ducas hated him, depised him as only the ungodly can. And he loathed Dar—was waiting impatiently to have done with him.

Why *had* Alton been murdered?

"I'm sorry, vicar, you said . . ?"

"Just that I'm concerned you're up and about too soon. After all, this is all new to you now—with the memory loss, I mean."

Ducas, laughing. "Well, I couldn't get that lost in the village, could I?" Dar said.

"Indeed, and you just head back the opposite way, and you'll be right on Manor land in no time."

Dar climbed onto the stallion's back. "I appreciate your candor."

"I'm happy to explain it to you, my lord. I hope I've laid your concerns to rest."

. . . deserves to die, the old gelding . . .

Ducas, insinuating himself into his thoughts. Ducas knew, Ducas sensed the door had opened . . . Ducas was laughing at the vicar's utter innocence in matters evil and banal.

Get out of here! The feeling of foreboding was overwhelming.

Dar couldn't find a thing to say in response; he was fighting every urge to leave right then, right there, wrestling every instinct that screamed at him to go.

He waved at the vicar, pulled the horse around by its

mane, and forced himself to canter away from the church-yard, down the road through the village, in the opposite direction from the sun.

Force . . . it was all about force and what was to come . . .

He pulled up under a tree, along a desolate stretch of farm road close by Sangbourne Manor land. He felt tired suddenly, as if his energy had been sapped from his body all at once.

Ducas.

Ducas was sucking it from him, figuratively, coming after him psychically. And there was nowhere to hide from Ducas. In the trees, in the woods . . . Ducas stalking him, aware of him every minute, every move . . . and he was so tired—and Ducas was counting on that . . .

This was the endgame, his destiny. He couldn't escape it even if he wanted to. So given that, he had to figure out how to combat Ducas, how to block him from his mind before Ducas pulled every life pulse from him, and rendered him useless.

All of that, and more, he must learn, he must do. And in the bright morning sun of a winter's day, it seemed like too much of a burden to undertake. It seemed like he was going insane.

Except for the fact that now he was conscious of Ducas too. The open door: it scared the hell out of him. He hadn't really focused on that or even absorbed the impact of his potential power. It was too supernatural. Too otherworldly.

A vampire, for God's sake . . . who fed on blood and war, trampling over the dead and wounded, relishing the gore.

The game had changed. This was a battle he couldn't win.

He hadn't really thought he had a choice about leaving; all he could choose was how he played the game. And watch as innocent people got killed along the way.

The price of war; but this was another kind of war, and he couldn't fight it as if he were in battle. Even so, Evil was always the enemy, and death and destruction, no more so now, only the adversary was an entity rather than a soldier. And how did you defeat that?

A vampire . . .

Alone—? Or with others . . . ? Why did he have no sense of what he was up against?

No other deaths . . .

No—don't forget the animals . . .

Whose son, really?

Don't forget Angene . . .

Oh, God, she was coming to Ducas this afternoon . . . Ducas who would eat her as soon as fuck her—

Why hadn't he? Why had he left her alone all this time?

Whose son?

Too many questions . . . no answers—

. . . Angene—!

She was the only thing about this that was real. And she was about to fall right into Ducas's arms, become Ducas's prey.

Or was she?

What was real, what was the lie?

Whose son?

The question jolted him, galvanized him. Too many questions. He felt like he was waking up from a dream.

Evil was real, in all its incarnations. Evil could not be allowed to live. Whatever the cost. Whoever was involved.

Whoever might die. Evil had to be vanquished.

Whose son? What was the answer to that question?

The answer was—everything he had ever wanted . . .

The answer was: *I'll kill them all . . .*

Ducas . . . !

He kneed the stallion's flank and spurred it toward the Manor.

He was too easily seen on horseback. Time to go on foot, now he was skirting Manor grounds. He slipped off the horse's back and slapped it to send it home.

Now he was alone, one on one, on the enemy's soil. It was no different from any other reconnaissance mission, except this adversary had extrasensory powers. This enemy lived in his mind.

He had to shut down his thoughts. As if he were in captivity, being tortured, he had close down his mind, his feelings, his emotions, because Ducas fed on them as surely as he lusted for blood.

And Ducas was on the hunt. Dar could feel him probing, trying to place where he was, where he was going. Ducas was prowling, waiting for him, somewhere on the grounds.

Block him out. Push him away, forcibly . . . he knew how to do it, he had done it some half dozen times in situations equally as dangerous and deadly, but never against an opponent like this.

But now he was this far from the house, he didn't know quite which way to go. It didn't matter. He only needed to walk east, away from the sun, and into a stand of trees that marked the property line that would shield him while he considered what next to do.

He felt Ducas seeking, prodding, reaching, but physically, he was nowhere near.

Now what? Close your mind. Go slowly, check your bearings. Move fast. Shut down your mind.

The trees gave way to a greensward, open, all of it, except for intermittent copses of barren bushes. That was a mean chance—if Ducas were following, he'd have him dead cold.

Had to take the chance. Run low. Go fast. Not in a straight line.

He angled his way across the field, going one way, then the other, making his way closer and closer to the house.

Ducas was out there, following him. *Can't hide.*

Close your mind.

Don't even try it.

He was nearing the stables; he could smell it. Hear it.

The last place he wanted to go. Too contained. Too dangerous. Did he really think he would come out of this alive?

He had to get to the house. Angene was coming, probably soon.

No, don't think about Angene—Ducas would pick the thought right out of his head. *She had to know—she* had *to.*

He circled around the stables, and cut across to the gardens. Ducas was circling around him out there, somewhere. The sense of him hovering, waiting, was so palpable, so strong Dar could almost taste it.

It was like being hunted by a shadow. Ducas managed to stay just out of range, just beyond his reach. He felt no rush, no compelling hurry. The confrontation was inevitable, written in the stars.

Dar wasn't ready to capitulate yet. Too many questions. Especially the one with which he planned to circumvent Ducas's mind intrusions.

Whose son?

Who knew what Ducas was? Veleka, Sir Eustace, Angene?

Whose son? How could he have fooled them all? But he had to have done. There hadn't been a false moment in the way they welcomed him home, took on faith that he had indeed lost his memory, did everything they could to try to help him.

What didn't fit?

Veleka's intensity? But that was a mother who loved her son to distraction, in spite of his foolhardy decision to fight in a war half a world away.

Was it? *Was* he Veleka's son?

Who? Was *who* Veleka's son—wait a minute, getting confused . . . had to get in the house. Angene coming soon, coming to Ducas—no, him . . . coming to him for one thing only.

. . . lust, pure naked lust feeding on itself—sexual vampires—they both had been, and what had she done with Ducas alone? *How* could she not know?

Ducas was coming for him, slowly, methodically, pushing him toward the front of the house. He moved in the shadows, in the trees, just out of reach of the sun, probing Dar's mind, seeking him, flaring with anger as he was thwarted, again and again.

Whose son? Dar chanted it like a prayer as he skirted the gardens, around the drive, hid in the bushes near the entrance of the house.

Now, only the steps and through the front door. It had been inevitable too. Ducas still wasn't quite sure where he was, not yet, even though he had pressured him toward the house.

He had that little time to duck into the house, to gain the advantage before Ducas came after him.

Whose son?

Who cares? Ducas, fighting him.

Whose son?

The devil.

Dar believed it. He slipped into the entrance hall. He wondered about Veleka and Sir Eustace, where they were, whether Ducas had revealed himself finally.

Revealed *what* about himself?

That he had been supplanted by a man who could be his twin, that he'd been faking his amnesia, pretending to be the duplicate pretending to be *him*—that he was in truth undead?

This was a nightmare. No one was around, Ducas was hovering, and if Veleka came into the hallway now, what would he say?

Whose son . . . ?

How much did Veleka know?

Whose son? What would she tell him?

What had Ducas told her?

Or had he told her anything? Had it been easier for him to let things lie until the final disposition?

He knew then where he was going in the house—up to Sir Eustace's and Veleka's room.

He climbed the steps on his hands and knees, hugging the wall, until he reached the landing, and then edging toward the door he had seen Sir Eustace enter—last night, was it?

The door opened easily. The air was cool, the room was dark, the curtains drawn. He didn't know quite what he expected, but there was nothing to differentiate this room from any other room in the house in terms of comfort and luxury. He took in the details in one lightning glance: the thick carpeting, the four-poster bed, the velvet draperies, a more massive fireplace. Beautiful paintings over the mantel and bed. A bigger dressing room. A hand-painted washbasin.

He threw open the doors of the armoire. Sir Eustace's clothes, neatly lined up, shirts, suits, all black, a dozen of them or more. Everything in the room belonged to Sir Eustace, he discovered as he rifled through the drawers, and the desk in one corner of the room.

Where were Veleka's things? There had to be a connecting door to another bedroom.

Whose son?

He tried them all. Where were Veleka's habitual green dresses and morning gowns? Where were the mirrors?

There were *no* mirrors in the room. And not a single personal item that might belong to Veleka in the room.

No mirrors. Whose son?

He was losing his grip on his thoughts. A mist shimmered upward from the floor. He felt the room begin to swirl.

You can never defeat me . . .

Ducas, floating at the foot the bed, larger than life, blanketing his vision, his consciousness, his world.

It was time. Revelations, chapter one, verse one. *Unto you, dear mother, your child is returned, never having left you in any way in the first place.*

How the hell could she not have known that?

The Other had made it supremely difficult. But that was to be expected, and in truth, he respected a worthy adversary. But he detested how much he and the Other were so physically alike, and there couldn't possibly be an explanation for that. He didn't even want to hear one.

It had been bad enough that he had put up a fight; it was like wrestling with himself trying to subdue him. But he'd gone down nevertheless, his duplicate, his Other. Overpowered, overcome, totally subjugated, in his fury that he even had to perform in this Punch and Judy show.

No help for it: the deed was done. The Other was bound and gagged and interred in his coffin under the bed. The only thing that remained was to reveal everything to Veleka, and to prepare the host for another feast.

With leftovers. He hoped. The damned host was getting more and more voracious, almost as if its body could not be slaked. It was time to get them off their asses, and send them to war, where they could feed their fill and fill the coffers.

After he took care of the Other. That was the last detail. Then he would plan perfectly how to accomplish that without any of the missteps that had bedeviled him. A little training, a little caution, and the host could gorge to their heart's content. And send a cask or two back for the body.

All right. That took care of two things with one strategy. A little judicious planning and all would be as it was.

The Other was the problem now.

And getting Veleka to his room. Although the damned Other might accomplish that all on his own, the way he was banging on the platform and making those ridiculous honking noises.

How could a man be so like him, and *not?* It defied all logic.

Who was he? *What* was he, who bore the mark of the Iscariot? He'd examined it closely; it was scarred into his flesh, the three X's, the mark of the clan. The host. And yet, the Other was not a one.

He couldn't be. Ducas knew them all, every last one of his clan. And this was a question only the Other could answer, and he was not prone to answer the question.

He was wasting time. This was *the* last one thing to take care of, and he could wipe that haunted look from Veleka's face, he could have his life back again, and all would be as it was.

Except how shocked would she be when he revealed that he had never been memory impaired, and that it was all a subterfuge, all in aid of rooting out his darkest secrets. And that it was all the colonel's fault, blast his soul, and when this was over, he was going to hunt him down and destroy him, suck the life, the love, the soul from his body, and relish every moment of it.

He savored the thought, as the Other pounded his boots relentlessly against the catafalque on which the mattress rested. Who did he think would come to his aid?

Damnation—he should've taken his blood kiss when he overwhelmed the Other, and had done with this insanity before it started.

Whose son, indeed.

"Ducas . . . ?"

Ah, perfect. Veleka, knocking. "What's that noise? I keep hearing a thumping sound . . ."

Well, the Other had done him a favor after all. He threw open the door. "Why don't you come in?"

She looked rather uncertain. Her face was pale, her hair unkempt, her dress slightly bedraggled. Not the Veleka who had been, before the advent of her amnesiac soldier son. Yet another score to settle with the Other—for keeping her so off balance and upset.

"Oh, it *is* coming from this room . . ." she said vaguely.

He closed the door. Locked it.

She looked askance.

"Shhh . . ." He grasped the bedposts, and she gasped, and fell back onto a chair. He turned them, the mechanism scraped and rolled, and the mattress lifted from the catafalque.

And there was the Other, his eyes blazing, his legs lifted in midair.

"Come and look what we have here . . ."

"Ducas?" She said it as if she couldn't believe it as she rose up out of the chair and moved to the bed on unsteady feet.

She looked at Ducas, looked inside the coffin.

Shrieked.

Ducas grabbed her, clamped her mouth, held her upright while her body convulsed with suppressed screams as the Other lowered his legs and absorbed her uncontrollable response with undisguised interest.

Finally, she shook her head wildly, pushed at Ducas's hands, covered her mouth, and stood at the foot of the coffin, her body shaking and rocking back and forth.

So maybe he had done the right thing, not desiccating the Other quite yet. That was some reaction. But Veleka didn't look like she was ready to tell bedtime stories, so he supposed he had to be the one to begin.

Where to begin?

"It's me, Mother. It's really me."

"Praise the moon," she murmured between her fingers. "Who has it been all these days?"

"It's been both of us, actually. It's a long story, but the short version is that I was found out, and I had to kill myself. There were just too many deaths, and the colonel was suspicious and couldn't let it alone—thus the imposter."

She looked at the Other. Shook her head wordlessly, as if there were something she couldn't believe, or didn't want to say.

"He thought I was a traitor, that this—this . . . thing, this duplicate would discover some . . . some treasonous plot, or a circle of spies operating out of Sangbourne Manor. I couldn't get out of Dundee to follow until a day or two later, and by the time I caught up—"

"Ducas had returned, without his memory," she said slowly. "Yes, yes—that explains everything—that Alton person was snooping around—now I understand—"

"*I* don't understand."

"I gave him the blood kiss and fed the host . . ."

"Hellfire." He felt himself steaming up. More complications. "Damn and blast . . ." He didn't want to tell her that the host had killed the guests. It was too much on top of the Other and the revelations. "Bloody bloody shit . . ."

And all the questions yet to come. Nothing was ever over until it was over. Damn blast hell . . . He felt like spewing curses, grabbing the Other and bleeding him to oblivion.

It took every ounce of will to cool down his blood, his temper, the tumult in his head, and to turn his attention to the Other. Because the sooner he had answers, the sooner he could feed, and then this chapter would be closed.

Veleka hadn't said a word during his tirade. But then she knew him well enough. And she was pale beyond white at this point, staring at the Other as if he were a ghost.

Maybe it was. Maybe it was haunting Veleka and himself. Maybe this was what he deserved for his carelessness, his vanity, his venal soul.

The Other was very very still, listening, thinking.

Could ghosts think?

Could it be he was going crazy?

"What *is* he?" he asked finally. And the wonder was, his voice was so calm, reflecting none of the turmoil he felt.

She knew, but she wasn't going to answer. He could see it in her face. She didn't want to answer, didn't want to account for all the damage the Other had done.

All the inconvenience *it* had inflicted on *him*.

And then she looked at him, and saw the lifeblood suffuse his face, the hot glowing spark in his eyes. The danger. The aura.

Whatever it was that galvanized men to fear him, Veleka

felt it also. And the fact she was his mother would not save her from him.

And she knew—from this she could not hide.

"He's your brother," she said in a dead flat voice. "He's your twin."

Chapter 14

His twin...! A nightmare—a phantasmagorical nightmare. It had to be. He couldn't be trussed up like this and lying in a coffin in real life. This had to be a nightmare.

His twin?

It was enough: Dar erupted, jackknifing himself up from the coffin bed in a frenzy of leg thrashing and mindless sounds, while Ducas implacably pushed him right back down with his foot.

"I feel the same way," he murmured. "A twin. A fucking bred-in-the-belly, line by line duplicate of me? What a bloody joke." And to Veleka—"How the hell—?"

"The Serb. The twin came, oh, five minutes after you were born, and it was immediate and obvious he was not Iscariot. I marked him for death instantly, but one of those Sir Eustace hired to assist me stole him away. Where she took him to, I never knew, nor could I hunt him. He was hours old, had no sentience with which I could conjoin."

Veleka stared down into the coffin. *So alike, so exactly the same. She had checked, snuck up to his room after deliberately spilling the coffee, and checked that he bore the mark of Iscariot. So how was that possible that her long-lost abducted son was able to sneak into her house and take Ducas's place like that?*

She still couldn't believe it. He had been living among them as her son, and she hadn't noticed any differences. He had been rooting around in their lives, and nobody saw a thing out of place.

It was the amnesia—an absolutely brilliant ploy that would account for every difference. She never noticed the differences. Had been consumed with wanting to repair him. Had gotten too comfortable, which made her the biggest sinner of them all, when she had been castigating the body for the very same fault. Thought she was immune to fallacy, thought she was the most observant, and so much more aware.

. . . and so the twin, and not even a mother's instinct could detect him . . . She would never get over it. That, and the way he had made a fool of her.

He had to die . . .

"Sir Eustace never knew," she went on, her anger building. "I hunted the kidnapper—I think *she* suspected—and I tried to make her tell me what she knew, what she had done with the child. But in the end, all I could get from her was my blood kiss and give her the most heinous death I could invent. And that wasn't even good enough for her, the bitch . . ."

She leaned over the coffin and smoothed Dar's hair. "I thought you were dead. I hoped you were dead. I've lived my whole life here, praying you were dead. . . ."

"Not dead," Ducas interpolated caustically. "And wreaking havoc from the moment he arrived. He's about to be dead, though. I just wanted to show him to you while there was still some stuffing in him. We've been playing fox and hounds for the better part of a week, the duplicate and I. It's time to end the show, Other of mine. I promise you, I have no compunction at all about giving my blood kiss to family . . ."

He looked at Veleka. *"How* could you *not* know?"

She shook her head. It was the mark of Iscariot, but that she was not about tell him.

"We're not *that* much the same."

Dar growled, and banged his legs.

"Even *he* doesn't think so," Ducas said. "By the way, that's the right answer, dear Other. You're getting into the game."

Dar growled again.

"But *who* is he?" Veleka wondered.

"Who cares? He's a dead man where he lays."

"When?"

"Leave me to him, Mother. I'll take care of it, just like I do everything else."

Such a cavalier assumption. Immediately Veleka lashed out. "Take care? Take *care?* Like your feeding on a body in the sight of the colonel? Oh, you definitely took care of things there. And look what it's gotten us into. Children coming back from the dead, faking amnesia, destroying our lives. And that Alton person . . ." She made a derisive sound and Dar went wild, heaving his body and banging his legs.

Veleka looked down at him in the coffin bed. "Well, what did you expect me to do? He discovered how to release the mattress; he found the coffin. What did you think would happen if someone got close . . . ?"

She stared into his eyes. She felt a twinge. Not regret. Just—something. "Oh—oh . . . almighty hell—they didn't know. Ducas, they didn't know."

Well, he knew that. And more besides. "No," he said without compassion, "they didn't know. Nobody knows. And we will keep it that way. The Iscariot will live, the host will thrive, the body will be nourished, and no one can stop us."

"That is my enduring purpose in life," Veleka reminded him, "to sustain the clan, but they've all become too lazy, they all expect their lifeblood to be handed to them and not to have to work for it. And now this—your ruining a perfectly good situation that provided the host with everything it needs. And *him* . . . bloody moon, I can't believe that you changed places like that and I never . . ." she trailed off. ". . . never—"

"That's right, you *never* . . . it does seem improbable when you look him now, doesn't it? Aren't the differences more plain?"

She stared at Dar. "No," she whispered. And then there was the mark . . .

Shit. His own damned mother. No matter.

"Wait—" she said suddenly, grasping Ducas's arm, "how do I know you're not *him?*"

His rage hit him like a bullet. Right in the stomach, boiling up to his heart. "I bloody well *am* your son, and that son of a bitch duplicate bleeding other bastard is going to die—" he lunged at the coffin, "—Now . . ."

"*No!*" Veleka screamed. "*Noooooooo*—Ducas—!"

Dar, howling behind his gag, bucking his body, fighting with his shoulders, his feet, his legs. That close to death—Ducas's eyes flaming with bloodlust, unfocused, going in for the kill.

"*Ducas!*" Veleka shrieking. "*Stop—Stop! . . .*" She threw herself onto Dar's body. "*Duuucaaassss . . . ! Stop! Stop!* You can't, you have to stop, you have to . . ."

His body slumped; the fire went out of his eyes. He stared at Veleka who was sprawled on top of the Other and under him, trying to comprehend what she was saying, where he was.

"Angene is coming," she whispered. "Listen to me—I saw her out the window. She'll be here in minutes. You have to come back. You have to get ready. You can't kill him now."

"*. . . let his blood turn to pustules . . .*"

* * *

He wasn't back yet—he knew it. He was still shell-shocked by the revelation the Other was his twin, and his waning bloodlust.

Twin. It sat oddly in his head and on his tongue. But he wouldn't give it any more thought than that. The Other was already dead, and his very last act of heroism would be to save the voracious and wanton Angene, about to burst in the door, eager for another grueling afternoon of hot hard fucking.

It rather amused him that the Other would be underneath the very mattress where *he* would be the one fondling and fucking her. The very mattress where the Other had taken her and used her, and where he would hear everything up close.

And he knew just how to keep the bastard under control too.

"If you make one sound, I will kill her, right there, right then, no compunction. She's a luscious thing, I've come that close to giving her my blood kiss. I always wondered how sweet her blood would taste, dear duplicate. And now that you've had your fill, I can finish the job—if you feel that you must make trouble . . ."

Dar shook his head. Madman. Vampire. God almighty—his twin—he couldn't absorb it. Couldn't begin comprehend it. Veleka his mother—Holy flaming hell . . . And now Angene . . . walking into the devil's den, at Ducas's invitation.

He watched as Ducas pushed down the mattress, by increments, felt his heart pounding like a hammer, watched as the light waned inch by inch, leaving him in darkness. In dirt. Like death.

"Enjoy the show," Ducas murmured. "You'll hear everything, you know. Every moan, groan, and scream of pleasure. Did I thank you for priming the cunt for me? It's always more entertaining to have a piece who knows what she's doing. Virgin flesh really is highly overrated . . ."

He was talking too much, he knew it. He just wanted to

make sure the Other could hear him, every goading word, every orgasmic sound. He wanted to gear himself up, make himself rigid with the sound of what he would do to Angene when she so willingly spread herself for him.

The Other growled, banged against the mattress.

"She's almost here, dear duplicate. Remember what I said—*I will kill her,* in the worst way imaginable if you make one more sound—and you will hear every scream for mercy."

Another menacing growl, and the Other went quiet. Good little duplicate. Very wise to know what battles to choose. Futile to fight one he must inevitably lose.

But Angene . . . he wasn't ready for Angene, hadn't shifted his consciousness over the business of lusting for her body with the intensity he had felt this morning. Bloody moon . . . There was too much going on. How could she expect him to concentrate on her when the only thing rising in his body was urgent need to give his blood kiss . . .

That bloody damned Other, screwing things up like that—

All right, now. Calm down. Angene at this moment was slipping in the kitchen door. Coming up the back stairs, in shuddering anticipation of all the delights to be had in his bed.

Dear Angene—*I am not delighted, not by you, not by this turn of events, not by the fact the Other is still alive because *you* had to come on time. You couldn't be fifteen minutes late. You couldn't let me wait. A good tart-tease would let a man wait . . . make a man beg . . .*

Well, no—he had trained her not to cross him like that, had exercised punishments for those petty infractions, and then salved them with lush-tongued kisses that soothed her crushed little soul.

Enough of this. No more games. He had to get rid of her, but how could he, when he had made such a fuss over *her* rejecting his penis. Shit. A man's rules always came back to haunt him. You just couldn't lay down the law anymore, because something would slap it right back in your face.

Hell and hounds, he wasn't nearly ready to deal with Angene.

Ready or not . . .

She pushed open the door. . . .

". . . may your bloodless body rot in your realm . . ."

It was like death, lying there in that coffin; it was as much a tomb as any burial vault or grave. He could die there. They could leave him there into eternity, and he would die and his mind, his body, his bones would fall away.

And it was torture. To know that Angene was in the room and that fiend was going to put his hands on her was pure, utter, killing torture.

. . . Angene . . .

His mind called to her. Futile. She didn't know to be receptive. He didn't know how to do it, or whether there was any other conjoining possible except with Ducas. And she didn't know anything except that she wanted so desperately to be Ducas's mistress. So what good were extrasensory powers now? He couldn't save her. He was going to die.

She could die.

It was a madman in the room with her. A beast. An unconscionable monster. There had to be a way, something he could do.

Calm. Down. Assess the situation. Take control.

Right. Everything by the book, right out of the covert operative's captivity manual. He took a deep breath.

Fine. Assess the situation.

Point one: he was as good as dead.

Point two: Angene was as good as dead.

And three: Ducas would go on pillaging battlefields to nourish his kind.

Good. Things were looking up. Definitely a way out of hell, given those considerations.

"Ducas . . ." he could hear Angene's breathless murmur as clearly as if she were beside him.

"You came." Ducas, bland, prosaic actually, not at all his usual implacable self. As shaken to the core as he was, and throwing up a wall in his mind so he could concentrate on Angene. And he wasn't doing a very good job of it.

He, Dar, could do better, even trussed up like a chicken. *Maybe he should . . .*

. . . the thought took hold. If Ducas could insinuate his sexual sensibilities on Dar's own, why couldn't he do the same to Ducas?

Angene now: "I want every minute you can give me, Ducas. Any time, anywhere, anything you want to do."

Ducas, angry, frustrated, his mind going like a wheel: Well, good. Just as he'd trained her. Except he didn't want her now, and he didn't want to do anything with her altogether.

Dar: *Good . . .* he didn't want Ducas even looking at her, or undressing her, touching her or kissing her. Stay away from her. Don't go near her . . .

Ducas: Dead was what he wanted her. Because the Other had plowed her first, had kissed her, fondled her, sucked her nipples. There wasn't a part of her the Other hadn't contaminated, and he didn't know how he was going to keep up the charade, even with the delicious bonus of the Other beneath the bed, listening, hearing, imagining . . .

You would think that would galvanize him, make him hard as stone, hard as he felt in his soul. But he felt nothing for her, about her.

Dar: *He felt nothing . . .* which meant he might be able to find a way to insinuate himself into Ducas's mind. He could direct the show—

Did he dare?

It was too quiet above. Ducas was doing nothing, in his

fit of pique. Angene was on the bed; Dar could hear her movements as she settled back, wriggling a little, trying to entice Ducas's interest, waiting for Ducas's next move.

Ducas: *Look at her. Trollop. Wanton. Gypsy whore. How could she ever have believed I'd want her for my mistress? Garbage like that. Shit. It's all the bleeding Other's fault, all of it. And he got the bloody first fuck too, after all my efforts to seduce her. Hell and hounds—it's the Other sapping my manhood. No wonder I can't get it up . . . Damn it to hell—Veleka is a dead woman—a twin, and never a word . . . springing it on me as heavy footed as a bullfrog . . .*

Angene, so softly: "Ducas . . . ?"

Ducas: *Why did I ever start this with her? Now I have a reputation to maintain, and the Other's prowess in bed to surpass. That should be a challenge instead of a burden. I should want to best that bastard in every way. If the little chit can't tell the difference between its penis and mine—by the bloody moon—I'll kill her too. But first—yes . . . starting to get interested. All kinds of lust rising in there, all ways and forms. Good. Hard now. Adam's arsenal is popping suddenly. Excellent—why squander a perfectly good hard-on? Let her trade her blow-off for my blood kiss. An equal and fair exchange . . .*

Movement above, Ducas walking toward the bed, floorboards creaking. But not climbing onto it, not going to mount her. *Stay away from her, you monster—*

Ducas: "So what are you waiting for, Angene? Here I am, rampant and ready and you're lolling on my bed like you're the queen of the manor. Get over here . . ."

Angene: "Yes, Ducas, of course—you're right . . ."

Don't touch him . . .

Angene, gasping: "I've never seen you like this."

Ducas: "Seen me—how?"

Angene, almost breathless: "So . . ."

Dar: *Noooooooooooooo . . .*

Ducas: "Show me . . ."

Dar: *Shrivel up and die, you bastard . . . don't touch him—goddamnit, Angene—Don't—Don't—*

Too late—he felt her touch, as surely as if he were in Ducas's body; felt the soft stroking sensation of her hands on Ducas's shaft—

Don't don't don't don't . . .

Ducas: "That's right, that's the way . . . I taught you well—that feels good . . ."

No power—no way to reach him now—lost in a sensual haze, building and spurting—that he felt, he . . . *felt all of Ducas's liquid life force gathering for the spill.*

Ducas pumping and guiding her every move . . .

Nothing he could do now.

He howled . . . a long silent primal howl deep in his soul.

Ducas was acting so very strangely today. He was with her, intensely, sensually with her—and he wasn't. His mind was on the business of pleasure—and it wasn't.

She felt as if he were performing by rote; he was saying the right words, his penis was a thick jut of luscious seed spume all over her hands, and yet his mind was someplace else.

Not a nice feeling for a mistress. She wondered if there were someone else—already.

Too soon for thinking like that. And anyway, she knew from her mother's liaison with Wentmore that there were times a man's mind just wasn't focused on sex. There were estate matters, family matters, financial matters—a man couldn't be a pumping machine every minute he was with his mistress, even though he could require that she always accommodate him.

This was one of those days. Ducas was just not with her, and she felt a billowing disappointment that nothing more might come of today. There was a certain unfairness in that: he could withhold his penis, but she must always be ready to spread her legs. He expected she would service him, but he didn't need to bother satisfying her.

She had agreed to that, after all. Whatever his terms. She had no business feeling let down. She had better stop thinking this way.

She wanted this, she wanted him, any way she could get him, and she had manipulated the unforeseen event of his amnesia to her advantage.

She must remember that she was the instrument of *his* pleasure, and by subsuming herself in that, she would insure her own. She had stored away a lifetime of memories already. So it shouldn't matter that he didn't feel like fucking her. That was just the way it was. Those were the terms.

And besides, it was early. There was a lot more time; however much time he allocated to her, she would be grateful. Even now, as he lay with her, idly running his hand down her neck . . . if only he would play with her nipples . . . but he was fingering the crisscrossed bites.

"What's this?"

"What's what?" Did he not remember? Maybe she ought not make a fuss over it.

"These . . . on your neck—" He wanted to know—but why, how could he not remember?

"I don't—wait . . ." She didn't want to say she didn't know what he was talking about; and yet, he didn't seem to remember.

"Let me go see—" She evaded his detaining hand and slipped out of the bed and over to her clothes, which she had dropped on the floor by the door. She knelt and withdrew, from the pocket of her cloak, the small hand mirror Gaetana had given her.

"The light is terrible this time of day . . ." she murmured, climbing back into bed, and seating herself with the right side of her face to the waning afternoon light. "There . . ."

Ducas went rigid. Surely the bitch didn't know what she was doing. He would kill her if she had even the slightest inkling what she was doing. He would destroy her where she sat . . .

"Oh, that," she murmured. How else to explain it? How could he not remember the thrilling sensual bites? "You—you did that, Ducas." She turned and crawled back to him. "Look—" She held up the mirror.

And froze. *No reflection . . . Dear heavenly Father—Ducas isn't there—*

Her hands shook. She tilted the mirror so that it magnified the bites on her neck. *Pretend nothing is wrong.* Her heart pounding, her hands icy-cold and shaking, her heart thumping in her breast so loud she was certain he could hear it, her whole body an icy block of denial . . .

What did she see?

Pretend she didn't see what she saw. That nothing nothing nothing was wrong. "See? You did that." God, how was her voice so cool, so calm? "All the way down to my breasts, Ducas." She tipped the mirror so her breasts were magnified, her nipples taut and quivering.

Take his mind off what you saw . . . you saw nothing out of the usual, nothing . . .

"You don't remember?" She tried to infuse disappointment into her voice. They were playing a game now, a different one from that before. And everything in this game was critical. Only she didn't quite know why.

"I don't have to remember," he growled, taking the mirror from her hand and tossing it over the bed. "I don't have to do anything. And *you* have to do everything, Angene. *Everything.*"

What had she seen? Bite marks, that was all. Bite marks he did not nip all over her neck and chest. Fuck the Other—fuck her . . . Dead, they both were dead already.

He felt the bloodlust roar up inside him. He was too kind, playing these games, giving her a chance. She didn't deserve it. She'd handed her body over to the Other and let him do this to her, moaned with pleasure as she let him mark her the way he, Ducas, would have marked her. She deserved nothing from him, nothing except her just due.

"I'm here," she murmured; she didn't want him to touch her, she wanted to slap his hand away, and it took all her willpower to stay still as he ran his finger down the bites on her chest.

Don't touch my nipples. . . . I imagined what I saw— what I didn't see . . . the future in my hand, Mother said . . . I didn't see anything—Mother knew—?

Act naturally—even if he touches you, swoon at his touch, pretend you want him, pretend—pretend . . .

"Yes," Ducas said, "you are, you are here for my pleasure, to spread your legs for me, to fuck me only."

Don't touch me . . .

"It's all I ever wanted," she whispered to conceal her quavering voice.

"Is it? When you question what I remember, what I don't? You don't ever question me, Angene. You have nothing to say. You are the cunt that I fuck when I need a good fuck. That's what a mistress is, what she does. I keep having to remind you, don't I? I'm beginning to think this arrangement is not going to work."

Send me away—please, send me away . . .

"But in my goodness—" he was playing games again; why was he doing this—oh, yes—because the hellacious Other was listening, was feeling every creak of the bed, every uncertainty in him and in the whore, because the Other knew that no matter what the bargain, they both soon would be received by the body and consumed by the host. Because there was no way out, and he, Ducas, had all the power.

And so it really didn't matter what fucking Angene saw in the mirror. She would not leave this room alive.

"—in my goodness, I am disposed to give you yet one more chance to prove that you can subsume your body and your entire self to my needs, and my desires."

"I can do that," she whispered—*don't touch me, don't come near me—I didn't see what I saw, I have to pretend—send me away, please, send me away—* "I yearn to do that . . ."

"Well, now you must prove it." He swung his legs over the side of the bed and got on his feet. Kicked off his trousers, which he had pulled up, and patted the bedside where he stood. "Right here, Angene. Come. I'm ripe and ready for you."

She averted her eyes as she crept across the bed to him, as she gave herself, cold and shuddering, into his hands so he could position her the way he would.

He has to see I'm shivering; that I can't abide his touch . . . he's doing this deliberately—lifting my legs onto his chest, pointing his shaft right between my legs—he's going to—he's going to . . .

Knock, knock . . .

"*Shit—who the fuck is there?*"

"*Ducas—*" Her voice was urgent.

Hellfire—Veleka. Oh, Veleka, enough of Veleka, and twins, and mirrors, and not knowing the difference—it was over . . . no more Veleka, no more Angene, no more Other—no more *anything* to get in his way.

"*What!*" He couldn't keep the fury out of his voice. Veleka's timing was impeccable. Only she would disturb him just as he was poised at the juncture of Angene's thighs, drowning in her huge, fear-glazed eyes, getting harder and harder as he fed off her terror, his penis throbbing with anticipation of his forceful punishing penetration of her—"*What?*"

"Croyd is here—"

What?

"Tell him to go to hell. Go away, Veleka."

"Ducas—it's about the guests—they never returned to London."

"How is that my problem?" Truly, there was never such a nagging woman; he was going to eat her alive, maybe tonight.

"The ticket master said they never left the station."

He felt his blood rising to the point of bursting. The bloody bloody host—another goddamned mess he had to fix—and he didn't know how . . . and Angene was waiting—and every part of him suddenly died. Just shriveled and died.

He thrust Angene away furiously, his mind running like a meter. She wasn't important; he could get at her and to her anytime he wanted. Tonight—it was a promise—after he took care of Croyd.

Maybe he should lock her in the room. Good idea. No, not such a good idea. The Other would know. Would use her to escape. Not that either of them could escape *him,* but why make double the trouble.

No, she could leave. She wouldn't get far, and more than likely, she would be with that gypsy bitch mother of hers . . . and even if the Other tried to attract her attention, she would never figure out where he was. He'd probably scare her to death anyway, one way or the other. Good. Ducas hoped he did. One less problem to deal with . . .

Why was everything falling apart like this?

"Get out," he barked, pulling on his clothes. "Go home. I won't hold it against you—this time."

Oh, God—could he see her whole body shaking with relief?

He threw open the door. Veleka was standing in the threshold, with a clear view of Angene, naked and shivering on the bed. Her expression didn't change.

Ducas shot her a cool, knowing, assessing glance. "Get out now, Angene." The one and only time he would gift her with her life. And then he closed the door behind him.

What did he know? What did he think she knew? It was a killing look. He was coming after her, soon, because of what she hadn't seen in that mirror. Pretending that she didn't know.

She felt the terror right down to her toes, she had to get out, and right now, she couldn't move to save her life.

She was so cold, so shivery, her body so rubbery with

fear, that her legs gave way, and she sank onto the edge of the bed and rounded her body into a protective ball.

... pretending that she didn't know ...

"*... let him come into the light and burn in the fires of hell ...*"

Chapter 15

She couldn't move. She was so scared, she just couldn't move. He could come back any minute, and she didn't know what would happen to her if he did, but for all her ravaging fear, she couldn't move.

This room . . . all the time she had spent with him in this room, on this bed . . . all those lessons in humility and sex play from him to hone her mind and body, to keep him interested, fascinated and eager for the ultimate moment he would take her . . .

No no no . . . she couldn't bear it—all the memories bombarding her, the exquisite pleasure of the first penetration, the triumphant moment of his capitulation to her dream and desire of being his mistress . . .

A lie—everything a lie . . .

What had she seen in the mirror? She didn't want to remember. If she remembered, he would come for her. Come sooner.

Because he saw what she saw—

—she remembered—

Still—another time, he'd said: No mirrors? *He'd been stunned.* No mirrors?

And so, she'd looked in the mirror as she pretended to examine her neck, and she had seen the future in her hand—her own face reflected back at her . . . and *only hers.*

Thump thump thump . . .

She jumped. *No mirrors.*

Dear God, what was that?

Thump thump thump . . .

Under her? No, under the mattress?

Thump thump thump . . .

Under the bed?

Thump thump thump . . .

Insistent . . . what if he came back, right now? She should have been gone already, racing down the drive and away from whatever it was—whatever he was, that his face didn't reflect in the mirror—

—no no no—it was an aberration, it was the light, it was something she did, and in the morning, everything would be all right . . . she would find it had been a dream, and everything would be back the way it had been—

Thump thump thump . . .

The thumping was loud, insistent, and *under* the bed. Something was *under* the bed . . .

Her heart started pounding. What if *he* were under the bed?

And she was still naked, so vulnerable—that point was the only thing that could make her move right now . . . she eased off the bed and edged toward the door where she had dropped her clothes.

All those hours ago . . . all that heady succulent anticipation—

Thump thump thump . . .

Took a surreptitious peek at the bed as she picked up her underclothes. The bed rail touched the floor, a deeply carved wooden bed rail, almost like a frame around the bed. There was no space beneath for anyone to hide.

Thump thump thump . . .

She jumped. She pulled on her clothes haphazardly, the

undergarments, the dress, the cloak, her shoes. The mirror—where had he tossed the mirror—?

Did she need the mirror? She needed it. She bit her lips. He could be on his way back upstairs at this minute, and here was this thumping noise, and her crawling all around the floor looking for the mirror, and what would he think, what would he do to her?

What is that noise?

"*Unnnngggrrrrrnnnnnnnngggghhhhhh...*"

She heard it plainly, as she crept around the floor. A human, almost animal sound beneath the bed. And that awful thumping in tandem with it, and suddenly now another sound—

Someone is under the bed.

But there wasn't an *under.*

Oh God oh God oh God—

Under the mattress then?

Hurry, hurry, hurry—

No under *under* the mattress—the thing was attached somehow to a platform beneath it.

Fine. Forget it. She had to go ... *where did he toss that little mirror?*

She needed that mirror and she didn't know why—no, maybe she did. Maybe she thought if she looked in the mirror again, she would see what she was supposed to have seen ...

Thump thump thump—

"*Unnnngggrrrrrnnnnnnnngggghhhhhh...*"

Her blood ran cold. There was a human being under that bed, trapped, had to be, and she could see no way to release him—and she *had to get out...!*

Maybe there was a secret lock ... Oh, God, I have no time to do this, I can't stay here. . . . She crawled to the bed rail, and ran her fingers all over the carvings, the fluted decorations, the flowers, pushing, pressing, hoping—

Something, something—anything—

All around the bed frame, feeling, touching, pushing,

nothing—her heart pounding, her blood pulsing in her ears, the thumping sound louder and louder, the human sound like a bear—desperate, roaring, close and yet enclosed as if he was in a cave—in a tomb . . .

What made her think that?

She was getting nowhere. She climbed to her feet, tried pushing the mattress, pulling it. It didn't budge. Somehow it was made all in one piece, immovable. Impregnable.

Now what? *Now what?* Hurry hurry—

What else could she push, or pull, or—or . . . She grabbed hold of the bedpost to steady herself, and she caught a glimpse of the mirror lying just beyond the edge of the bed near the wall.

She pulled away from the bedpost, and it gave in her hand. Just the most imperceptible of movements. She stopped, startled—*mirror first and then, and then*—she snatched it up and put it in her pocket. *Time to go. Time to* go!

Thump thump thump . . . "*Nnnrrrrrggggnnnhhh* . . ."

Oh, God, there's someone in there and how can I go— how can I not go?

Wasting time, Angene—

She stared at the bedpost that had moved in her hand. Now what, now what . . . ? Try it try it—

He's coming for you—no, not yet . . .

I've got to get out of here . . . !

"*Nnnrrrgggnnnngggghhhh* . . . !"

Desperate—oh God, oh God, what if what if what if . . . ?

Thump thump thump . . .

She grasped the bedposts, she took a deep, heart-stopping breath, and she twisted them.

And they moved . . . they *moved*—and there was a creaking sound . . . something rumbled . . . and the mattress lifted, slowly, slowly . . . up up up . . .

His legs were in the air, his arms were bound behind him, and he was twisting and howling behind the gag on his mouth.

Was he human? She didn't know. She only knew it was already too late.

She was looking at Ducas Sangbourne in the flesh.

And she started to scream.

It was the blood. Or lack of it. A half dozen people gone missing and not a sign, not a clue, not a witness, not a shred of anything to prove they had stayed on in Cheshamshire, or had gone somewhere else.

The station master hadn't seen them. Which didn't mean they hadn't boarded the train. It just meant no one had seen them. And they had arrived nowhere since. So it seemed logical to begin at the departure point.

Not that Mr. Ducas was making it any easier.

"Yes, Constable, they left here making for the five-thirty train. Yesterday evening." Ducas was bored; Ducas was in a flaming fury, but only Veleka knew that. "After we buried Alton. Sir Eustace can bear that out."

Sir Eustace nodded. "Yes, indeed, we gave them a basket of food and off they went, and where they might have gone after that is only for them to know."

Croyd was making notes. "And the coachman took them to the station."

"That is my understanding," Sir Eustace said, looking perplexed, looking at Ducas, who shrugged.

"And yet their families report that they have not seen them since."

"I'm sorry to hear that, Constable."

"They didn't return here?"

"They did not." Sir Eustace was emphatic.

"Did the coachman perhaps drive them someplace else?"

"You'd have to ask him; we assumed they were let safely on the five-thirty train."

"And yet no one has seen them. . . ."

"Constable, they are my good dear friends, just what are you getting at?"

"No one saw them leave Chesham Station is what I'm getting at, and the families are fairly upset. It has been two days and a night and no one has seen or heard from them."

"I'm sorry to hear it, but they left from that front door—" Sir Eustace motioned to the entrance hall "—at approximately five o'clock two days ago to take the five-thirty train to London, and we know no more about it than that."

"I see," Croyd said. "Mr. Ducas?"

Ducas started. "Constable? . . ." Stopped short. Had to think. Just because he had now revealed everything to Veleka didn't mean he could become Ducas again. As far as Croyd was concerned, he was still memory impaired. He had to think for a long moment about whether he had already made a slip or if, when the guests had departed, the Other had been there.

Bloody damn hell. There was no end to this assinine pretense. And Angene skulking around upstairs—

He reined in his temper. They would die, all of them, Croyd included, they would die. "Yes, Constable?"

"You can corroborate that the guests left the Manor as Sir Eustace has described?

Ducas looked at Veleka who imperceptibly nodded her head. "I was right there," he said.

"Very well, then. That's all for the moment." Croyd pocketed his notebook. It was ever the same.

No blood. No bodies. Nothing. Again.

He howled that awful gag-stuffed sound. And he struggled to get upright, and Angene backed away, her eyes shot with terror, her screams melting down to a mewling whimper as she almost collapsed in horror.

Ducas—who had left the room with Veleka—no, that didn't make sense, how could he be immured in a . . . in a . . . it looked like—

She edged closer—swallowed hard, swallowed another scream—it looked like—a coffin . . .

"Rrrnnnnngggnnn . . . !"

He was emphatic, banging his legs against the side of the coffin, making those awful animal noises behind the gag.

No time. She'd gotten the coffin open, he could fend for himself now, whoever—or whatever—he was . . . *get out now . . .*

She made a move toward the door and he howled again: *"Nngggg!"*

She pulled up, and turned. Looked into his eyes. Something in his eyes—

Take off the gag—

Did she hear the words, did she imagine them? No—she wasn't going to be manipulated by the likes of Ducas Sangbourne anymore. No. Not after tonight. After the mirror.

Oh, God, she had to get out of there!

"Nggggghnnn . . . !"

He was raging to tell her something, but he had told her enough before he left the room. She knew too much—*She had to get out of there . . .*

How could Ducas have tied himself up and imprisoned himself under the bed in that short a time?

Dear God, now she was feeling sympathy for the creature?

"Ngggnn!"

He could see her wavering, she knew it. She was torn between leaving him, and at least removing the gag. Maybe the gag, maybe she could salve her conscience by giving him his voice.

She had to get *out* of there. . . . She edged toward the coffin—Lord almighty—a coffin . . . toward the back of it, where she could just . . . no she couldn't. Her hands were shaking so badly, she was so terrified, horrified—who would imprison someone under a bed in a coffin?—someone who looked like—

. . . oh . . .

There's dirt in the coffin . . . oh, my God . . .

This can't be—this is Ducas . . .

Looking at her the way Ducas always looked at her—

Take off the gag—we have to get out of here . . .

I know. Did she think it, did he catch it?

Do it . . . He leaned forward so that she could get behind him and loosen the knot and pull it down.

Her fingers were ice, her body was shaking out of control. He was sitting in a layer of dirt in a coffin under Ducas's bed, and he looked like Ducas . . .

She felt like fainting from the ghoulishness of it.

Get out of here . . .

Her fingers were so cold she kept fumbling with the knot, and finally, she just pulled the gag down, over his mouth, around his neck.

He sagged with relief.

"*Ducas . . .*" she whispered—testing him?

He shook his head. "Dar St. Onge . . ."

"No . . ." She edged away from him. "No. It's because of what I saw in the mirror, isn't it? It's a punishment, isn't it? You trying to scare me. Terrify me . . . I'm getting out of here. . . ."

"Angene—*don't leave me*—I *am* Dar St. Onge." He felt such desperation, and no way to prove it to her. It was bad enough she had almost screamed the house down. They had so little time to effect any kind of escape. "You've got to untie me."

"No."

"At least my legs."

"*No . . .*"

"They are going finish up down there very soon. Croyd isn't getting the answers he wants, but he can't do anything about it. Ducas will be up here in minutes. You *have* to untie me."

She stared at him. "No. Ducas isn't downstairs. Ducas is here."

He shook his head. He had to convince her. "Look—the mirror—"

The mirror. Her hand snaked into her pocket and she closed her fingers around it. *The mirror. No mirrors.*

. . . who . . . ?

"Do it," he challenged her. "See for yourself."

She swallowed hard. This was all too much, all the things he knew about the constable's inquiry downstairs, the mirror, how he looked exactly like Ducas—he *had to be* Ducas, playing games with her—

Maybe—

"They have nothing else to tell Croyd, he'll be leaving in a moment and Ducas will come . . . Hold up your mirror— we *have* to get out of here. . . ."

She pulled her hand from her pocket, held the mirror up in front of his face. Held it up so that she could see herself, and him. And she saw—herself . . .

And him . . .

And she almost fainted.

"Who are you?" She started fumbling at the ropes, her fingers still encased in ice.

"There's no time. I'll answer every question after we get away from here. You need to get my legs free. Break the mirror—quickly—"

Oh, God "It's bad luck—"

"Worse luck if Ducas catches us here—" *Break the mirror . . .*

She felt him compelling her to do it, in spite of her ingrained superstitious impulse. She watched, almost as if she were outside herself, as she slammed the mirror facedown on the edge of the coffin, as she picked out the largest piece and started to saw at the rope binding his feet.

It wasn't thick rope, but it took an appreciable effort for her to make her boneless fingers exert enough pressure to cut through the tight weave.

"Just my legs. Quick. They're seeing Croyd out the door now. . . ." He had the sense of them moving, the murmur of voices, Croyd's deferential tones, Ducas's testiness . . .

The door into his consciousness was nearly open now—lying in that coffin could do that to you—make you expand your mind and see outside wherever you were confined. He didn't want to go in there, but now it was imperative that he did, alone and on his own.

Angene was terrified enough; and the urgency that coursed through him was as raw and red as blood.

The rope gave way. He scrambled to his feet, and she helped him over the edge of the coffin.

"Take the mirror pieces. Out the door—*now* . . ."

They scrambled out the door and into the hallway. They heard Sir Eustace's last good-bye, heard Ducas's footsteps in the hallway veering toward the steps.

This way . . . barely a whisper in her mind. No time to unbind his hands. They raced across the landing, while he tried to figure out which doorway led to the back stairs.

That door . . . At the opposite end from Ducas's room . . . concealed by a small wall, and tucked into the northwest corner of the house.

Ducas's footsteps echoing ominously, as he made his way upstairs.

Angene opened the door. A narrow winding staircase, up and down.

Down . . .

He headed down first and she barreled after him. Not a minute more until Ducas would discover they were gone. She needed two or three minutes at least to cut the rope, and they couldn't take the time.

Down to the lower floor—and they could go even farther down . . .

What did that mean? Cellars. Hiding places.

Dar halted, whispered, "Undo my hands."

It was dark on the stairwell; she groped for the shard of mirror, felt for the rope. She could kill him, she thought, slice into his wrists and he could bleed to death.

Not Ducas—she sawed at the rope. This was the moment of truth—*not Ducas*—giving him his hands meant giving him control. Meant trusting him. Meant—he wasn't Ducas—she had seen *his* face in the mirror—

. . . the ropes loosening strand by strand—he flexed his arms, felt the rope fraying, giving, slipping from around his hands.

He grabbed Angene's hand, whispered, "Quick—choose now: come with me, or leave the grounds."

"Where—?" A breath of a question.

"I don't know—down there—"

She couldn't be alone, not now, not here. His hand was warm, enveloping her cold one reassuringly. Ducas was overhead, discovering, even now, the open coffin, and both of them gone. No other protection, not even Gaetana and her powerful incantations. Nothing to trust except his warm hand grasping hers. Maybe, in this horror, that was enough.

"With you," she whispered. "I'll go with you."

". . . let the evil ones turn to dust . . ."

Damn fucking hellfire . . . you couldn't count on anyone doing what they were supposed to do . . . damn Angene's gypsy soul to hell—had she gone? Had she just left the manor as he ordered her to?

No. Never. Stinking gypsy bitch . . . what did she do instead? The stupid little bitch had to poke and prod around and stick her nose into things she wasn't meant to know.

That bloody mirror—as sure as his father was Iscariot, that hadn't been Angene's idea. Angene had no notion, none. It was the mother. It was the very thing he had been trying to circumvent by using Sir Eustace to distract her.

And now the mother knew . . .

And why? Because that damned old fart Sir Eustace had chased her out of his bed. Made her go home. Had no conception of the kind of vindictiveness her kind was capable of.

And now look—yet another disaster to contend with. By the bloody moon, that ass deserved to die.

As if he needed another reason to kill the old bag.

Well, it was going to stop here. And now, Croyd's visit had cemented his resolve. The question of the guests was the straw on the house of cards, and he wasn't going to sit by and watch them tumble down.

He could have dealt with Angene. He could have pretended to be the Other to allay the colonel's suspicions, and then have disposed of them both. He could have pacified the gypsy and compelled Sir Eustace to make it up to her.

But there was no way to avoid the question of the guests, once Croyd got started on a formal inquiry. He hadn't said when that would be, not yet. But it would be soon, if the families kept pressing for answers.

And then Croyd would come hunting for explanations, and everything would fall apart like a sand castle on the shore.

It would be just like that too. Messy. Muddy. Mucky, trying to get past an investigation.

Well, that was what happened when you let *people* into the mix.

They got too much in the way, and then he had to fix things, and that made everything worse. Well, he couldn't do it any longer. Didn't want to. Was ready to hoist up the body and move it somewhere safe—safer—because the effort of sustaining it was draining his energy faster than water over a dam.

He needed it settled, nourished and at the ready.

It was time to give all of this up. All of it—the Manor, the mother, the marginal pleasures of fucking Angene. She and the Other were beside the point now; they would be consumed in the conflagration.

It was the only solution. Send them all to perdition at one blow.

Kill all of them.

All—and no regrets . . .

Soon. Tonight. Tomorrow—this minute . . .

Only he just might have waited too long . . .

Chapter 16

It was dark as a tomb in the stairwell. Dar edged his way down the narrow steps by feeling along the gritty stone wall with his one hand, and pulling Angene firmly behind him.

"Don't speak," he cautioned her in a whisper. "He senses everything."

As *he* should have been able to, but he didn't at all sense that there was a door at the bottom of the steps. Locked.

Shit.

The aura of evil was so palpable, Dar could taste it. Evil, above them, around them, and beyond the door. No choice, no chance now—

This he felt, this he knew—Ducas had crossed some kind of threshold.

The door suddenly swung open.

You can know all the secrets . . .

Ducas, taunting him.

But he already knew them. From time immemorial he knew them, they were written on his soul. Secrets of the blood, and death everlasting.

Dar pushed open the door. Darker than dust in there, dank as the grave, and not a sliver of light to guide them.

No matter; he had his newborn feral senses, still feeling, still reaching, not quite there . . . and he had his unquenchable determination to conquer Ducas, and his fierce desire to protect Angene.

A warrior's puny weapons against a fulminating evil. And yet—it had to be enough.

They stepped into what felt like a passageway. No storerooms here, as he had expected. Nothing but stone walls, a dirt floor, and, he gauged, as he experimentally stretched out his arms and touched either wall, a narrow tunnel. To nowhere . . .

"We have no choice," he whispered, "we have to keep going."

Angene took a deep breath. This was scariest thing; there was no other safe haven but this man who looked like Ducas. Ducas who would kill them both if he could find them.

Who was already on the prowl.

Unless this man, this *Dar* was not who he pretended to be.

The darkness was all encompassing. It was as if they were the only two people in existence, and this raw dank space was their whole immediate world.

Dar pressed on, his senses at full alert.

You cannot escape me . . .

Dar ignored him.

You are going to die.

Block him out. Shut him down.

You can't get away . . .

I'm getting away—ah, that was a mistake, giving him that.

Are you . . . ?

Was he?

He felt a waft of cold air streaming around them. He saw the faintest whisper of light in the tunnel ahead of them. He felt the telltale prickles inundate his body.

He stopped short, pulled Angene close to him, whispered in her ear: "Ducas is here."

She started shaking. The space felt even closer suddenly, the smell of death infusing the air.

He could tell her anything. They were the only ones here . . . how did she know, how could she know anything?

And—the thought slammed into her suddenly—what if she had done . . . things . . . with him?

She wrenched away from him. She felt numb. Unreal. This was a horror story, a nightmare, she'd wake up and find everything just as it used to be. She *wanted* it just the way it used to be. Otherwise, she might just be going crazy. "Where, where is Ducas?"

I'm here.

"He's there," Dar murmured. "He's that little glimmer of light, waiting for us in the tunnel."

How very perceptive of you. . . . Come into the light, Other mine. Let us get this confrontation done.

Dar moved in front of Angene and edged forward toward the light. There was choice, this was his destiny.

There was a small kerosene lamp set on the ground, its light flaring upward, illuminating the craggy rock wall, casting deep lingering shadows everywhere.

It was icy cold, and Ducas was nowhere to be seen in the flickering smoky light.

Dar picked up the lamp, and the meager firelight spewed a misty haze that swirled all around them.

Here I am, dear Other. What can you do to me?

Ducas was the mist, winding himself all around Dar's body as if he would choke the very life out of him.

But it wouldn't be enough. Dar sensed it, felt it. Ducas wanted the blood kill, and he wanted it badly. The end was near. He had made up his mind that everyone must die. The host had set the table.

"Show yourself, then," Dar goaded him. "Make yourself whole. Come and get *me* . . ."

The mist spiraled down to the dirt floor, and coiled upward as Ducas began to reconstitute his body in human form.

I'm coming after you now, hellacious interfering Other—prepare to die . . .

No—you will— Dar tossed the lamp at him, Ducas howled, Dar grabbed Angene and pushed her away from the conflagration, back the way they had come, running, running fast, running not fast enough, away from the evil that was burning, its vile perfume permeating the tunnel, reaching for them, choking them.

But Ducas wouldn't die. Dar sensed it instantly . . . already he was one with the smoking fire. One with the evil on earth.

Up the steps, frantic now, coughing, hacking from the ingestion of smoke. There was no escaping him. They had inhaled him, swallowed him. There was nowhere to hide.

The host had set the table.

Everyone would die.

Out of the stairwell, and into the downstairs hallway they tumbled, out behind the main staircase, hidden from sight. They flattened themselves against the stairwell wall, listening, the scent of death still in their throats, their eyes watering at the effort to suppress the urge to gag.

There wasn't a sound, not a movement. No servants. No sign of Veleka or Sir Eustace. The house was preternaturally quiet, and yet there was a thrumming in the air that Dar felt reverberating in his very bones.

"The host is waiting," he murmured. "However much they've fed, it wasn't enough. They want everything, everyone. They want it all."

Angene went icy cold all over again. This was insane. From the moment Ducas had abandoned her in his room, she had pitched into an appalling nightmare. It had to be a nightmare—otherwise . . .

"Dear God, what are you *talking* about?" . . . otherwise, she was going out of her mind.

"I have to get you out of here."

Not the answer she wanted to hear from this duplicate of

Ducas. And Ducas—in the tunnel—no no no—she'd imagined that, it was part of the dream. It *was*.

"I'll get myself out of here," she snapped. And end the cryptic conversation, the phantasmagoric dream. She waited, hoping she would wake up, hoping she would find herself in Ducas's bed, cradled by his side.

Dar listened for a moment. "You can't—they're hunting."

"How do you know?"

"I just know."

I just know—like he had some kind of otherwoldly power. *Wake up, wake up . . . !* "You're saying there's nowhere we can hide."

He shook his head. "Not here. You have to get to the church."

"You're crazy," she said flatly.

"You don't understand the situation. They'll kill you. They're vampires."

Her heart slammed right up into her throat. A crazy dream. *Wake up, time to get up—!*

"How—what?" She could barely squeeze out the questions over her rising hysteria.

"God, I don't understand it all yet. But Ducas, yes . . . and I don't know who else. They killed my aide, Alton. If I had to guess, I'd bet shillings to sovereigns they killed Veleka's guests . . ."

"*Killed . . . ? Killed . . . ?*"

"Fed on . . . ?

Her legs gave way at the thought—*fed on . . . ate . . . bloodied . . .*

He pulled her up, and for one moment, it could have been Ducas with his arms around her. Ducas who was revealing these horrific things to her. Ducas who looked so much like the one *he* had called Other, that Other might well be him.

Pure unadulterated terror washed over her. For all she

knew, this *was* Ducas, after what she had seen in the tunnel, and she did not want to wait around to find out.

Whatever might happen to her without him, she felt an equal horror of what might happen to her if she stayed with him.

She went limp again, to give herself a moment to pull her wits together. It was too much to comprehend. *Vampires* . . . She could not allow herself to think about the possibility of dementia. She was here, she was whole. It was a dream, and one she had to escape from. And she had to keep thinking like that.

. . . *Vampires* . . .

Or had she been afraid of that when she'd held up the mirror in her hand?

"Angene—"

"I know," she muttered. "The church." *Right. If she could get away from him, she'd race for home, and then the church where the vicar would explain how it had been just an awful nasty dream.*

"If we could get to the stables . . ."

"If . . ." she murmured, slanting another look at him. Too much like Ducas, enough to be his twin—enough to be a vampire too—

The fear raced through her body all over again. She reared back and kneed him in the groin so hard, she thought she had crippled him. He went down, hard, on his knees, and she wrenched away from him, and ran.

Running, running—into the night, into the shadows, running, not looking, not thinking, into the danger, into the stables, into the night . . .

Now he was alone. Better that way. Hampered having her with him. Couldn't explore, investigate. Discover what could be done.

God, she had almost maimed him, put him prostrate on the floor, and it was too late now to try to follow her. Better this way.

Too late for everything. Bloodlust all around him. He could feel it pulsating, hungry, hot, seeking . . .

Swallowing bile, slumping down to the floor again, crawling inside the door, onto the steps, sprawling there, agonized and depleted.

Run, Angene—run . . .

Cold outside, the wind howling through the trees . . . Ducas pacifying the host . . . Angene at the stable door . . . another minute more, and she would be safe . . .

". . . let the evil he has wrought redound against his kind . . ."

He pulled himself down the steps and into the tunnel. In the dark, the scent, the bowels of hell.

It was all around him as he stumbled down the passageway. Hands on the wall, he could feel it, touch it, taste it. For all his life, he had lived without this knowledge, without this sense, and yet it was part of him all the same. He marveled at it; he loathed it.

He came closer to the acrid smell of burnt cloth. Stepped over the ashes. Stumbled on the little lamp. Picked it up. Carried it with him, went on into the black hole of the tunnel.

Something drawing him in? Ducas, waiting?

No, Ducas was with the host, placating the seething body.

The time was near.

He was functioning solely on intuition and gut. Deep into the tunnel he went, slowly, easing out of his pain and pulling his body, his senses into a coherent whole.

Curiously, he wasn't afraid. Ducas was nowhere near, though Ducas was aware of him.

Always, my Other . . .

He was almost there. The tunnel walls widened, and he had a sense of space. The air wasn't as close, but it reeked of a metallic scent. It smelled of blood.

He felt along the walls, and no longer touched stone.

Now it was wood, rounded wood, metal staves. Casks, mounted on racks. Small, portable casks, stored in the walls.

Rows and rows. He rapped his knuckles against one. A hollow sound. Empty. And another. Empty still. And a third, farther down the row. No more full.

All of them empty. A hundred blood soaked casks empty . . .

He felt dizzy suddenly in a wave of utter comprehension of what it meant.

Ducas—he was bringing it from the battlefield; from the sick, the wounded, the dying and the dead, he had siphoned out their lifeblood into these casks, and returned it to the host . . .

Clever Other . . . Ducas, following his every thought, his every deduction. *You can't stop me—you can't stop it. The host will live* . . .

Hundreds of racks, niched into the stone wall, some of the racks empty; and every cask he tapped, that awful hollow sound. The host has set the table. Not even a half dozen deaths could sustain them all.

How much more blood did they need to sustain them? There would never be enough. And they would pillage the countryside. They would go into battle, hundreds strong, and they'd ravage the living troops, and the wounded and dying. And still it would not be enough.

Dar saw it all in his mind's eye, and he knew with every fiber of his being, that it would never be enough . . .

And that *he* was the one who had to stop it, *now* . . .

Try it, most intrusive Other. Just try . . . *and you will see who was born to die* . . .

Ignore him. Keep on going.

The tunnel was endless, racked with casks in the wall. Empty, empty, empty . . . he kept rapping them, a wave of pure terror spiraling into his soul.

Clear your mind. Nothing has changed. The mission is the same. Ducas is the source of everything.

Ducas, your *twin*—

* * *

Black night, black soul. Sentient quiet. Silent as the moon.

Angene crept into the stable from the back door, into the waning warmth of the stove that hadn't been stoked for hours. The horses restive. One calming voice going from stall to stall. A dog howling in the distance. The hooting of an owl. The caretaker listening, pulled by its call.

No other one in the stables. *They're hunting . . .*

Her mind ran riot, her heart dropped to her feet. *They're hunting . . .*

Don't. If you let yourself think about it, they'll get you. Ducas *will get you. You have to get out of here. You have to get out of here . . . !*

She crept into the stable. It was so quiet. Too quiet. No one around. Good. All to the good for her. She waited. Not a soul challenged her.

She edged her way toward the nearest stall. Some of the horses were feeding, others, their ears pricked, their heads lifted as though they sensed something, moved nervously in place.

That would make it harder—the agitation over something not seen, an enemy not known . . . but then, those were her fears too . . .

She had to get out of there, no matter what she had to do. She slipped into an empty stall, sank to the ground, and waited for the moment she could safely run.

Darkness, unceasing, never-ending darkness as he felt his way through the tunnel, and the rows of empty casks lining the walls.

And then suddenly, it seemed as if he were veering around, and the tunnel path was off in a different direction.

But where? There had been no juncture where the storage tunnel gave into the entranceway. He followed on, warily. Maybe this led to another entryway, a place where the host could access the tunnel away from the house.

The walls were narrower now; there were no more racks

with casks, just the cold, hard stone walls, and the dark, and the blood scent, and the aura of death.

The floor inclined upward suddenly, a subtle change, and only noticeable farther on in the tunnel as the air got cooler, fresher.

There *was* an outlet here, he felt it in his bones. Here was where the host hid, lived, fed, waited. . . . The host was always waiting. . . .

Not too much farther—it was colder now, the blood scent had diminished, and he could almost feel the sky beyond the tunnel lit by a full moon.

No rush. Be wary. Ducas is with the host . . .

But ever nearby, my own insidious Other. It was I who led you through the tunnel, you know . . .

Dar made a sound—he felt Ducas slamming his thoughts down—good. He needed every ounce of concentration now to determine where this tunnel led out.

Coming to the end of it now . . . the sky midnight blue in the wash of moonlight. The air so icy and sweet, he just gulped it in as he emerged from the tunnel.

"So—you will fight my son at every turn," a voice said somewhere above him.

He wheeled. Veleka, on an outcropped rock just by the tunnel entrance; Veleka, floating in the moonlight.

Veleka . . . ? He didn't think, he reacted instinctively.

". . . Mother?"

She let out a harrowing shriek, and she leaped at him— and she vanished into the moonlight.

". . . *may her body fester in the moonlight, and the black earth rot her soul . . .*"

He had to find her. He had to know everything. Nothing made sense. His life seemed totally disjointed suddenly and he felt as much the Other as Ducas had named him.

What *was* he, if Ducas was what *he* was? And what was she?

He didn't even know where on the grounds he was—he just followed in the moonlight, a pulsing urgency spurring him on. He had to find Veleka. *Had* to.

Mother.

Dear God—how he had wished to know his mother.

Veleka, his mother—who had spawned him and an unholy vampiric twin . . .

Shit. Where the hell was he?

He started running—toward the hulking shadow of the house in the distance. He had been on the opposite end of the property then, not far from the village road.

Down through the fields where Ducas had led him yesterday, over toward the stables, and around to the back door.

Slow. Stop. Think. He was out of breath anyway, drained by his exertion, wouldn't do himself any good out of breath like that.

Couldn't spare but a thought for Angene . . . holy hell, Angene . . . he'd think about her later.

For now—he eased his way in through the back door. Into the silence. The darkness. The peculiar scent of the grave.

Through the rear of the house toward the entrance hall, no one about. Ducas, pacifying the host. How many of them were servants in the house? The thought made his skin crawl.

But no more so than the glowing apparition of Veleka, waiting for him, at the bottom of the stairs.

". . . holy light, burn this evil from the darkness, excise it from the grave . . ."

"Mother . . ."

"You will die," she intoned, raising her hand over him like a benediction. "It is written, it was foreordained."

"Tell me how, tell me why."

"He is Iscariot, and for the host to live, you must die."

"Why? How? What is Iscariot?"

"It doesn't matter now. It only matters that you have

harnessed your powers and you are the only impediment to the host. You will die."

"What powers? What is Iscariot?"

"He will turn you when you die."

"No— *Mother*—"

She shrieked at him then, an otherworldly howl that sent shudders through his body. "Listen, you. He is descended from the Judas, the last of his clan, born to sustain the host and insure the survival of the body.

"He bears the mark of thirty, and he will live forever. . . ."

"He'll kill you." It was a desperate shot, but instantly Dar knew it was true, that Veleka was not safe from Ducas, not her, not Sir Eustace . . . not Angene—

"But I am of the undead already. . . ." Veleka said. "And dear gullible Sir Eustace is gone—I took care of him—so the only one who remains is *you* . . ."

The words hit him like a punch—Eustace dead? And Veleka—?

"Mother?"

"Yes, I sheltered you in the womb; yes, you were born of my body, but you are not Iscariot, you *are* an ongoing danger to me and mine, and you *will* die." She looked up for a moment. "The host has set the table. Their will be done."

She held out her arms; she beckoned to him as she floated down the steps. "This is your destiny. As it was mine when my first child was taken from me in my native land, and I was transfigured. It was my destiny to bring the last of the Iscariot into this world, never aware there was yet another babe growing in my womb, the duplicate of my son in every way but one. I wish you had died. You must die so that he may live . . ."

"*Mother* . . ."

"*Never call me that* . . ." She reached for him and he ducked out of her way. "I am *not* your mother. I am *not* . . ." She came after him, and he evaded her unholy hands. "Your . . . mother—" Her voice rose into a scream as she came after him, her fingers curved in a death grip. "Die die die . . ."

Dar dove onto the floor, crawled under her suspended body as she shot out into the hallway, raced up the steps as she halted and veered around to come after him again.

"Diiiiieeeee . . ."

She was faster, but he was that little much ahead of her. He dashed down the hallway to Sir Eustace's room, threw open the door, and, just as she came at him and reached for him, he pushed it in her face.

She screamed again, as she bumped up against the door; Dar locked it, and whirled—no Sir Eustace—wherever he was, Dar couldn't save him now.

Could just barely save himself, he thought sardonically, as Veleka wafted through the closed and locked door.

Split second decision—he had nowhere else to go but out the window; he rammed his elbow against the glass, and dove into the darkness . . . again . . .

Chapter 17

"So I was right. Do you think I like being right? Do you think I don't know the danger we're all in?"

Oh, yes, Gaetana knew; Gaetana had figured it out, and had never flinched from her conclusions. Gaetana had warned her more than once, and now Angene huddled by the fire once again, utterly distraught, totally ashamed she hadn't taken those warnings to heart.

What had she done?

She'd lusted after a man who was a ravening monster, who would as soon kill her as kiss her. She'd played sensual games with him, lied to him, teased him, goaded him, eaten him, and allowed him to engulf her virginity—had given him every inch of her body inside and out—

And all the while it might not have been *him* . . . and now she knew what he was and how dangerous he was, she was desperate to know if it *had* been him . . .

. . . *or the Other—*

Which answer would salve her soul?

Her body went cold; and then a hot wave washed right down from her head to her feet. She burrowed deeper into the blanket that Gaetana had provided her. She was not going to get any sleep.

Whose mistress *had* she been?

She felt sick, remembering all the things she'd said, all the things she'd agreed to, all the things she'd done, and the way she had suborned her body to his demands.

Whose demands? *Whose* pleasure? Ducas the damned or the duplicate named Dar?—she could never know, and she had to live with the consequences.

. . . *Vampires* . . . and Gaetana had known.

She still couldn't quite comprehend it. A duplicate of Ducas and Ducas, unholy and forever damned . . .

He had fucked her—*who* had fucked her? Back to that— she couldn't get away from it, in her thoughts, in her life. *One* of them—or both—? And she'd never been aware . . .

No, that wasn't so either—had she not felt something was different? Hadn't she? Noticed it but ignored it in the heat of his wicked seduction? Something had been different. And yet so much the same . . .

Who . . . who . . . who?

She was so hot, so cold, every memory tainted . . . she would not believe Ducas was unholy. She couldn't. It was out of the realm of anything she knew. It was still the nightmare—she hadn't woken up.

There was no duplicate. Ducas was up at the Manor, dining with his parents. The guests had arrived in London— they would get word of that in the morning. The duplicate didn't exist—Ducas was playing games.

Ducas was waiting for her, up in his room . . .

. . . She was burning up, hallucinating, dying for all her sins.

And Gaetana knelt before her altar, steeped in her revenge.

Angene was not at the church. Dar felt an instant overwhelming panic. Where the hell was she?

Danger was rife, the air was humming with portent. The body was hungry. And Angene was nowhere in sight.

He had to rouse the vicar from his sleep.

He came, rubbing his eyes, to the rectory door. "My dear boy, what—?"

What . . . ?" God, Dar hadn't even thought about how he would present this to the vicar. And he had to get to Croyd, Croyd who was so suspicious of Veleka and about what might have happened to those six missing guests. And the minute he started speaking, he knew convincing the vicar was a lost cause. "There isn't much time; you have to listen and you have to take this on faith, vicar . . ."

"I do that for my living, my lord. What is it? What troubles you?"

"Not *my lord,* sir. My name is Dar St. Onge, and I came to Cheshamshire to investigate why a disproportionate number of men were dying on the battlefield under the care of a certain hospital ward attendant named—Ducas Sangbourne."

The Vicar looked shocked, utterly disbelieving, protesting all at once, "No. No, My lord—what on earth are you . . . ?"

"Let me finish. It's what we talked about, vicar. The thing you never believed. Vampires. That they're here. But they are—and Ducas Sangbourne is one of them—the unholy, the undead . . ." He heard himself then, the disjointed tone in his voice, the urgency; he sounded crazy.

"No—no . . . you're Ducas Sangbourne, clearly—you don't remember, that's all—your mind—your injury—let me . . ."

"You are the one person whose help we desperately need. They're hunting, vicar."

"My lord—who is hunting? Maybe you're just remembering the spring hunt, you know—the one Sir Eustace sponsors every year . . ."

"Sir Eustace is dead; they've fed on him, *and* the guests who were at the Manor this weekend; their stores are gone, and they're on the hunt . . ."

"My lord—you must, *must* let me call the doctor—he'll . . ."

Futile. Fool. Why did he think approaching the vicar was the way? He sounded demented. He should have gone to Croyd. Croyd would be more open-minded. And Croyd would definitely want to know . . .

"Listen to me. He felt it then, Ducas, probing, seeking him. And he was so open—he had to get out the information quickly, *now*. "My name is . . . D—" Too late. Ducas was inside him, compelling him, and twisting his words. ". . . *Ducas . . . St. . . . Sangbourne . . .*"

"Well, you see, my lord . . ." the vicar looked distressed. "You do know who you are. Come," he took Dar's arm, "stay with me tonight. Lie down. Let me send for the doctor. . . ."

Dar removed his hand forcibly; he felt Ducas coursing through him, pushing his words. He fought him, hard, tight, fierce. "Du-Ducas . . . Iscariot—last . . . of his clan . . ."

"What?" The vicar looked stunned as Dar broke for the door.

Ducas was reading him. Compelling him. He fought for the words. "You have to help, vicar. They're hungry . . . they never have enough—"

He pulled open the door. "Iscariot, vicar—whatever that means . . . and they're moving in for the kill."

It was all he could do. Ducas was too much in him, on him.

Close down your mind. Leave the vicar to grapple with it. No more you can do here. Out the door now. No matter what he says, you have to go.

Angene . . . he could not forget about Angene. Not at the church, not a good sign. She hadn't believed him—couldn't comprehend. Was too intensely wrapped up in Ducas Sangbourne, and too unwilling to believe what was before her eyes after everything she had said to him and done with him.

No, with *him*, Dar . . . but he would probably never be

able to convince her of that. For one moment this night, she had thought it was possible he was still Ducas, in spite of everything she had witnessed.

How insidious was the Judas . . . betraying everyone with a single blow.

The air was thick with heat, the sky yellowed with rising storms. He stood at the edge of the cemetery, listening, seeking . . . and the scent of bloodlust came to him—thick, in his mouth, in his consciousness, Ducas triumphant: he inhaled the aroma, the taste, the passion for blood—and he knew, they'd found a victim—they were feeding on their prey . . .

And then his heart went stone cold. Ducas, taunting him, revealing who it was.

Veleka . . . Father in heaven almighty—his *mother* . . . attacked, taken—absorbed into the body of the beast—her life, her memories, everything—anything she could ever tell him . . . forever gone . . .

Grief hit him like a cannonball. Suddenly, urgently, so overwhelmingly it sent him to his knees amid the gravestones and statues of saints and crucifixes.

Grief—for her? She, who was of their kind? Of all the things he had experienced on this quest, he never thought he would feel this blasting eruption of grief for the . . . *entity* who had given him life.

The entity. Not a mother. No maternal feelings. No love, no regrets.

She had wanted him dead at birth, and only fate had interceded to save him, and for that, someone else had had to die. Death piling all around him, up to the sky.

Even so, he shed tears for her. His *mother* . . . it still sat strangely in his mind. She who had given birth to both a hunter and a fighter . . . *her* time on earth was done.

And his was just beginning. There was power within *him,* he had yet to fathom. The power with which Ducas could access his mind, and he *his.* A potent strength he had not yet tested. That telling prickling feeling—was it when he sensed Ducas—or when the unholy were near?

Now? As dawn crept slowly over the horizon, were they circling the cemetery, dripping in bloodlust, ready to kill? No one was exempt—not the vicar, not Croyd, not Angene—and they were the ones most dangerous to the body, they were the ones who could identify the host . . .

But dangerous to whom? To whom would it matter, other than those whose loved ones had been sacrificed to the host? Who would help, who would care?

It struck suddenly that he was alone. That it was he and Ducas and the knowledge between them of the bloodlust of the host. And it was he alone who would fight Ducas to the death.

And only one of them could win.

The vicar was awake all night, rooting through his books, praying for his sins, asking forgiveness that he had let that poor delusional boy run away. No, he had to be realistic, he couldn't have detained him. And truthfully, the vicar hadn't wanted to after he'd had said the one word that made his blood run cold.

Iscariot.

No, they didn't exist. He had pretended to believe that because he didn't want the taint of them around him. He had given lip service only to the notion they were anywhere near. And that, for his parishioners. He believed it not.

And yet—if the boy were to be believed, they had come, they were among his people, and all his piety, sanctity, and certainty had not been enough to keep them at bay.

Nor would his questions be answered in books. He knew what he knew, but whether the boy was who he claimed, or whether Ducas Sangbourne was what the boy said he was, he would not find the answer in a book; there was only one way—that was to go up to the Manor himself, to see Sir Eustace and Lady Veleka.

A simple thing. He was fairly sure they were perfectly all right.

If only the boy hadn't said what he'd said. . . .

Now, everything was colored by that one word. The air felt thicker, the sky looked ominous, there were no birds singing, and clouds drifted across the sun.

Iscariot . . . descendants of the Judas who had betrayed the world . . .

A folktale. Superstition. Ignorance. Myth.

Hysteria.

The Iscariot—it had been written, had been denied reparation for that betrayal and from that, and the suicide of the Judas, had arisen a clan of vengeance-bent demons, who roamed the earth draining their victims—not with a bite on the neck or body, but by a blood kiss to the heart with their long, barbed tongues.

A monster story, wholly without merit or crediblity. And besides, Ducas Sangbourne did not have red hair, as it was said of the Judas.

A man can put vegetable dye in his hair—women sometimes did . . .

He was looking for what—an excuse to believe or a reason to deny?

The stigmata then, of the three X's, said to represent the thirty pieces of silver . . . supposedly they all bore the mark on their chests . . .

Well, it was not for him to demand that Ducas Sangbourne remove his clothing or to confess to any sins. No, he only wished to ask after Sir Eustace and his wife.

His books couldn't tell him everything, he told himself; and that was why he had come.

And there, Ducas answered the door. Cordial as ever. Inviting him in, telling him his mother and Sir Eustace were called unexpectedly out of town.

Perfectly fine explanation. No matter that the air in the house seemed close, hot, metallic. No matter that he was squirming in his skin, because Ducas—this Ducas?—had none of the anguish and urgency he had exhibited yesterday.

Ducas was well, thank you, everything was fine, thank you. And did I thank you for the service for Mr. Alton? He assured him he had—but why didn't he remember? His visit to express exactly that sentiment was but a day ago . . .

And are things going any better? the vicar asked him. *Any better how?*

Your memory. I was concerned about whether your memory was on the mend, and praying that things were going a little better now.

Oh, yes, things are much much better . . . is there anything else, vicar?

No. Just . . .

He peered over Ducas's shoulder. *Just*—was that a spray of red drops on the wall?—*concerned about you, and Sir Eustace and your mother . . . it's been a trying time . . .*

But things are better now. I'm definitely more at home here now, thank you for coming, vicar, thank you for asking.

And he firmly closed the door.

And when the vicar, still uncertain and unconvinced, returned to the church, Ducas was waiting in the hall.

"*. . . may their bones rot and their marrow congeal, and feed the worms to eternity . . .*"

"They have killed again." Gaetana uttered the ominous words as she leaned forward and blew out the candle. She looked old suddenly, the lines on her face etched deep, her skin pale, white. "No one can stop them, no one is safe."

"Your incantations were always futile," Angene said. "He told me to go to the church."

Gaetana leaped on that. "He? Who?"

Angene stared at her. "Ducas—no, the other Ducas . . ."

"What is this?" Gaetana pricked up. "You said—another Ducas . . ."

"I—he . . ." How to explain?

"*Angene*—" Gaetana grasped her shoulders. "Tell me . . ."

She wanted to. Desperately She had rehearsed it in her mind. . . .

I was with Ducas, making love with Ducas, was it Ducas?— and Croyd came, and Ducas left, and he—the other Ducas— was making so much noise, I had to find him—he was tied and gagged in a coffin of dirt under the bed. And then Ducas came after us, or maybe he was really Ducas and it was all a lie, except I saw Ducas walk out of the bedroom at almost the same time the other Ducas started pounding from underneath the bed . . .

It sounded insane. Two Ducases, one in pursuit, the other claiming the real Ducas was a vampire.

She had given herself to a *vampire* . . .

Where to begin?

"Ducas . . . he has a . . . there is a . . . the . . ."

"There is another," Gaetana murmured. "Yes, yes. That too he did not want me to know. . . . Tell me, the Other—he was there?"

"He was there. He has been there—he is the . . . the twin, he said."

"Yes, yes . . . another—" Gaetana murmured, her excitement rising. "And so you know now . . ."

"I know now," Angene whispered. "I held up the mirror and I saw . . ."

"And the Other?" Gaetana breathed.

"He was reflected . . ."

"Ah!"

"I couldn't believe it; I attacked him, I ran. Before that, he had told me to go to the church."

"Yes . . ." Gaetana closed her eyes. Mercy was here. The savior had arrived. "And so we will go. Come." She began gathering up her icons, all of them, religious and secular, and the silver dagger. "We mustn't lose a minute. They are hunting; the kill doesn't satisfy their hunger as much anymore. They need more and more . . . Come . . ."

She had everything piled and tied in a large shawl, and she stood looking expectantly at Angene.

Angene stared at her, tears welling in her eyes. "I don't know which Ducas . . . made love to me . . ."

Gaetana touched her face, smoothed her hair. "It was the one who told you to go to the church; I will see him, and I will know . . ."

It was the blood. All this time, all these games, Croyd thought. He was tired of playing hound and hare. Something was going on up there, up at the Manor. Something.

He had found not a clue to the missing guests; he had no just cause to search the premises, and yet his every instinct screamed that there was something to be found.

It was the blood. Found on the farmstead road, a big splotch of blood, just where an aimless traveler could see.

As if Ducas were taunting him.

So he'd gone to the Manor anyway, demanded to speak to Sir Eustace, and what did it prove but Sir Eustace and the lady Veleka had suddenly gone away.

"Really, my lord?"

"Really, Constable. Up to London, in fact, to check with the families of those friends you seem to think are still missing. Your brutal questioning and accusations distressed them very much."

"Did they indeed, sir?" He tried to peer over Ducas's shoulder. Was he seeing drops spattered on the wall?

"Indeed. They decided to put paid to all your speculations, Constable. As they shall when they return."

"Rather sudden, wasn't it?"

Too suddenly to his mind, with all this blood business going on. But there, he couldn't press things with Mr. Ducas. Not to that extent.

"They didn't think so," Ducas snapped. *Bloody nuisance.* "Now if you'll excuse me . . ."

Drops it looked like, red spattered drops . . . spattered blood even, but from this distance Croyd couldn't really tell. And Ducas was not about to invite him in.

More bloodiness, and he didn't know quite what to do, where to turn with Ducas pretty well shutting the door in his face.

No one would believe his theory anyway. Everyone would laugh in his face.

. . . well, maybe not everyone—

Maybe it was time to lay all this out for the vicar. The vicar would tell him if his thinking was out of place.

Angene saw him before he saw her, and her heart started pounding painfully. How could it not be Ducas? Everything about him was the same, *everything*.

She couldn't go in that room, couldn't be in the same room with him. Couldn't.

Could still feel his hands all over her, in her, feel him sliding inside her, pumping, pushing, demanding her all.

To whom had she given her mouth, her nipples, her breasts, her soul?

What was he plotting, sitting there so close to the vicar? How deep, how devious was the vein of evil in him that he would toy with such a trusting old soul?

Could he fool Gaetana?

Gaetana was staring at him, murmuring, nodding, whispered, "It is as I said. We are safe. It is him."

And so they were five, five against the unholy, five to fight the host.

They were gathered on the altar, the vicar, Croyd, Dar, Gaetana, and Angene, the shadow of the cross falling over them, protecting them from the pervading evil.

Dar felt it. Even in the holy confines of the church, he felt it. Ducas outside, testing, probing, raging.

"There are not many paths open to us," the vicar was saying. "Not much is known about the Iscariot in terms of how to kill the body of the host. From the beginning of time, the vampire has always been staved off by just the sight of religious icons. We must assume that they have the same meaning and the same power over the Iscariot. Dar, you said you are thinking they must hibernate in the tunnel at night . . . ?"

"It's the only place they could be," Dar said, "The only place they can get sustenance and succor."

"Then let us bury them there with a flaming cross. Let us sear them into the ground," the vicar said, not at all shocked at his thirst for revenge.

"We can do that, yes, but remember, Ducas is the key. He is the last of his kind, he of all of them must die. And I must be the instrument of his death." He held up his hand as the vicar protested. "It is done. This is my destiny."

"Then we'll do what we can do," the vicar said. "We'll build the cross, perhaps two, and fire them up in the tunnel."

"And this . . ." Gaetana said suddenly. "This—" She pulled apart her shawl and removed the silver dagger. "Silver. What would wound an Iscariot more than the thing with which he betrayed all of mankind?"

"Vicar . . . ?"

"What do we know of the Iscariot? We must use every weapon we can conceive of against him. Silver . . . it would make sense . . ."

"Thirty pieces," Dar said. "If we could melt it down— use it as a weapon."

"The blacksmith," Croyd said suddenly. "Fires hotter than the devil—could melt a stone in there . . . ?

"Good. Good thinking. Now—we need to gather thirty pieces of silver—anything . . . quick—Angene . . ."

"I'll take it, I'll get it done before the time comes . . ."

"The time is tonight, " Dar said. He knew it, he felt it. "We have no more time. We need to start—now."

They worked the entire day after that, Gaetana and Angene gathering wood, and Dar and Croyd pounding together two wooden crosses that measured seven feet high and three feet at the crossbar.

Dar had scant hope that Ducas didn't know what they were doing; nevertheless, the power of the cross was magical. It was calming, it gave him hope, it gave him peace.

They finished late in the afternoon, and the vicar then commandeered a wagon, and Dar brought them to the entrance through which he'd escaped by the outcropped rock near the tunnel.

He entered the tunnel, he listened. A murmuring of sound, the rustle of bat wings, a hunger gnawing hot and heavy beneath the earth . . . the host was waiting, the host was restless . . .

He signaled to the vicar, and he and Croyd laid the crosses in the tunnel entrance, pacing inside as far as they dared to go, silently, prayerfully, placing them top to top, and sprinkling them with kerosene.

They jumped back into the wagon as Gaetana lit the fire and ran.

The crosses ignited with a whomping roar. The horses reared as Gaetana made for the wagon, and as she climbed in, they took off, the wagon careening crazily as the horses dashed out of the field and down to the road.

The grasses around the tunnel entrance caught fire, as flames consumed the tunnel entrance and the sound of deep haunting howls followed them all the way down the road.

"Back to the church," the vicar urged, but even as the wagon barreled into the village, there was a crowd milling on the square.

"Fire—fire—look, the Manor—"

And they weren't pointing out of town toward the fields. They were pointing toward the house.

"He's luring me," Dar said. "This is his trap, his ploy."

Ducas came through to him, clear and loud. *So right you are, dear Other. Did you think you could defeat me by annihilating the host? Naïve Other—I don't need them—they need me. . . .*

"You can't go." This from Angene, quiet, horrified, beautiful Angene.

"He's mine to take or to die for," Dar said.

"I don't want you to die. . . ." She hadn't even known she would say that. Or that the thought of his death would make her feel so bereft.

"I won't die. Not if you kiss me."

And here was the test—he wasn't Ducas, he wasn't. He was himself, the Other, the twin. And he might be going to his death.

She lifted her face to him, and he lowered his head. And it was the kiss, the stunning, delicious, unbelievable kiss . . . a forever kind of kiss—one to build dreams on, affection, futures, lives—

Her whole body was bombarded by that kiss, little darts of pleasure pricking her everywhere . . . his kiss . . . not— not—she wouldn't even think it, say it. This kiss. The first kiss on his return, his memory impaired.

But not. This was the kiss—and why she had thought deep in the back of her mind that something was different. But there was no more time to examine that thought. He was going, up to the house, to confront the evil, and they could just see from where they stood, a lick of hellish flame.

Dar mounted the wagon, drove to the blacksmith shop, and then by the light of the raging fires, headed toward the Manor, straight into hell.

Chapter 18

And now he was without protection, but for the cross around his neck, the silver dagger, and a small pail in which they had melted down thirty pieces of silver.

The fire from the tunnel was spreading in the fields beyond the village, lighting up the night sky. As he got closer to the manor house, he could see the flare of flame within.

Clever Ducas. No big conflagration for him. No, Ducas would have it all under control. Just that subtle pull and tug to bring his nemesis to his door.

His twin. The life he might have led, had Veleka not been one of them, being consumed before his very eyes.

And Sir Eustace—had he known? How could he not? That kind old man . . . It didn't bear thinking about.

He needed all his energy for the battle ahead.

The silver at first so molten and flowing, was hardening in the bucket, and the fire was creeping along the back of the house.

And where would Ducas be?

In your tomb . . .

Ducas's voice, clear as a bell in his mind . . . Dar jumped from the wagon, pulled the pail, and ran into the house, into the spuming smoke scent and the crackle of flames suddenly too nearby for comfort.

Or had Ducas planned that too—to take them both down in a holocaust of flame?

Where would he be? The only place Dar knew to find him—his resting place. Up the steps, then—and into the bedroom, pulled by Ducas's aura, and the evil steeped in and around this house of doom.

The mattress was aloft, and Ducas was sitting in the coffin weakened by curses, radiating evil.

"Well, so we come to the final confrontation. You've murdered the host, you've severed the body, and now you've come for me. Such a clever Other—maybe—" Ducas stood, priming himself for what was to come.

"This is why you must die. Because all these years, we were so comfortable. Everything was going so well. The host was happy, sustained. Veleka had found for us the perfect situation, when you think about it—haven't you thought about it, intrusive Other—this beautiful house, and my pledge we would never decimate the peasants to feed the host—

"And then, Veleka was very good at pulling the veil over Sir Eustace's eyes. He thought what she made him believe—that she was young, beautiful, sexually voracious, needed variety to keep her sated; he never knew she slept apart, under his bed; never knew about the Iscariot. Could never have conceived of you—but then, that was *her* secret, and for that, and a litany of other transgressions, she really had to die.

"And he had to die—the host was hungry after all, and what good was he to us? So of course the manor house must burn. It's the only way to hide all the secrets. And to hide your tomb, you bloody bastard . . ."

He was in such a rage. Dar girded himself, poised his body, canted his hips to take a blow, had his weapons at the ready. This had to work—it had to . . . as Ducas ranted on—

"*You*—You've taken everything from me; you even took Angene. Took her virginity, took her adoration, took my place—*took my place!*—And for that you *will* die, you will die—and *I will survive.*"

He lunged at Dar then, sprung from his life force in the dirt, as smoke began billowing up around them; he leaped at Dar over the coffin that would entomb him, and Dar moved his arm, and aimed for his heart, and shoved the point of the silver dagger dead on as Ducas came flying through the air.

He fell on his back into the coffin, appalled, astounded, his eyes glazed with astonishment. And Dar took the pail, the silver now annealed to molasseslike thickness, and he heaved it over the dagger wound.

The heat of it was fiery, staggering, seeping into the wound, into his heart, spreading like wildfire through his vitals, burning like coals.

Ducas knew what it was. It was thirty pieces of silver, it was circular, it was destiny. The Other, his judge and jury, denying him reparation, sealing his fate.

He who was so like him killing him—it was like *him* taking his own life.

He felt his body shriveling as the silver seeped slowly through his body, and melted into his bones. He felt the heat of the fire, saw his reflection in his own face, and then the mattress platform closed over him, and he knew no more.

Dead dead dead, all of them, dead, and the manor burned to the ground, the tunnel caved in and swallowed by the fire. All of the evil dead, burned, buried.

And now they had to deal with the aftermath. The explanations, how much to tell; the calming of the villagers. The ongoing litany of masses and prayers. Croyd's decision in the case of the missing guests. The black hole that had been Sangbourne Manor, and the public version of what had happened to the family.

It was not an easy thing. To scare the villagers with the knowledge that there had been vampires living among them didn't seem politic. A horrible accident that had taken the lives of the Sangbournes one and all seemed a more believable story. More to the point. Less likely to cause a panic.

The sane thing to do, when there never had been evidence of vampires in their midst. The cows and chickens—he would tell them it had been a roaming wolf, Croyd decided. The deaths of the guests, which was not common knowledge to begin with, would be accounted for by misadventure—far and away from Cheshamshire and Sangbourne Manor. The truth would serve no one well.

There were so many truths. Dar was dizzy trying to sort the truths. They all muddled into one big disaster, predicated on his birth, his path, his powers.

It was Gaetana who finally explained it all to him. "You were born of the moment when Veleka was human and warm. It is said of those Malaysian women, that they *can* have marriage, family, and a normal life, in in their vampiric state. At that moment, when she was in that state, she mated with one of her kind, and you were made—of her muted blood and his Iscariot line. And you were born to be a *dhampir*—a vampire hunter. It was you they always feared. That is why she wanted you dead. They always knew someday you would come."

If he believed in fate. If he believed in predestination. But there had been none of that in his life. Only poverty, punishment, isolation, and loneliness.

Until he came to the army. Until he took on the missions other men shunned, and waded into the depths of evil incarnate—man's inhumanity to man. Then he found acceptance, camaraderie, structure and a sense of control.

But nothing could have prepared him for this. Nor was he prepared to continue in battle, even as he felt his powers ballooning—his senses stretching and reaching, almost beyond his control.

And then, there was Angene.

What could he say to Angene? She had wrapped her heart around Ducas, had lived for Ducas, had pinned her every dream on his making her his mistress.

And he had made mockery of those dreams, he had taken her without compunction, everything she was willing to give, he had used her, fucked her, and then walked away.

It struck him suddenly that there could be a child. It had been perhaps a week, but it was conceivable there could be a child.

And he was a man who had always yearned for a home and family. Beyond anything else in his life, he had always wanted a family.

If there was even the possibility of that with Angene, how could he ever walk away?

So it was over. Ducas was dead, and a week of searing sensuality was about to become a memory.

She felt like a fool. Ten times a fool. For just handing her body over to one or both of them so cavalierly. For reveling in all that lust. For wanting what was above her touch. For not knowing . . . not seeing, not feeling the differences.

She would never ever be sure—which of them had taken her virginity, which of them might be the father of a child . . .

She had never even thought of the possibility until this moment. Why should she have thought of it? It had barely been a week.

But even a week was enough time: there could be a child. She could have conceived—Ducas the *vampire* might have spawned a child.

A monster like him.

Which of them had fucked her? Who? Who?

After that final fiery night of retribution, she had run from him. Run from her sins and her stupidity. From her dreams and her transgressions. She couldn't go to face him, after that stunning, consuming kiss. She didn't know what it meant. She didn't even know who he was.

So how could she ask him? She wasn't really ready, but

they said he was leaving—soon—and now, on the heels of the thought about a child, she really had to know.

He was staying at the rectory. The good vicar had offered him everything. He had a soft bed, a warm room; he had knowledge that deep inside him, there was an unfurling certainty of who he was and what his burgeoning powers meant.

And that he could use them—or not. That there was a future—or not. Or maybe, for this moment, there was just Angene. Angene and that kiss. Angene in his bed. Angene, his. Not . . . the other's.

His, whether she knew it or not, she was his. He had marked her, he had claimed her, and banked as it must be, his desire for her was still out of control.

But—a thought nagged at him: had it been *his* lust, *his* desire, or had all of that always been filtered through . . . the other?

Did it matter—especially if there was a child? *This* child, this *possible* child, would have *him.* He was determined on that already. No matter what he had to give up—the military, his so-called powers, even his life—this child would have him. Would have a father, a family, a life . . .

The die was cast. He'd leave the military special services. He would make a home for them. He would have Angene and her luscious kisses. They would have the child.

He would not leave Cheshamshire without her. He began stripping off his clothes. He had to see her before he left . . . to make things right, to make them complete.

Which one, which one, which one . . .
The words thrummed in her head as the vicar showed her into the parlor at the rectory.

"I believe the boy is bathing."

"Can I wait?" Her voice was steady, her body a bundle of raw nerves.

"As you wish, my dear."

She settled on the sofa as he left the room, then jumped up and began pacing. Fidgeting. Picking up objects and putting them down. Trying to parse out before she saw him what she would say.

Well, here's the thing—Dar or whatever your name is— whoever you are—are you Dar? I don't know who . . . which of you I . . . I mean—which of you—did what . . . and how I know Ducas is really dead . . . or if he might have fathered a monster . . .

Oh God, oh God, oh God—*a monster* . . . a little vampiric child, weaned on mother's blood . . .

The wash of horror almost brought her to her knees. Where was he? She couldn't wait—she couldn't. She ran from the parlor into a hallway, frantically looking for a bedroom, *his* bedroom.

There was short hallway that gave onto another, perpendicular to it. She thrust open doors. The office here, the library there. A small bedroom on this side; the vicar's bedroom on the other—and then . . . a room with a door ajar.

She edged toward it, silent as a cat. Yes, he was there, toweling his head, pulling on his shirt. Over his broad chest. Over the telltale identifying stigmata of the three X's.

. . . Ducas! . . .

She ran, she fled, she could not get away from the rectory fast enough, she could not contain her utter terror. It was Ducas who had survived. Ducas who was alive . . .

Oh, God, she had to hide. She had to leave the village, run for her life—*Ducas was alive . . .*

And now he had to find her. She was not in the parlor, not anywhere in the house or on the grounds.

The vicar gave him directions to Gaetana's house, and gave a brief account of her history.

Pretty little house, he thought as he came up the garden path. A percent interest on the funds out of the Earl's pocket, and he got the fiery Gaetana in exchange.

Now he knew that, it was perfectly clear what had been Angene's true desire, her real intent.

Gaetana met him at the door.

"Where is she?"

"She is totally unnerved, Dar. You have to talk to her."

"I'll talk to her. I'm not leaving Cheshamshire without talking to her."

Gaetana patted his arm, led him into the parlor where Angene was huddled, staring at the fire, and withdrew.

Angene looked up as he entered, and pure terror flashed in her eyes. God, he was so tall, he had such a presence. Why hadn't she noticed before? But the other one had been like that too . . . how could she know? *How?*

"*Who* are you?" she whispered, pulling her shawl closer as if it could ward off whatever evil spirits he had brought into the room.

"You know who I am."

"No. I don't, I don't know. I don't want to know. I want you to go away, whoever you are."

"Angene . . ."

"It's not over, is it? The demon didn't die, and now I have to live with the horror of knowing what I did with him, all the things I did, all the selfish things I wanted, and what the consequences might be. You have to leave. You have to leave me alone, do you hear? Just . . . just go away—"

She wasn't angry, she was petrified, scared of him, paralyzed by the possibility that Ducas hadn't died, and that *he* was Ducas, and he had lied.

But why? How in the world could she come to that conclusion?

"Angene . . ."

"You scare me."

He drew up a chair. "I'm not *him.*"

"I don't know that. I don't know anything. I don't know which one of you I . . . I don't want to know, except . . ."

"Listen . . ."

"No!" She turned her head, she who had been so fearless with him—with *them?*—her body cringed—on *every* level.

He said it first. "There could be a child."

"A monster, you mean. Spawn of a vampire. Blood-sucking demon, you mean." Her voice cracked. "If there is—" she could barely get the words out, "—if there is, Gaetana will take care of it. She knows things to do. You'll have no responsibility, you won't even have to think about it, because I've been thinking about it . . . and that's what I'm going to do."

He let the words sit in the air. Horrible, awful words, and yet—if the possibility existed that the child—the yet-to-be-confirmed child—had been Ducas's . . . what would any woman do?

"*If* there is a child," he said, keeping his words measured and calm, "*if*—it is not Ducas's child."

"How do I know that? How do I know you're not Ducas when you bear the same mark on your chest as he does—did? . . . How do I know?"

"Everything about me had to be exactly as it was on Ducas," he said patiently. "We went over his body. Noted every scar, every mole. Everything was reproduced surgically on my body, down to the X's. I promise you, Angene. Ducas is dead."

"And yet, he could be you and you could be him, because you were, you did change places, and you both fooled everybody, especially me. How can I know? I've been so gullible, so steeped in my own cupidity and selfishness. I won't take your word. Not this time. Tell me—how can I know?"

"How did you know before?" he asked reasonably. "You looked in a mirror. Look in the mirror, Angene. See what you see—"

The mirror. Of course, the mirror. "*Mother . . . !*" Right. The mirror. The other hadn't reflected in the mirror. He'd been furious at what she'd done, and near to the kill—if Croyd hadn't come.

"I've been listening," Gaetana said. In her hand, she held a small wall mirror framed in gilt. "Sit next to her. See what you see . . ."

Dar moved to the sofa; Gaetana handed Angene the mirror. She stared at her own pale, haunted expression. *What would she see?*

She tilted the mirror slightly, so that Dar would be reflected.

And she saw his face.

"See what I see," he said gently, taking the mirror from her hand and holding it directly in front of him so that his head and his upper torso were wholly reflected. And then he turned it toward her so that she was now in the reflection with him. "I see a future, Angene. I see that incredible, unforgettable kiss. I see we could be a family, with the possibility of a child. I see all the things I've ever wanted and never had. And all the things you yearned for and hoped to have found in *him.*"

She started crying, the tears shimmering just on her lashes. "Exactly—it was the both of you," she whispered. "How do I know . . . ?"

"*I* know," Dar said firmly. "I *know.* You never . . . not with him."

"*Not* with him . . ." she echoed faintly. All that pleasure, all that she had given—not with him. Only with Dar? All that sumptuous pleasure—?

She believed him. Did she believe him? Maybe . . .

. . . *maybe* . . .

Could she see the differences now? Was he just little bit taller, was his face more lined? Was he stronger, more decisive, more—more righteous? More elegant, more loving, more kind?

"This is what we'll have, if you will have me," Dar said. "We will have time. Time for you to get used to seeing *him* in me. Time for you to learn, I am not him, and he was not me. Time for me to find my way in the secular world. Time to determine if we will have a child. And then after, we'll have time to explore everything we already know about each other. And time to build on that, make it lasting. Make it more."

Now she was crying.

"I want this, Angene. I really do. I want a family, I want marriage. I want everything I was ever denied. And I want you. Make no mistake about that. I haven't forgotten one minute of our time together. I want *you*."

Her tears spilled over. He hadn't forgotten. Neither had she. And it had been him. She had to believe that. Every time, it had been *him*.

She nodded, and she let him enfold her in his arms; she raised her face to his to accept his kiss.

"He is the goodness and the light," Gaetana said. "He will make everything right."

The differences . . . they were evident now, and so transparently clear. They were in this kiss, this forever kiss.

It *would* take time.

But she would take him, in time, in love, in marriage, and—she felt it was already so—as the father of her child. . . .

Magersfontain Hill, South Africa
December 1899

It was the tail end of yet another bloody battle, this time one in which the Boers were kept contained—for this hour. But more immediately than that, the colonel had before him the letter from Dar St. Onge recounting the disposition of Ducas Sangbourne, in the all the gory detail, and tendering his resignation.

Perfect, the colonel thought as he changed his uniform this raw December morning as his unit prepared for the second stage of the battle.

It was over. Ducas Sangbourne was no longer a danger. There would be no more carelessness, no more negligence, no more vain, self-serving lunatics.

Finally.

He had waited so many years. It had taken him too many years to set up the right situation to instigate sending Dar St. Onge to Sangbourne Manor. All those years, working beside him, planning his fate.

But it had worked out. He had fulfilled his promise and the prophecy, and they all would move on.

It was over. . . .

The colonel touched the scarred three X's on his chest.

And now—it could begin again. . . .